GW00467480

Th Ship Sailed On

A colourful thriller set on a 1960s cruise ship, with boozy parties, diamond smuggling - and murder.

By
Valerie Lawson

First Edition, 2024.
Published by Winter & Drew Publishing Ltd.

ISBN: 9781739184964

CONTENTS

ACKNOWLEDGMENTS

This book is dedicated to all my friends that have helped me along the way, especially my late sister Brenda, who was such a great source of advice on the early drafts.

Also, I would like to acknowledge my friends in the Exeter SPA who have provided such encouragement and feedback as the book progressed.

Finally, I would like to thank Jonathan and his team at Winter & Drew Publishing Ltd for their help and advice in shaping the book for publication.

CHAPTER 1

On a cold November day in the late-1960s, a white 25,000-tonne cruise liner, the *SS Ocean Star*, was berthed at Pier Head in Liverpool. A taxi pulled up alongside the ship and a slim red-headed girl with a face full of freckles jumped out and waited while the driver lifted her suitcase from the back of the cab. She paid him, then made her way towards the gangway.

Margaret Hargreaves looked up at the massive side of the ship.

I've actually made it, she thought. *I'm only twenty-three and about to start work on this boat. Who knows, I might fall in love with the chief officer, or even the captain!* She was bursting with excitement.

When Margaret finally reached the gangway the master-at-arms asked for her boarding pass.

"I'm joining the ship," she said proudly, handing him her discharge book. "I have to report to the Laundry Manager, Freddy Brown."

He smiled, handing back her book.

"So you're the new Steam Queen, eh? Not bad either. Just go through the bureau square and turn left at the second door saying Crew Only, then down the iron staircase until you reach G deck. Once you get there, anybody will tell you where his office is."

Margaret thanked him and, still clutching her heavy suitcase, made her way in the direction of the bureau.

Inside, the ship was as impressive as from the outside. The bureau square was covered in oak panels, and the handrails leading to the various decks were made of solid brass, which shone with the reflections of the chandeliers. Margaret had read that it held ballrooms, a cinema, a hairdressing salon, an attractive shopping centre, a nursery and also an indoor swimming pool in addition to the one on the outer deck.

She opened the heavy door leading to the crew quarters, where an iron spiral staircase led down to the working alleyway. A drab-looking passage with a well-worn dirty deck suggested many feet had trampled over it. She was to find that it stretched from one end of the ship to the other, and that it was vastly different to the passenger decks. She went up to the first person she saw, a man of about thirty, with hair redder than her own. He was short and stocky and wore gold-rimmed glasses.

"Excuse me," said Margaret. "Where is the Laundry Manager's office please?"

"Keep going that way and you will see it on the right," explained the man. "By the way, what's your name, my dear?"

"Margaret."

"Well, Miss Margaret, I'm Ginger." He waved his hands in the air. "If you need any help, don't hesitate to ask me. Us girls must stick together, dear!"

Margaret gave him a puzzled look and thanked him.

At last she arrived at Freddy Brown's office, which was situated above the laundry. He was talking to a woman in her early forties. She was small and rounded, had jet-black hair and a pink face with a turned-up nose.

Margaret was thinking how much the woman resembled a pig when Freddy Brown turned to her and asked her name. He was of medium height with a huge beer belly, a red face and a mass of white hair.

When she told him, he said to the woman next to him, "Lil, show the girl to her cabin."

Margaret followed Lil back along the alleyway still clutching her suitcase. They came to another spiral staircase, which led to the female quarters.

Lil turned to her and spoke for the first time. "You'll be cabining with Betty, Eve and Owd Rosie. Rosie hasn't turned up yet, she'll be along later."

In a short while they came to a cabin. The door was open and two women sat on opposite bunks smoking and drinking beer.

"Want a drink, Lil?" asked one, dragging a case of beer from under her bunk.

"Thanks, Betty." Lil nodded and sat down next to her, taking the beer and also the cigarette, which was being offered. Both of the women were in their mid-fifties. Betty was a big woman with grey hair and Eve was small with bleached blond hair, too much smeared red lipstick and a pair of skinny legs covered with varicose veins.

"What about you?" asked Betty. "Want a beer?"

"Thank you but I don't drink," replied Margaret.

"Have a ciggy then."

"I don't smoke either."

The three women gave her a peculiar look and carried on drinking and smoking. Lil took a big drag from her cigarette then turned to Margaret.

"While you're here I'll tell you the score," she said. "You must wear a white uniform at all times with white shoes. You're not allowed in the passengers' accommodation; only if you're required to, when on duty." Her chubby pink legs dangled from the bunk, with bright red fluffy slippers swinging back and forth. "You mustn't be in the Pig later than eleven at night or you can get logged if you're caught."

"What's the Pig?" asked Margaret.

"To put it posh," answered Lil, "it's the crew bar. We start seven thirty in the mornings and finish at noon. Start again at two and finish around five. In port we work through lunch so we can get finished early. Once you get to know the score, you'll be okay."

7

After hearing the word 'score' for what seemed like the hundredth time, Margaret realised that it meant a kind of routine.

"The other girls in the laundry are Eileen and Kitty. I cabin with them. Anyhow you'll meet them later They're all good skins. The stewardesses live around the corner from us. We call it Fluff Alley. Always be quiet when you come back from the Pig, they get a cob on if you disturb them, because their hours are longer than ours."

Lil took the last gulp of her beer then stood up.

"Well girl, leave your case here, you can unpack later. I'll take you down to the laundry now and show you the score."

The laundry was a huge room situated in the bowels of the ship. With the boat just coming out of dry dock, it was empty apart from the machinery and some dirty linen dumped in a pile on the deck.

"I suppose you'll be on the calender," Lil said, indicating a huge machine with rollers. "You'll be putting through the sheets and pillowcases, with Owd Rosie and a couple of the boys, Billy and Joe. The other lad is Johnny; he does all the odd jobs around the laundry. Betty and Eve work the presses and the girls iron the passengers' clothes, such as shirts, dresses, and what have you. I help Freddy with packing the passengers' laundry. I'll tell you what?" said Lil, pointing at a pile of white linen, "There's some officers' shirts to iron. Do them, then I'll see you back in the cabin."

---0---

After Margaret had finished the shirts, she made her way back to her cabin where she found the three women were still drinking beer.

"By the way, Maggie," said Lil. "We thought you'd be better with the younger crowd, so I'll swap cabins with you. Here's the cabin key, it's number twelve across the way. I'll collect my gear from there later."

Whew! What a relief, thought Margaret to herself.

She smiled at the women.

"That's very thoughtful of you all. Well I'd better go and get my things unpacked. See you later." She could hear them cackling in the background as she made her way to the other room. She unlocked the door of her new cabin to find the room in total darkness, so naturally she switched on the light.

"What the hell do you think you're doing?" yelled a voice from the top bunk. "Can't you see we're trying to sleep?" Two more figures emerged from the bottom bunks. "Who the bloody hell are you?" cried the one on the right. "If my feller was here," screeched the one on the left, "he'd wring your bleeding neck." Margaret switched off the light with a shaking hand.

CHAPTER 2

The following afternoon, the ship set sail for a 38-day cruise to the West Indies and Rio. It was one of the most exciting days of Margaret's life. Officers with gleaming gold braids on their uniforms were busy around the decks. There was the sound of excited passengers and crew members pushing their way to the side of the ship. Hundreds of people stood on the quayside waving the ship goodbye. Thousands of different coloured streamers, held by passengers and their loved ones, gently broke as the liner left the side. The band was playing. People shouted above the music, wishing each other well.

Margaret's mother stood waving. She was with Anne, her other daughter, and Anne's husband. "Look after yourself, love. Don't forget to write," she cried, looking as if she was fighting back the tears.

"Don't do anything I wouldn't do," joked her brother-in-law.

Margaret waved back. It was so strange how life could change in the matter of two years. At that time she was about to become engaged to Jim. 'Her lovely Jim' she called him.

They had first met when Margaret joined a local judo class, after her father had suggested it.

"It's a hard world out there, Maggie my love," he observed one evening over supper. "You're such a little slip of a thing. You should learn how to defend yourself. I'd get some judo lessons, if I were you."

So she had gone along, more out of curiosity than from a wish to learn. But the moment she walked in, she knew she was going to stay.

It was the teacher. He was tall, with wavy dark hair that fell onto his forehead, a cheeky smile and a soft voice.

"Hello," he said, giving her a firm handshake, "I'm Jim."

From that moment they became friends. By the time Margaret had earned her orange belt, they had progressed to a romance, and by the time she had her blue belt, they were engaged.

They had gone around to different jewellery shops, when at last she saw a ring she really liked. They both entered the shop and the assistant brought out the ring. It was set in a circular cluster of tiny diamonds. Jim put a small deposit on it until he had enough money saved to pay for it in full. Coming out of the shop the pair of them were so excited that they popped into a little coffee shop and started a discussion about when they were going to be married, who would be best man and bridesmaids, and of course how many children they would have. "A girl and a boy," Margaret had suggested.

Then fate struck a terrible blow. His death. Not only his, but her father's too. About a week after that wonderful day, Jim and her father had gone to a football match. On the way home, a drunken driver had crashed into them head-on. They had both been killed outright. Over the following months, her mother was walking around in a trance and kept bursting into tears. Her devastated sister kept coming over to console her mother.

For Margaret it all became too much. She ended up having a nervous breakdown and was in hospital for a few weeks.

In time they had learned to accept the tragedy and to get on with their lives. Margaret had gone back to her job in a shoe shop.

It was about a year after the tragedy that Margaret got talking to a customer who was trying on a pair of shoes, telling her of the accident and that her life felt meaningless now that Jim had gone.

"Why don't you go away to sea for a while," said the woman. "I'm a stewardess and I have travelled all over the world. I'll give you an address to write to, and just mention my name. I can't guarantee a stewardess job, but I do know that they are always looking for laundry staff. You must be willing to take anything that they offer."

"Oh I would!" answered Margaret eagerly. "I just feel that I need a fresh start in my life. I know Mum would miss me, but she has my sister and brother-in-law living close by."

Margaret did write to the shipping company. Their reply informed her that they had no jobs going at the moment, but would put her name on the waiting list. Now it was a year later and a position had come up. So here she was, waving goodbye to her family as she started a 38-day cruise to the Caribbean and South America.

The ship gave three loud whistles. The ropes were freed from the bollards and the tugboats began to pull her from the quayside, tooting in response to the whistles. Finally the *Ocean Star* let out one last whistle.

Margaret watched the sun set on the Liver Building as it receded into the distance, then turned slowly and made her way below deck.

---0---

Margaret was soon to find out that working on the calender was a hot, boring job. It was a huge machine with massive rollers that flattened the washed linen. Two people at one end put in anything from damp sheets and pillowslips to napkins and tablecloths, while two others folded the extremely hot, pressed linen that came through to the opposite side.

It was when the ship was rolling in all directions to the force nine gales that were hitting the Bay of Biscay that Margaret turned to Owd Rosie. "I feel sick!"

"You what, kid?" Owd Rosie turned her pale thin face with its short bright dyed-red hair towards her. "I can't hear you. I'm a bit deaf." She was also toothless, having told Margaret earlier that she'd left her false teeth out that morning because her gums were sore.

It was too late for Margaret to reply. One second later she was sick all over the napkins that were piled up in the tub beside her.

"Oh! I think I'm dying," she moaned.

Owd Rosie called over to the two laundry boys, Billy and Joe. They came around to see what was the matter. When they saw Margaret, they both burst out laughing.

"Johnny will have to wash all the napkins again. You'd better go to your cabin, Maggie," said Billy. "Joe, go and get Lil and tell her to take over Maggie's place for a while."

Needless to say, when Lil came down from the linen room she was none too pleased about having to go on the calender.

"These new people that can't take a bit of a rolling make me want to spew, too," she muttered.

Margaret, who by now was past worrying, dragged herself back to her cabin and flung herself onto the nearest bunk in sight.

After jumping up every five minutes to be sick, she eventually dozed off, only to be awoken a little while later by Eileen, one of the laundry girls, coming in. She was a tall girl in her mid-twenties with light brown hair; pretty, though hard-looking. The girl had swung open the door and switched on the big lights.

"Listen luv," she said, rather sarcastically, "Next time you lie on anybody's bunk, choose your own."

"I've only lain on the top of it," stammered Margaret, "my bunk was too high to keep going up and down to be sick."

The girl just glared at her.

"Well, make sure you change the sheets and pillow slips, Margaret," Eileen said. "Oh, and by the way, we're having a party tonight, so don't expect to be getting an early night. Kitty and Chris will be getting some ice and glasses, and Bob the cook said he'd make us some sarnies. You can give them a hand if you like. I'm just going down to me feller's cabin. See ya later."

At that she left, slamming the door behind her.

That's goodbye to my early night, thought Margaret.

It had been quite a hectic day for her, what with a lifeboat drill that morning, her long day in the laundry, and then only to end up being seasick. Maybe the party won't go on too late, she hoped optimistically.

But her hopes were not to be fulfilled.

At 2am the party was still in full swing. There were stewards, waiters, deck crew known as 'top-siders' and galley staff pushing their way into the tiny cabin. Some sat jammed tight on the two bottom bunks, others sat on the top and the rest sprawled on the deck. Empty beer cans were scattered all over the place. Cigarette ends had been stubbed out on the carpet.

One of the waiters got out a guitar and the singing began; anything from 'Your Cheating Heart' to 'Old Shanty Town'. Chris looked as if she were ready to flake out after all the alcohol she had drunk. Eileen sat in a corner necking with Tom, her fellow. He was running his hand up and down her thighs. Kitty wasn't at the party, but Margaret was informed by one of the stewards, who was breathing beer fumes all over her, that Kitty was 'officers' material' and would be out most nights with whoever fancied her, for a bit of the other.

Lil was the only woman from the other cabin who came to the party. She had staggered back to her room about half an hour prior, much the worse for drink, stumbling in the alleyway and being picked up by somebody who pushed her through her open cabin door.

Eventually to Margaret's relief, a stewardess from Fluff Alley came in a tattered-looking bright pink dressing gown, with hair full of rollers, to complain about the noise and how she had to get up earlier than anybody else. So if they didn't all shut up, she would go first thing in the morning and report them to the captain.

"Stupid old cow," said one of the waiters as soon as her back was turned. "Trust old Molly to go and spoil everything. Them old Tabbies are all the same. Don't like to see anybody enjoy themselves."

At last the drinks were beginning to run out, so one by one the crowd began to disperse. Chris was fast asleep on her bunk, while Eileen slept on the other one, cuddled up to Tom.

---0---

No sooner had Margaret fallen asleep than it seemed time to get up for work. The loud trill from Eileen's alarm clock woke her up. To her surprise there was Kitty in the top bunk opposite, snoring her head off. She had obviously made it back to the cabin.

Margaret climbed down from her top bunk. The cabin looked like a bomb had hit it. The other two girls were also fast asleep. Tom must have left earlier.

The laundry seemed to be hotter, but at least the ship was not rolling as much as the previous day. Somebody at the party had said, "Rough in the bay, calm out, and vice versa."

At morning break, they all sat around in a group, some drinking tea, others drinking beer around the ironing board, which Kitty was sitting upon, She was wearing a pair of dark glasses, after her late night. A very pretty girl of about twenty-six, she had jet-black hair, dark brown eyes, and an olive complexion.

"There's a cabin inspection at 11 o'clock," said Eileen, who had just finished off a can of beer. "We take turns to do the cabin. I suggest you do it today, Maggie, and one of us will clean it next time."

For the first time since Margaret had joined the ship, she decided now was the time to stand up to them.

"I don't see why I should clean all the mess up on my own, and especially after a party you organised," she said.

Eventually they compromised. Eileen suggested Kitty and Margaret would do it today, and she and Chris would do it next time.

Margaret still did not think that it was fair, but by then Eileen was turning really nasty; effing and blinding while Chris and the other women agreed with every word she said.

"Oh aye, girl, she's right, you know," interrupted Betty, "we all have to take our turn."

Kitty was oblivious to the argument, seeming to have to keep stopping herself from dozing off and falling off the board.

Cleaning the cabin was a job in itself. Margaret hardly knew where to start. Kitty was neither use nor an ornament. She just stood there yawning her head off, saying she didn't see why she had to help when she wasn't even at the party.

Margaret ended up doing the job on her own.

CHAPTER 3

Eileen's boyfriend Tom was with Mick, the head barman, in the Meal Bar. This was situated in the galley, just outside the Atlantic restaurant.

Mick was a tall, slim, suave man in his late forties. He had taken the chance to go over with Tom their plans involving smuggling some diamonds. These had been stolen in a dive on the wreck of a cabin cruiser, after it had sunk in a storm off the West Coast of Africa. Mick was planning to get them on board from his contact in Sierra Leone.

"After we leave Freetown," he said, "I'll give you the stones. I know we've gone over it a hundred times in England, but remember it's still up to you and Paddy how you get them off the ship and through customs. My job's done till we get back. Any cock-ups and you and Paddy will face some pretty serious consequences."

Tom gave a breezy smile. "No problem," he said.

Tom was a distant relation to Mick's wife; the brother-in-law of her sister's husband. Although they were never really close friends, Tom only lived a few roads away from Mick, so they used the same local pub and would sit together occasionally, especially as they both worked on the same ship.

Once he had set up the plan, Mick thought that it would be a good idea to get Tom involved, as he wanted someone to take the diamonds ashore, and didn't want to risk it himself.

"And this chap Paddy; he'll help you out?" Mick asked.

The Irishman had become involved when the two of them had been discussing the diamonds in the bar of Mick's local pub in England before the cruise.

They were so deeply involved in their conversation that by the time they knew Paddy was there, the tall, thin man had heard enough for his participation to become a necessity.

The first they knew was when he said, "By Jesus, Tom, do you mind if I come and join ye?"

"Yeah, Paddy," Tom said, "sit down and I'll get you a drink. Oh and by the way, meet Mick, the head barman from the *Ocean Star*."

Full introductions were made. Paddy was also a seaman. He was aged around forty-five, and a good friend of Tom's. They lived in the same street, and had even sailed together, but for the last few years, Paddy had been on another liner. Now he was home on leave, before joining the *Ocean Star* for the world cruise.

Mick was interested to learn that Paddy had done a year's apprenticeship in engineering, and was very handy with his hands. He'd given it up to join the Merchant Navy, and had been on various ships ever since.

After the three of them became more involved in the discussion and had had a few extra drinks, the more it made sense to Mick to let them do the dirty work of getting the diamonds ashore safely. All he had to do was to use his and his contacts' money to get the stones in Freetown, then pass them over to Tom and Paddy to get them off the ship in England. Then they would return the diamonds to him so he could turn them into plenty of cash. Tom and Paddy would get a share, of course, but nowhere near as much as Mick and his contacts.

Mick had done smaller jobs of smuggling in the past, and had always managed to get away with it. But this one was big, and there had to be no mistakes. If there were, he would carry the blame. It could even mean his life. He was dealing with the underworld, some very hard people.

People who did not tolerate failure.

And now they were all on board the *Ocean Star*, and the plan still needed to take its final shape.

Tom finished his drink and stood. "I'll get off up to the Pig now. See you tomorrow."

It was about ten-thirty when Tom reached the crew bar, situated at the forward end of the ship. He ordered a couple of pints of beer, and then went over to Paddy, who was sitting on his own.

Tom put the drinks down on the table and sat next to his friend.

"I've just been talking to Mick," he whispered. "He's all set to get the diamonds in Freetown. God only knows how we're going to get them ashore."

"Wait till we get them first," hissed Paddy, swilling down the last drop of ale from his pint.

"Maybe we could plant them on somebody?" said Tom.

"What about your bird?" Paddy suggested.

"Leave her out of this. Anyway I don't reckon I'll be seeing her once I'm back home. She's okay for a good screw at sea, while I'm away from the missus for a few months. What we need is somebody who looks innocent. A person that the customs would least suspect."

"Eileen certainly wouldn't fit that picture," smirked Paddy. "Anyhow, I thought that you were going to take them off yerself?"

"That's what Mick thinks. He doesn't know I've had trouble with the customs before."

"He'd bloody kill ye if he knew that," Paddy said, swilling his beer.

"Yeah, I know," Tom replied. "But I couldn't let a golden opportunity like this go." There was a silence, then he continued. "Just think though," he said, "once we get them ashore, we'll get a good cut out of the money. It's worth taking the risk, and if we can get somebody that the customs wouldn't suspect, well hey presto, our problems are over, and..."

"Well, can ye think of anybody?" interrupted Paddy.

"Wait a minute! Maybe I can," exclaimed Tom. A smile came over what would have been a handsome face, if there had not been a big gap in his teeth. He was a huge man, his jet-black hair sweeping away from his face. "That new steam queen. You know, the one that cabins with Eileen. She's so naive, it's unbelievable."

"Hey! Guess who's just walked into the Pig," said Paddy, roaring with laughter, "Your bird and Miss Innocent."

Some of the crew turned around, looking at Paddy.

"Why don't you fucking shut up!" snarled Tom. "Do you want to draw attention to us?"

Paddy's laughter subsided immediately.

At the table nearest to where the two men were talking sat Ginger, the bedroom steward, who had half an ear to the conversation. He was sitting at what was referred to as the 'Queers' Table'.

At that moment there was only him, a male waiter known as 'Lola' and young Peter, a bellboy. With being underage, he wasn't really allowed into the bar late at night, but most of the crew turned a blind eye and usually the barman was too busy to notice.

Ginger usually felt it was up to him to protect the lad, and never let him stay too long. He would always chivvy the boy out before any of the masters-at-arms did their rounds.

He sipped his pint of beer, only half-listening to Lola. He could have sworn the men had mentioned something about diamonds. What were they up to? He never had much time for the two of them, as they were always running homosexuals down. But why had they been whispering? Also the new girl, who worked in the laundry, had been mentioned. He only heard snatches of the conversation. What was Paddy laughing at? He had laughed even louder when Margaret and Eileen had walked through the door of the Pig.

"I'd better go, Ginger," said Peter, standing up. "I don't want to get caught in here. See you tomorrow."

"Yes," said Ginger.

"Bye dear," smiled Lola, holding a cigarette holder in his right hand, and making affective gestures with the other.

Ginger went back into deep thought, as the ship sailed on.

CHAPTER 4

After a few days at sea an atmosphere of excitement seemed to fill the air. The ship was to land at her first port of call the following day.

Margaret was busy on the calender working with Billy. She had swapped sides with Joe for a change. Owd Rosie seemed quite happy where she was, feeding the linen through the rollers.

"We're in Lisbon tomorrow, Maggie," said Billy. "Fancy coming to the Texas Bar tomorrow night with Johnny, Joe and me? I think some of the girls are coming as well."

Margaret smiled at him and nodded. "Okay," she answered, "but mind you, I don't drink."

"Oh don't worry about that, we'll all put money in a kitty and drink whatever we like."

One of the waiters had asked her out, but she didn't really fancy him. He was rather egoistic. Then a bald-headed little greaser – a worker whose main job is to oil machinery – asked her. She politely declined. There was one person whom she did have an eye on though. She had seen him the other day working on deck. He was tall and dark and had merry brown eyes. He just nodded at her and smiled, then disappeared through a nearby door. He must have been a deckhand because he was wearing a sailor's uniform. She did not see any more of him. Possibly he was working on some other part of the ship. Now if *he* had asked her out, she knew what the answer would have been.

"You'll have a right laugh with us at the Texas Bar," Billy was saying. "There's music, the lot."

What he did not tell her, though, was that it was also a brothel.

"Hope you like dancing because they have that as well."

"Oh I love dancing," answered Margaret, "I'm sure we'll have a great time."

The following morning the ship sailed slowly into Lisbon harbour, passing under the big Salazar Suspension Bridge. Across the water from the dock was a beautiful big white statue of Christ with his arms outstretched. The sun was just beginning to rise and the rays fell onto the calm water, lighting up the little ripples of waves made by the ship, as she slid towards the quayside.

Margaret had popped up on deck with Owd Rosie during their morning break. She felt as excited as when the ship first sailed.

The statue strangely reminded her of Jim, welcoming her with open arms to his judo class. She would have been married by now if it hadn't been for that horrific accident. How life can change at a flick of a finger.

"Come on, kid," said a voice, bringing her back to the present. Owd Rosie tugged at her arm, and they made their way down to the laundry.

The laundry staff had finished work about twelve-thirty that afternoon, so Margaret and Rosie went ashore for a couple of hours. Lisbon was a beautiful old city. They walked around admiring the buildings and churches.

Margaret felt a little disappointed that the shops were closed for siesta. They looked in a few windows, but everything seemed to be so expensive. Finally they both sat at an outside cafe sipping coffee, and watched the world go by.

---0---

That evening Margaret put on a pretty blue dress and made finishing touches to her makeup. She was quite pleased with the way she looked. Eileen and Chris were coming out too. As Eileen pointed out, "Her feller was working late in the dining room that evening." Margaret often wondered why Chris did not have a boyfriend. She was over six foot tall, and quite attractive. Her long blond hair fell over her broad shoulders.

Maybe it was her height? Yet there were quite a lot of tall men amongst the crew. Margaret knew she would prefer to be tall than small.

A knock came on the door, and when Margaret opened it, there stood Billy, Joe and Johnny, all looking very smart. When Billy saw her he blushed to the roots of his hair.

"You do look nice," he said, with a cheeky smile.

"Are you all ready?" asked Joe

"Hold your horses!" yelled Eileen. "I haven't finished my hair yet. Help yourselves to a beer while you're waiting; there's a case under my bunk."

At last they were all ready to go ashore. Margaret felt a shiver of excitement as they stepped down the gangway and jumped into the first taxi that would carry six people.

Billy instructed the driver to go to the Texas Bar. It was tucked away in a side street, which the crew called 'Barbary Coast'.

They all scampered out of the cab into a crowded street. Music was blaring from various bars. One fellow was sprawled out on the pavement drunk, while his shipmates were coaxing him to get up.

"Well, here we are," said Billy. "Try and keep together."

They pushed their way into the bar. It was packed with seamen and sailors, and plenty of women with too much make-up and not enough skirts. A band was playing in what looked like a rowing boat suspended above the dance floor.

"We'll order three bottles of Mateus Rosé," Billy said as he made for the first vacant table. "We'll share them between the six of us."

"Don't forget," said Margaret in a low voice, "I don't drink."

At that, they all turned on Margaret. "Oh come on, don't be so miserable!" Billy said, punching her on the arm. "One won't hurt you."

"Don't be such a fucking spoilsport," snapped Eileen. "If my feller was here, he'd make you drink it."

"If you won't drink it," said Chris, putting her hand on Margaret's shoulder with a smile, "I will."

They all sat down and the waiter came and took their order. Later he returned with the bottles and poured the wine.

"Well, cheers everyone. Here's to a good cruise," joked Billy. They all raised their glasses.

Margaret just sipped her drink until Johnny started filling up the others' empty glasses.

"Come on, Maggie, get it down you, there's plenty more where that came from."

Not wanting everybody on her back she drank it in one gulp and Johnny, laughing, filled her glass up again. In fact she felt quite nice after it. A warm relaxed feeling came over her, and suddenly everyone seemed so friendly.

"Want to dance?" asked Billy.

"Okay," laughed Margaret. "This seems like fun."

They danced amongst the rest of the crowd. Margaret was remarking on how pretty the girls were and how some of them looked too young to be out at night. They ought to be in bed by now.

"Don't worry about them," said Billy with a wink. "They soon will be!"

They sat down and more wine was ordered. By this time, Margaret was drinking as freely as the others. That was until she suddenly lost her balance while dancing and fell flat on her back, with Johnny falling on top of her.

She couldn't remember being escorted back to the ship by Billy and the girls, nor could she remember Eileen and Chris dragging off her dress, and pushing her into the top bunk. But one thing she would always remember – the next morning, she woke up with the most enormous headache.

CHAPTER 5

George Bowder, the second engineer, sat back in his chair, and drew a puff on his cigar. He was sitting in the comfort of his own cabin, which was vastly different from those of the crew. His was on the upper deck where all the officers lived. The porthole was a big square window that gave a lot of light to the room. He also had his own bathroom and toilet. Looking at the man sitting opposite him, he smiled then lifted the lid off the ice bucket. "Running out of ice," he said, "I'll get the steward to fill it up."

"Don't worry, George," said his visitor. "There's enough for me here. I must go soon and get some more work done."

"Now as I was saying, I have it all planned out. About the diamonds."

"Yes," interrupted the other man, "but how do we get them ashore?"

"That's what I'm trying to tell you, if you'll only listen to me for a minute," hissed the second engineer. "I was in the ship's shop yesterday, looking for a birthday present, when suddenly I had the answer. They have these fancy hair combs with imitation diamonds. You know, the type that women wear when they have their hair up. Now if I put the diamonds in there, no one will ever know the difference. Well, not the ordinary person."

The other man looked at him hard. He chewed on his lip, which made the scar under his chin more prominent.

"And who will be taking this comb off the ship?"

"You!"

"Me! Why me?"

"For the simple reason as I've told you before, I have to sail with the ship again. Anyway I've been doing all the buying of black-market diamonds in Freetown, and also setting up the sale

31

in England. So you have to do your share at the other end. Remember, we are splitting the difference." His big, heavy body leaned forward again as he put the last ice cube into his whisky.

His visitor stood and swallowed the last of his drink. "Well, I must go. I've work to do. Heaven only hopes I don't get caught with them. You know what these customs officers are like."

"That's your problem, not mine," came the grim reply. Then he sighed. "Leave it with me. I'll think of something."

The younger man gave a grunt, and walked out of the cabin.

George Bowder finished the last drop of whisky and pressed the button for the steward to refill the ice bucket. A few minutes later a knock came at door, and when George called out, "Come in," a bellboy entered.

"Where's Lenny, my regular steward?" he demanded.

"Sorry sir," stammered the young man. "He's busy in another cabin and asked me to answer your bell."

"Huh okay. Just get me some ice." George looked again at the bellboy. "What's your name, son?"

"Peter, sir."

George smiled. Even though he was a married man in his early fifties, this boy was just the type he fancied; medium-height, skinny and with blond hair. Just the thought of Peter's body next to his was a turn-on.

"Did you want anything else, sir?" asked Peter, interrupting his thoughts.

Did he want anything else? You bet he did.

"No, no, not at the moment."

The bellboy turned and walked out of the room, muttering what a big fat git he was.

George paced up and down. He must try and get the boy in his cabin some evening. At that age many of them would do a few favours if the price was right.

---0---

Las Palmas had certainly been a busy morning, Ginger thought, what with scrub outs, linen changes, and to top it all, lifeboat drill for all crew members. They even had to go down in the boats. That wasted another half an hour of their time. He couldn't wait to get ashore.

He knew that most of ship's crew were off duty; many of them went ashore for their tax-free bottles. If you wanted cheap spirits, 'fire water' as it was called, then Las Palmas was the place. At the top of the gangway, the master-at-arms would be checking the bags as they came on board the ship. Well, he was supposed to be checking them. Nine times out of ten, he turned a blind eye and only checked if he had it in for that person, or if an officer of high rank was watching. Ginger had always been one of the lucky ones up until now.

---0---

Margaret was ashore wandering around the market on her own, deep in thought, when she bumped into Ginger.

"Getting your bottles?" he asked her.

"No, just looking at some of these handbags," she replied. "Are they actual crocodile skin?"

"Should imagine so," replied Ginger. "Aren't you going to get some booze in? You'll need it for the long journey across to the Caribbean. As you know, they only sell beer in the Pig. The officers are the only ones who have a spirit allowance on board the ship." Then he added, "And all the deckhands get is rum."

"I don't really drink much of the stuff," replied Margaret.

"Well, what about your cabin mates? I bet they do. And if anybody throws a cabin party you can contribute your share of the drink. Or maybe get one to take home for your mum?"

"I suppose you're right." she said, smiling back at him. "I never thought of that."

33

"I'll tell you what, Miss Margaret, come with me and I'll show you where to find the cheapest place, then we'll pop into one of the bars for a drink."

"Okay," she laughed. "I'm off duty for the rest of the day."

"Lucky you," Ginger said. "I've got to be at back at six to do my turn-downs."

When they had finished all their shopping, Ginger escorted her to the nearest bar that was on the way back to the ship. It was a dull, shabby-looking place, with low lights and music coming from the jukebox.

"Why, half of the ship's crew is in here," exclaimed Margaret. "I didn't expect that."

"Don't sound so surprised," laughed Ginger. "A good seaman knows all the bars in every port. What are you drinking, anyway?"

"Just an orange juice, thank you."

"Oh come on, have more than that," he insisted. "What about a gin and tonic?"

"No thanks," she replied. "I don't want to wake up with a bad head."

"Well, have a beer, at least."

After a bit of persuasion, she settled for half a beer.

"How are you liking sea life?" he inquired.

"It's okay so far, thank you," she answered as she looked around the room.

Suddenly, she saw him; he was sitting at a table with a few of the other deckhands. He looked so handsome.

Ginger carried on talking; knocking back his vodka and tonic. Then the dark, handsome young man caught her eye.

He smiled directly at her.

She smiled back, then shyly turned her head away.

"You alright?" asked Ginger. "You look a bit flushed."

"It must be the beer," she said, going redder than ever.

"My word, it doesn't take much drink to affect you."

She wished that Ginger would shut up. He was making her feel more embarrassed than ever.

After a while the young man got up and sauntered towards the door, turning and waving goodbye to her as he went.

Ginger, not missing a trick, looked at Margaret and said, "You fancy him?"

"He seems quite nice. What's his name?" she asked, feeling a little more relaxed, now that the young man had left the bar.

"Ricky, I think. Don't know much about him. I can always find out though."

She didn't say anything, just shrugged her shoulders and offered Ginger another drink.

On the way back to the ship, she was still thinking of Ricky. He was handsome, and had actually smiled and waved her goodbye.

"Well, here we are, back at the old ship," said Ginger, "Better go and get my shower and start on the turndowns before all my passengers get back from ashore. They'll all soon be screaming at once for something or other."

"I'll just stop and have a look at these stalls here on the quayside," answered Margaret. "I want to get my mum a Spanish doll. Thanks for a nice afternoon, Ginger. Hope to see you again soon."

"Goodbye Miss Margaret, and don't forget to bargain them down."

She turned around to a nearby stall and picked up a little doll. Her thoughts were still on Ricky.

---0---

Ginger stopped by his pantry on C deck, before making his way back to his cabin. He wanted to put a bottle of vodka away in his locker for a drink later on. Martha, an old stewardess in her late fifties, was sitting on one of the stools in the pantry.

"Been busy?" asked Ginger.

"No, just a few calls for a pot of tea." she answered, "apart from that it's been fairly quiet."

She was holding a cup of what looked like water. Her eyes looked very glazed, and her heavy makeup accentuated the wrinkled face.

"You okay?" inquired Ginger, "not drunk, I hope."

"What do you mean *drunk*?" she asked in an indignant tone. "Never touch the stuff." At that, she nearly fell off her stool. She sat herself back on it again, trying to place the cup on the bench she was leaning against. It fell over and the liquid spilled all over the flat top. The smell of neat gin oozed over the pantry.

"I'd get yourself off to bed if I was you. Give me twenty minutes and I'll be back to cover for you," said Ginger.

"Hic! What d'ye mean? Ye don't think I'm drunk?" Her voice was really beginning to slur now.

"Don't answer any bells until I get back. Do you hear, Martha?" Ginger left the pantry hurrying along the deck, when he bumped into Peter.

"You seem in a rush," said the bellboy.

"It's old Martha, she's bombed out of her mind. I'd better get down quickly and change. The silly bitch will only go and upset one of our passengers and then that's goodbye to our tips at the end of the cruise."

He then looked more closely at Peter, who did not seem his cheerful self.

"You okay, Peter?"

"Yeah, I suppose so," the boy replied."

"You don't sound very happy. Nothing wrong?"

"No, not really, just busy," Peter muttered. "That stupid old engineer keeps wanting something. The other day he even rang the Bureau asking for some writing paper. Too bloody lazy to get it himself. So you can guess who they sent up, can't you?"

Peter gave a hollow laugh. "Well, I'd better get on my way. See you later, Ginger. Best of luck with old Martha."

Peter went on his way, giving Ginger a thin smile.

CHAPTER 6

A few days later in the early hours of the morning, the *Ocean Star* moored outside the harbour of Freetown. It was the last port the liner called at before the week-long cruise to the West Indies. Margaret went up on deck for a few minutes before starting work.

She was leaning on the ship's rail, watching the quartermaster standing by the helm of the launch that was carrying passengers from ship to shore. The second engineer stepped into the first launch, and a few minutes later, another boat pulled alongside the ship, and the head barman did likewise.

Later that day, Margaret stepped into the launch herself, helped by one of the deck department. She could feel the sun beating down on her head and shoulders. She was glad when the boat started moving, stirring up a small breeze.

When it reached the quay, a shuttle bus was standing at the quayside, so she followed the rest of the passengers onto it, and into the town centre.

She felt rather disappointed wandering around, as it turned out to be a shanty-looking place – people with beautiful, ebony skin sat in the shade, flies swarming around them. Poverty seemed pervasive. Young boys with their big pitiful eyes offered to escort her around town, others begged for money. She decided not to stay too long and was glad when she got back to the safety of the ship.

At midnight Margaret was awoken by the grating sound of the anchor being raised, as the *Ocean Star* set sail for the Caribbean.

The atmosphere was hotter than ever down in the laundry, as the ship was sailing on the equator. Margaret noticed that all the officers and crew had already changed from their blue uniforms into whites.

She had heard from Tom, Eileen's boyfriend, how the passengers were getting themselves ready for the Crossing of the Line ceremony, one of the highlights of the cruise. About four different passengers would be chosen as King Neptune's prisoners. The ship's band would beat on the drums to the loud music and King Neptune and his assistants, who were in reality officers dressed in vivid coloured clothes, would march the passengers to the top deck. Each person would be escorted in turn to sit on a chair at the edge of the swimming pool. They would then be accused of having done outrageous things on board the ship. This would lead to having raw eggs cracked on the top of their heads, shaving foam painted all over their bodies, and a big cream cake pushed into their faces, followed by being thrown into the pool. The onlooking passengers would laugh and scream at the poor old culprits.

Below decks it was a different story. Greasers and engine room workers, and of course the laundry staff, would be sweating in over a hundred degrees Fahrenheit.

Margaret felt she could stand the heat no longer. The steam from the calender was burning her face. There was hardly any air coming through the vents. She had taken loads of salt tablets, but that didn't seem to make much difference. Freddy had insisted that his crew were given jugs of fruit juice to quench their thirst.

She looked at her watch. Another hour to go. Would she last? Looking at all the other laundry staff, she noticed how they were wiping the sweat from their foreheads, but still carrying on with their work. She felt like a slave from the old days. She liked being on a boat, but oh! If only she had a different job. The only consoling thought was that many people would give their right hand to be in her position. And it was worth it for the excitement of visiting different ports.

When the working day eventually finished Margaret went straight to her cabin and climbed up to her top bunk. The peace did not last more than a few minutes, as Kitty flung the door open.

"One of the officers having a cabin party tonight. You're invited."

"I don't think I'll have the strength," answered Margaret.

"It doesn't start till about nine. Have a kip and then you'll feel fine. I'll take you up there. By the way, don't tell the others or they'll get a cob on because they're not invited."

"Won't we be in trouble if we're caught up there?" inquired Margaret.

"No, I'll take you around the back way to their quarters. We must still wear our uniforms though."

Margaret gave it a thought. She wouldn't get much sleep even if she did have an early night. There would be Tom, Eileen's boyfriend, coming around for a drink after he finished second sitting. That would be about ten-thirty. Also there had been a party every night since Las Palmas, either in their cabin, or one nearby.

"Okay," decided Margaret, "I'll go."

---0---

Kitty took Margaret partly through the passenger accommodation then up the back spiral staircase, until they eventually came to a heavy fire door. This led through the officers' accommodation.

Margaret could hear music coming from one of the cabins. As they approached, they were greeted by a young man wearing an officer's uniform.

"Coming to the party?" he asked.

"Yes, we're invited," answered Kitty, naming an officer.

"Come on in then," he smiled.

The room was bigger than theirs, with a single bunk situated under the porthole. There were quite a few officers, all dressed in their white uniforms, their epaulets displaying distinctive gold bands. Most of them were standing and talking with refined accents. A couple of stewardesses were sitting on the bunk chatting to each other.

The young officer offered both the girls a drink, then, making polite conversation, asked Margaret how she liked working on board a ship. Margaret felt rather uncomfortable; it was as if he was looking down his nose at her. After a while she excused herself and went and sat beside the two stewardesses. Kitty was already chatting away with another officer.

"Mind if I join you?" she asked.

"No, move over Mary and let the girl sit here," said the younger on. "I'm Liz, and this is Mary."

"And I'm Margaret."

"I haven't seen you before," said Liz, "where do you work?"

"In the laundry," replied Margaret.

"Oh, a laundry maid. You look very young. I bet that's why the officers invited you up here. We both work in the nursery."

Margaret felt her face flush. *I'll just finish this drink, then see if Kitty will show me back to my quarters.* But before she had time to finish her drink, the young officer who had showed her and Kitty to the cabin, took her glass and started filling it up again.

"That's enough, thank you," she said, "I won't be staying too long."

"Really?" said the officer. "Why, you've only just arrived."

"I feel a bit tired," said Margaret. Even to her it sounded a weak excuse.

"Get this down you. It will help liven you up." At that he passed her a glass of beer, then walked away to offer somebody else a drink.

After a while Margaret was desperate to use the loo. She turned to Mary and whispered, "Excuse me, but is there a toilet around here?"

"If you want the loo," answered Mary, "there's one in the cabin here."

"I don't like using the one in the cabin," Margaret whispered again.

"Why not?" inquired Mary, looking surprised. "They're as good as the ones down below."

"I know, but I don't want them to hear me."

"Is something wrong?" asked an officer leaning over the three of them.

"It's Margaret here, she wants to go to the loo, but she's frightened of anybody hearing her having a piss," said Mary, shouting over the noise of people talking.

One second later the whole room fell silent, then everybody burst out laughing. Margaret wished could be anywhere else on earth but here.

A kind-looking older officer came to her rescue. "Don't worry, use my cabin. Just turn left from here, then right, and right again. It's on the opposite side to this one. I think it's the fourth door on the left, and it's unlocked."

Margaret thanked him and made her way out of the room. She had never felt so embarrassed in her life.

She eventually found her way and counted four doors. She slowly turned the handle; it was unlocked. She opened the door to find herself in a dimly lit cabin. To her surprise a very fat man in a dressing gown was standing by an open window with his back turned to her. He seemed to be pushing something through the porthole; something that looked a bit like a pair of feet. Before she had time to think, the man turned around and saw her.

"What do you want?" he snapped at her.

"I... I think I'm in the wrong cabin," she stuttered.

43

"You've no right to be in officers' quarters. What are you, a stewardess?"

"No, I… I work in the laundry."

"Laundry! Well, let me tell you something, Miss, if you tell even one person that you were up here in my cabin, I'll see the captain, and make sure you get instant dismissal from the ship. Do you hear me? Now get out of this room, immediately!"

Margaret scurried out the cabin, closing the door behind her. Shaking from head to toe, she found her way back to the party.

"Oh, there you are, did you manage to find my cabin alright?" asked the officer, with a kindly smile.

Margaret just nodded.

"Are you okay, my dear? You look a bit pale. Would you like another drink?"

"Could...could I have a whisky, please?"

"Going on the hard stuff now, eh?" he laughed.

Margaret accepted the glass and nearly drained it in one gulp. She just wanted to get back to her cabin.

At last she saw Kitty through a crowd of people, and made her way towards her.

"Kitty, could you please show me the way back, I don't feel very well."

Kitty looked at her as if to say, *why have I bothered bringing you to the party at all?*

"Okay, come on then, I'll show you back." She turned to the people whom she had been talking to. "I'll be back in a minute, just taking Maggie to her cabin."

When they left the room, Kitty turned to Margaret and said, "Remember not a word to any of them. They'll only get a cob on if they know where you've been."

She left Margaret by the toilets in the crew quarters, which Margaret made use of immediately. When she returned to her cabin, to her relief the other two girls were asleep. She quietly undressed and climbed into her bunk. She put out her sidelight and tried to get the tension out of her body. *At least she was back safely in bed.*

As the ship sailed on.

CHAPTER 7

It is a terrible thing when you have so much on your mind and nobody to talk to.

Margaret clambered out of her bunk the following morning with one dreadful thought above all others; *what if I lose my job?*

The shame of it.

How would she face her family and friends at home?

All because of that horrible man and his threat of instant dismissal! And from the look on his face, he really meant it.

"Come on, luv, are you going to stand at that fucking sink all day?" snapped Eileen. "I want to get a wash as well."

"There are other people in this bloody cabin, you know," butted in Chris.

Kitty was still fast asleep.

Margaret just looked at them, and got her uniform from the locker.

She was glad to get out of the cabin. They were an awful bunch of women. She decided to go to the crew mess. She needed a cup of tea before going below.

The mess man didn't greet her with his usual friendly smile.

"Hello, Tony," said Margaret, "You don't look very happy today. Suffering from a hangover?"

Her attempt at a joke fell flat. "Haven't you heard the news?" he asked.

Oh my God! she thought, *I bet it's about me. I bet that awful officer has told them about me being in the officers' accommodation. I've got the sack!* She could feel the tears welling up in her eyes.

"It's poor Peter, the bellboy."

"Peter?"

"Yes," continued Tony. "He's gone missing. The night steward went to call him this morning, but he wasn't in his bunk. They're searching the ship for him."

"Oh, I bet they'll find him somewhere," said Margaret with a forced brightness. At least it was not anything to do with last night.

She gulped down a cup of tea, then made her way down to the laundry.

When she entered the hot, damp room, Betty, Lil, Eve and Freddy were there already.

"I think they'll have to turn the ship around," Freddy was saying. "There's still no sign of him."

"Poor kid," said Eve, "I hope they find him alright."

But Peter was never found. The captain did turn the ship around, and after hours of searching for the boy, he was then declared as Missing Overboard. A short service for him was then scheduled for a few days' time in the ship's cinema, with all crew members expected to attend.

It was very quiet in the Pig that evening. Most people sat with sad faces, talking amongst themselves in hushed tones.

Ginger was in tears at his usual table, nursing a glass of vodka. He had spent most of the day being questioned about Peter by the chief purser and chief steward. When had he seen the boy last? Was Peter depressed? It had been question after question.

Ginger turned to Lola and a few of the other crew sitting at his table. "They almost accused me of having sex with him," he sobbed. "I might be queer, but by God, I'm not into young boys. I know he was a bit fed up, but we all get like that. I'm sure he wouldn't do anything stupid. He wasn't that type of person."

He drained his vodka in one go, then poured himself another large one. "I loved that kid, I took him under my wing. I was more like a mother to him." A tear fell into his glass. "If I ever find out that anybody's done anything to him, I'll kill the bastard!"

"Come on Ginger," said Lola, lifting his friend to his feet and steadying him as he swayed side to side. "I think it's time we got you to bed."

---0---

Another person was upset too.

The murderer.

Three days had gone by since the bellboy's death. And although nothing suspicious had been found, he was still worried.

Why had the stupid kid panicked when they were in the midst of making love? Surely the lad was getting as much pleasure as he was?

Things had been going so well, then suddenly the boy had begun sobbing and shouting, "Stop this! Stop! How can I face my mum and friends after all this? I'm just another queer like them I sit with in the Pig!"

The murderer grimaced. He'd had a sudden flash of anger at being left on such a high. So he'd put his hands around the boy's throat to quieten him. No pressure, really. None at all… it was only to shut the boy up… but then the bellboy had made a choking, rattling noise, and gone all limp.

He had slowly released his grip and shaken out the tension in his hands.

Was the boy dead?

There was no movement. No breath.

Blue lips.

What was he going to do? If a man in his position were ever to be found out, the consequences would be disastrous.

Then he noticed the partly open porthole.

Big enough for a man to go through…

49

The next thing was to lift the body up. It was heavier than he thought, but after a bit of manoeuvring he finally pushed it through the porthole.

Then suddenly there was a young woman standing behind him. A bloody laundry maid! *How the hell had she got into the room?*

He'd had the damn broken lock fixed! Hadn't he?

What had she seen?

And it was not just her. Had anybody seen the bellboy coming into his cabin? Had anybody heard him? And had anybody seen the body fall from his window? Even though the cabin was nearer to the aft-end of the ship, it was possible for any person standing on the open deck by the railings to have seen something. The ship was always lit up at night, with the reflection shining on the water.

And that steam queen. Had she seen him pushing the body out?

Bloody nosy woman!

Women at sea were loathsome at the best of times, but the laundry ones, they were nothing but sluts. Scum of the earth. How could the other officers entertain them? As officers, they were always told never to mix with the crew. Except for sex. Yes, like that bellboy, all they're good for.

But how to keep the bloody girl quiet?

What had she really seen?

Had he scared her enough not to tell anybody that she had even been in his cabin?

But knowing the crew, after a few drinks, they would open their big mouths to anybody willing to listen.

He gave a sudden cold shiver. Had she noticed the bellboy's shoes on the deck, and his clothes piled upon the chair by the bunk?

He shook his head. She was a laundry maid. A nobody. Her word would count for nothing against an officer's.

But what if it became a murder investigation?
The police wouldn't worry about any class distinction.
He frowned. Something had to be done to keep her quiet.
Whatever it took.
Even if it meant another murder.

CHAPTER 8

Margaret was leaning over the rails of the funnel deck watching the flying fish and also a school of dolphins following the ship. Watching the way the dolphins kept up with the speed of the ship fascinated her. She just hoped that they wouldn't get tangled with the propellers.

Freddy had told his staff during their lunch break that they need not bother starting work until four o'clock. It was fairly quiet in the laundry that day so they could have a bit more free time to themselves. Margaret decided to go and get some sun. She could have gone on the fo'c'sle head or well deck, which was for the crew, but decided to take advantage of the top deck. This was allocated to the stewardesses and laundry women, for sunbathing only.

There was a lovely breeze on deck that made her burn more with her fair skin. She had been warned that getting sunstroke or too burnt was a logging offence at sea. She wrapped her beach robe around herself, so as not to get any more sun on her body.

She was self-conscious about her freckles. They seemed to stick out a mile after being in the sun.

Chris and Eileen had come up with her to sunbathe, but had just gone down to their cabin to get a quick kip before turning to in the laundry.

Margaret had too much on her mind to be able to sleep. So much had happened over the last few days. What with going into that officer's cabin, and, worst of all, poor Peter the bellboy. Though she didn't know him very well, she had spoken to him on a couple of occasions. She couldn't get him out of her thoughts.

Another thing that bothered her was she could have sworn when she'd entered that cabin she had seen a pair of bare feet disappearing through the porthole.

What if they had been Peter's?

Who could she confide in? And would they think she had gone round the twist?

Yesterday in the mess room she had been sitting with Owd Rosie and had just summoned up the courage to confide in the older woman. Except that when she started, Owd Rosie stopped her with a raised hand. "You'll have to wait a minute, girl, but me gums are killing me." Then, to Margaret's horror, she took out her false teeth and laid them on the table.

Margaret took one look at them, grinning up at her, and nearly threw up.

"What's that were you saying again, Kid?" Owd Rosie mumbled through her gums.

"Oh," Margaret squeaked, "it's not that important." Then she made a hurried exit.

If anyone would listen to her concerns, it would be Ginger. But the only time she could get to see him was when he was in the Pig. She couldn't go to his pantry because officially she was not allowed in passenger accommodation. And in the Pig, he always sat next to somebody, usually one of the other feminine men.

Not to mention that he had been bombed out of his mind with drink lately.

Her thoughts seemed to be going around in circles, when suddenly a voice spoke in her ear. "Enjoying the sun?"

She spun around to see *him* standing there.

Ricky.

Her heart missed a beat.

"Just watching the dolphins," she heard herself say, as she felt her face flushing even redder.

"You look like you've caught the sun," he said. "Be careful not to get too burnt. Your freckles will show up more."

Trust him to notice her freckles. "I can't stand them," she said.

"Oh, I think they look nice."

She looked up into his face. He had lovely brown eyes, dark hair, and a deep tan that he must have acquired over the years of working on the open decks. He was carrying a paintbrush in one hand and a tin of white paint in the other.

"What's your name?" he asked. "I've seen you around a few times but never knew what to call you."

"Margaret," she whispered. "And you?"

Even though she already knew his name, she was not going to admit it to him.

"Ricky." He flashed a smile of even white teeth.

Margaret felt her heart beating faster. She was suddenly stuck for words.

"Fancy coming around for a drink tonight?" he asked.

"Where?"

He laughed. "My cabin, of course."

"I'm not allowed in the men's accommodation," she pointed out.

She didn't want another scene like last time.

"I'll tell you what, I'll get some beers and we can sit at the aft-end ."

Her face lit up. "Okay then, that'll be fine with me."

"Eight-thirty alright?"

She nodded. "Alright."

In a matter of minutes her whole life seemed to change. She forgot about the officer, even Peter.

All she could think of was of Ricky.

---0---

At eight-thirty that evening, Margaret stood on the poop deck. She wore a pretty blue cotton dress with her red hair hanging over her shoulders.

Ricky was standing over by the ship's railings, waiting. He called her over. He had set up two deck chairs overlooking the aft-end of the ship. There was an icebox filled with beer.

"So you managed to make it, eh?" He looked even more handsome, having changed from his working clothes into a red t-shirt and a pair of white shorts, showing off his tanned, well-shaped legs.

"Here's a beer," he said, as he prized a hole at each end of the can with a spanner. He had even brought her a glass. Usually at sea they drank straight from the can.

"Thank you," she said, sitting down in one of the chairs. The smell of salt in the air, and the taste of it on her lips made the evening feel romantic. It was dark by now and she could see the silvery moon shining on the white foam. It mingled with the deep blue sea which had been churned up by the propellers, falling on the smooth, black water.

Suddenly a shiver ran down her spine at the thought of Peter falling over the side.

"You okay?" asked Ricky sounding concerned.

"Oh, I'm fine, thank you. I suppose I was just thinking about poor Peter the bellboy falling over the side of the ship."

"Yes, it was very sad about him. Poor kid. Did you know him?"

"I only met him a couple of times. He seemed such a nice boy.

They both sat and chatted for a while. The few other crew members who were sitting over by the bollards eventually drifted away. In the end they had the deck to themselves.

Ricky poured Margaret another beer. "You always look like you're deep in thought," he joked. "A penny for them."

She looked deep into his eyes, and then began by saying, "I suppose I do, but I don't want to bore you with my problems."

"Go ahead. I'm a good listener," said Ricky with an understanding smile.

She began by telling him about the officers' party; how she went to the wrong cabin and how she saw this man with his back to her. She could have sworn she saw him push a pair of bare feet through the porthole, and how horribly he spoke to her when he swung around and saw her standing there.

"You see, Ricky, I'm wondering if that could have been Peter."

He gently took her glass and placed it on the deck, then put both of his hands over hers, holding them tight.

"Have you told anybody else this story?"

"No. You're the first person I have ever spoken to about it."

"Margaret, I know what you're saying sounds feasible, but will you please make me a promise?"

"Well yes, I suppose so."

"Don't mention a word about this to anybody. I can understand how you feel, but other people won't, and if that officer or the chief steward finds out you have been spreading rumours like that, they would fly you home immediately from the nearest port. Besides, from what I knew of Peter, he did seem a depressive sort of kid."

"I suppose you're right," she said.

"I am right, and if it's the officer I think it is, he's a nice chap when you get to know him. I bet he got a right shock when he turned around and saw you in his cabin." At this Ricky roared with laughter.

Margaret joined in with him, nervously at first, then more openly, as the funnier side of the situation became clearer.

"Now again, Margaret, I do beg of you not to mention another word over this to anyone. Besides, who will I have to take ashore if you're not here?"

57

Take her ashore? She could hardly believe her ears.

"I promise you, Ricky," she breathed. "I won't mention another word about it."

"Good girl!" He gently took her in his arms. Then he brought his lips to hers and gave her a kiss.

It was only brief, but Margaret thought her heart would explode.

As the ship sailed on.

CHAPTER 9

The *Ocean Star* was only a couple of days away from Trinidad, the most southerly island in the West Indies.

Margaret could sense the atmosphere of the Caribbean amongst most of the ship's crew. Record players could be heard from all areas of the crew's quarters – Harry Belafonte singing 'Island In The Sun', and other calypso music.

When she arrived at the Pig to meet Ricky, she found it was packed. The room was decorated throughout with synthetic palm trees. Arrangements of coloured lights shone dimly from the deck head and red and white chequered tablecloths adorned the tables.

Margaret went over to sit with Ricky and the deckhands. They had put a few tables together, making it the longest in the bar.

Eileen was sitting over with the waiters, jammed between Tom and Paddy. Lil, Betty, Rosie, and Chris sat with the laundry boys. A few of the stewardesses were also there.

A couple of waiters began strumming on their guitars, accompanying a waiter on the piano. They began to sing 'Jamaica Farewell'. The next was, 'Day-O'. At that all the deckhands, including some engine-room hands and greasers, who appeared to have already had too much rum and beer, started to join in. "DAY-O! Daaaaaaay-O, daylight's come and I wanna go home!" The singing was so loud that the waiters put down their guitars. Then the whole crew joined in.

Ginger was still drowning his sorrows over Peter, but even he managed to join in with some of the songs.

The singing was to last till the early hours of the following morning.

---0---

Tom had his arm around Eileen, when Mick the barman came into the Pig, and made his way over. He leaned over and whispered in Tom's ear. Tom excused himself and followed Mick out of the room. They found a place to stand where they could talk without having to shout over the singing.

Tom frowned. What did the man want this time?

"I've been looking for you everywhere, Tom, just to let you know everything's gone well. I'm going to pass the diamonds over to you tomorrow night. Eleven o'clock in my cabin, alright?"

"Alright," answered Tom. How he was going to get them off the ship? He still had no idea.

"Just make sure you look after the stones. Okay?"

"Yeah, I've got a safe place for them."

"You better had, or you know the consequences," said Mick, giving Tom a sinister look.

Tom did know the consequences. Many an unknown body was found in the River Mersey. Mind you, he wouldn't lose them. Look what he would gain when they were safely ashore the other end. Yes, it was worth the risk.

He made his way back into the Pig, where he had to push through a crowd of people standing in the doorway of the Crew Bar, and eventually managed to get seated again next to Eileen.

"Where the hell have you been to? You're missing all the fun. What did that snipe Mick want, anyhow?"

"Oh, nothing much to worry about. It was about a bottle of wine that one of my passengers ordered from the wine waiter. Anyway we've got it sorted out." At that he put his arm around her, gave her a kiss on the cheek and offered her another drink. Eileen seemed satisfied with his answer, and snuggled closer to him.

Paddy looked across with a questioning look.

Tom winked back.

---0---

The whole table was covered in empty beer cans. Even Margaret had drunk a few, and she was enjoying every minute of the singing. Especially she was enjoying being with Ricky. He was very attentive towards her, which made the evening all the better. She also discovered that he could sing, and later he told her that he played the guitar.

Life couldn't be better.

When the singing finally came to an end, old Alfie, a little Irish greaser, decided he wanted to give a song. The other men hushed the rest of the crowd while Alfie made his debut. He was just able to stand up without falling over. He was in his late fifties, skinny, with grey hair and a face that looked like a shrivelled prune. When he opened his mouth to start singing all that could be seen were a few dirty brown teeth, with big gaps in the gums.

He sang, 'I'll Take You Home Again, Kathleen', a song that had nothing to do with the Caribbean, but when he had finished the whole crew gave a loud clapping and cheering.

This then encouraged him to sing more songs.

After about another six, one of the other greasers came up to him and literally dragged him back to his seat.

"I think we'd better be going," said Ricky, turning towards Margaret. "Do you want to come back to my cabin for a quick drink?"

"Won't I get into trouble if I'm caught in your accommodation?" she asked.

"Nothing to worry about, I know Martin, the master-at-arms. He won't say anything."

"What about your cabin-mate, won't he mind?"

Ricky smiled, "Being a bosun I'm classed as a Petty Officer, so I have my own cabin. You are a funny girl, Margaret. You do make me laugh. Come on, you'll be okay with me."

A few minutes later they got up from the table to leave, only to be teased with, "We know where ya going!" Ricky laughed again, but Margaret felt herself going red with embarrassment.

He led her down the iron spiral stairs away from the Pig. They eventually ended up in crew accommodation, which belonged to the deckhands. He opened up a heavy fire door, which led to a small passage of cabins. His was the last one at the end. Ricky quietly opened the door and led her into his room. It was a small V-shaped cabin with a sidelight shining over a single bunk. There was a day bed underneath the porthole, which looked like a narrow settee, and beside it stood a table. Every movement of the ship could be felt, as the cabin was under the bow.

"Like a gin and tonic?" he asked, as he reached for the gin bottle.

"Just a small one, thanks. I think I've had enough with all the beer."

"One for the road." He flashed her one of his charming smiles.

She sat down, and Ricky passed her drink over, then he sat beside her and lifted his glass. "To us," he said.

"To us," she answered him back. They both took a sip of their drinks, then he took her glass and laid it on the table. He put his arms around her and began kissing her lips, his hands moved down towards her breast. He found the button of her blouse and started trying to unfasten it.

She slapped his hand away.

He jumped back with a look of surprise.

"I'm not that type of girl." she snapped.

"What, are you frigid or something?" He frowned. "You're not a lesbian?"

Margaret felt herself shaking "No, I'm not."

"Well, what's the problem then?"

The problem was that she didn't want to lose Ricky, but on the other hand she didn't want him to think she was cheap. It was the first time that he had made a real pass at her, apart from that brief kiss on the deck.

"I thought we liked each other, Margaret. It's natural for a man and woman to make love, you know."

"I know that, Ricky, and I do like you a lot, but I don't want to turn into a slut. I mean, look at most of the women on this ship, they'll go to bed with anyone who wears trousers."

"Does that mean you'll never sleep with me?"

"I… I don't really know. I've got to get to know you first."

Ricky scowled as he handed back her drink, then took a gulp of his own.

"Please Ricky, don't be annoyed, I do like you, but just give me time."

He looked at her again, and then seemed to have changed his mood. "Okay, Margaret, I suppose you're right. You're a decent kid. Certainly a change from the other women. I like that." He took her back into his arms and kissed her tenderly. "I'll tell you what. We're in Trinidad the day after tomorrow. Do you want to go ashore with me?"

This was not what Margaret expected; rather that it would have been the end of her romance with Ricky. "I'd love to," she replied with an enthusiastic smile.

"Right, meet me at the bottom of the gangway at four o'clock. We'll take a taxi to the Seamen's Mission, then I'll show you around the town of Trinidad, and maybe onto a night club. How does that sound?"

"Wonderful."

"Well, it's nearly three in the morning," he said, looking at his watch. "Time I got you back to your cabin. I won't see you tomorrow as I'm busy, and up early Wednesday morning to tie the ship up."

He led her from his cabin until they got to a big heavy door, which led through to the passenger accommodation.

The master-at-arms was standing by the door, giving Margaret a nasty start.

But Ricky was unfazed. "Evening, Martin," he said. "Can you do me a favour and let my friend through?"

"Yeah, no problem." Martin unlocked the door and gave Margaret a wink. "Don't tell anyone, or you'll get me shot."

"She won't," assured Ricky. "Don't forget, Martin, any time you want a beer, you know where my cabin is. There's always one in the ice bucket."

"Cheers, mate," Martin answered back.

Ricky left Margaret outside her cabin, gave her a quick kiss goodnight, and went back the way he had come.

Margaret hardly slept the few hours left. All she could think about was Ricky. When she did eventually drop off, it seemed immediately time to get up and get ready.

Outside the room she bumped into Betty, Lil, and Rosie, each of them carrying a white pillowslip filled with *dhobi* – or washing. Their milk-bottle coloured legs matched the linen.

"See you've got yourself boxed off, girl," said Eve, who still looked drunk from the night before.

"You mean Ricky?" exclaimed Margaret.

"Well, he was the only person you seemed moonstruck over last night. Yes, him."

Margaret looked at her then said in a proud voice, "Yes. I suppose you're right, I am."

"Watch yourself, girl," butted in Betty. "You know he's a married man?"

"Married?" She could hardly believe what she had just heard. "Are you sure?"

"Oh aye girl, of course I'm bloody sure, his wife has been on board a few times to meet him."

Margaret's heart dropped a mile. She could hardly hold back the tears. Why didn't he tell her? She must speak to him as soon as possible, and then she realised that she wouldn't be seeing him until late tomorrow afternoon.

She followed the three women to the laundry; her head held down.

CHAPTER 10

That evening, Mick was relaxing in his cabin. It was quite a big room, consisting of one bottom bunk, a large day bed, a table and a couple of chairs. It was situated on C deck at the aft-end of the ship.

There was a knock on his door.

"Who's there?" he asked suspiciously.

"Tom here," said a soft voice.

Mick unlocked the door and let Tom in. "Sit down," he instructed. "What's your poison?"

"Oh, just a beer will do me."

Mick took a beer from his ice bucket, opened it, took a clean glass from the shelf above and handed them over to Tom.

"Have you thought yet how you're going to get the diamonds off the ship?" He looked straight into Tom's eyes.

"Paddy and I have thought of a few ways to get them off in Liverpool, but we still haven't come up with anything positive yet." Tom took a gulp of his beer. "Don't worry, Mick, we will think of something. I promise you."

Mick took a sip of his brandy. "You had better think of something, these diamonds are worth thousands of pounds, and I don't want anything to go wrong. You understand?"

"I understand, Mick, and believe me, we won't let you down."

Mick stood up, went to his wardrobe and unlocked the door. He took a small black velvet pouch from one of his coat pockets, closed and locked the door again.

"The ball's in your court now. You lose them, or make any stupid mistakes, and you know the consequences."

"You can trust me, Mick," Tom replied.

Mick looked at Tom again. Could he trust him? At times he thought he was as thick as two short planks. What with that stupid laundry maid he was seeing, there must be a screw missing. Tom had a lovely looking wife at home and two young kids. How he could go with Eileen to replace her, God only knew. He himself always managed to get an attractive woman passenger for the trip. One could satisfy one's needs without having to get involved with any stewardesses or laundry maids.

He also knew that a lot of the crew would get a dose, especially with all the beautiful women in Rio. The men would all be lined up at the doctor's after a week or two. They would each be given an injection, and hopefully by the time they got back to England, everything would have cleared up for when they met their wives.

Anyhow as long as Tom and Paddy got those jewels off the other end safely, that was all that mattered right now. They would get some money out of it, but not half as much as he would. In addition, his contact in England had given some money towards the scheme so they could get enough diamonds, which would make it more worthwhile.

"Well, Tom, I've got to go back to the bar and see if everything's okay. Make sure that none of my staff has done a disappearing act."

Both men stood up, and he escorted Tom to the door.

"Put them in a safe place immediately," said Mick in a low voice, as he was closing the door behind him.

On his way to the bar, Mick took a moment to lean on the ship's rail. The silvery moon shone brightly on the black, calm water.

Tomorrow they would be in Trinidad.

---0---

68

Margaret had been unable to sleep all night, and now her luminous watch said it was four-thirty in the morning.

There was the sound of the anchor lowering into the water. They must have made landfall at Port of Spain, Trinidad.

Her Ricky would be on deck, bringing the ship into port.

Her Ricky!

Why was she daft enough to think of him as that? He was a married man. She had no right to him. If only she could have seen him before going ashore this afternoon. She wanted to tell him that it was all over between them. She could have gone down to see him if he was in his cabin, but knowing herself she would have lost her way, and felt foolish asking someone where he lived.

Yesterday, working in the laundry, she thought the day would never end, and now, when she should be feeling excited at the thought of being in the Caribbean, she just wanted to cry.

Life just wasn't fair.

She had met the man of her dreams, and they would have had a wonderful time ashore.

If only he hadn't been married.

Later that morning she was folding a damp, hot sheet with Owd Rosie.

"Going ashore today, girl?"

"Yes," answered Margaret, forcing a smile. "Ricky is meeting me at four o'clock and taking me for a drink. I think we're going to the Seamen's Mission."

"I might just have a walk on the quayside and see what they're selling on them stalls," said Owd Rosie. "Want to come with me? It'll only be for a few minutes."

"Okay Rosie, I'll pop down with you."

Freddy Brown let his staff finish at noon that day, so they could spend more time ashore. After lunch Margaret and Owd Rosie descended the gangway. There were lots of colourful stalls, selling bongo drums, coconuts with faces carved all over them, beads, and many pretty dresses. A steel band was playing in the background.

Even though Ricky's marriage was like a thorn in her side, there was still a tinge of excitement in Margaret's heart. She had never seen anything like all this before. She was handling some beads made of shell when a hand tapped her shoulder. She turned around and her heart missed a beat. It was Ricky.

"Hi, enjoying yourself?" he asked.

"Yes, yes, thank you," she could feel her voice going hoarse.

"I've been looking everywhere for you, Margaret. Can you make it four-thirty at the bottom of the gangway?"

"Yes." That was all that would come out of her mouth.

"Good! See you then."

She watched him turn away. He even looked lovely from the back, with his broad shoulders and long tanned legs.

Margaret went over to Owd Rosie, who was browsing through a few things on one of the stalls. "I'm going back to my cabin now. I want an hour's kip before going out. See you later."

At four-thirty on the dot, Margaret stood at the bottom of the gangway. Ricky was waiting for her. He put his arms around her waist and escorted her to a taxi. She was wearing her favourite pale green minidress, which she knew would show off her well-shaped legs. Her hair hung over her shoulders and she felt that she looked nice. In fact she felt even better when a young native boy came up to Ricky and asked, "Is this your lady?"

Ricky looked at the boy and said, "Yes."

"She is beautiful," replied the lad, gazing up at Margaret.

When they both got into a taxi, she noticed that the little boy was still gazing in their direction as the taxi drove away.

They reached the Seamen's Mission and went into the bar for a drink, then ventured outside to sit by the swimming pool.

"This is the life, isn't it, Margaret?" said Ricky, sipping at an ice-cold beer.

"Yes," said Margaret, who was drinking a piña colada.

"You don't look very happy. Something up?" he asked.

"Well yes, there is." Margaret looked straight into his eyes. "I believe that you're a married man."

Ricky looked taken aback for the moment, and then put down his drink. "Yes, Margaret, I am."

Her heart dropped again. She was hoping he would say that he wasn't married, that it had all been a mistake; the woman had got it wrong. She said in a trembling voice, "I'm sorry, Ricky, I can't see you again, I don't go out with married men."

"Margaret, I never told anybody this before, and promise me that you won't say a word of what I'm about to tell you now?"

He looked so sincere that Margaret said, "Okay, I promise."

"Well, my wife and I are putting in for a divorce. You see, Margaret, she never did really understand me. We have had so many arguments over the years, and also I'm sure she has got herself a lover while I'm away from home." He hung his head down as if he was about to cry. "Please, Margaret, don't repeat what I have said. You're the only one who really knows. Please trust me."

She looked at Ricky, one part of her heart gave a sigh of relief, and the other felt sorry for this man. "I won't say anything, Ricky. I do trust you."

His face seemed to light up. "Will you still see me, now that you know the truth?"

"Well, now that I know that it is over with you and your wife, and you are going to divorce her, yes Ricky I will see you again."

He put his hands on her cheeks, drew her close and kissed her lips. "Margaret, you will never know how happy you've made me. I think we're in for a lovely evening."

It did turn out to be one of the best nights Margaret had ever known.

One she thought she might remember for the rest of her life.

71

They walked through the streets of Trinidad holding hands. Someone was playing Louis Armstrong's 'What a Wonderful World'.

How perfect! she thought, as she squeezed his hand.

Ricky bought a coconut from one of the locals selling them in the street. It was cut open with a large knife and they both drank the juice from the shell.

Later as the night drew darker, Ricky took her to a little restaurant with calypso music playing softly in the background, then on to a nightclub where they danced the night away to a steel band. The last piece of music played was, 'This is a Lovely Way to Spend an Evening'.

That was when they were dancing cheek to cheek, and Ricky whispered in her ear, "I love you".

CHAPTER 11

Barbados was the next port of call for the *Ocean Star*, and it was also linen change for the bedroom stewards.

All along B-deck alleyway, Ginger had neatly hung clean sheets and pillowcases over the rails outside each passenger's cabin.

At quarter to seven that morning, he was pacing up and down waiting for them to get out of their rooms, so he could go in and change the beds. A couple of cabins had 'DO NOT DISTURB' cards on their doors. He could hear others moving in the rooms. Old Martha had already been around with cups of tea.

Thank goodness nobody had ordered breakfast in bed that morning, In addition, out of his twenty cabins, he only had four second sittings.

The gong sounded over the Tannoy for first sitting breakfast. Out popped a couple of passengers from their cabins, followed by more people heeding the call. As each passenger opened his or her door, a little piece of folded white paper fell onto the deck. Ginger would slip them in between the doors, so he could tell if they had gone out.

"Morning Ginger," said one of his passengers, as he locked up his room. "What time do we get to Barbados?"

"Good morning, sir," answered Ginger. "I think we should be docked for about eight o'clock. Going on one of the ship's tours?"

"Well, seeing we're in this port for two days, we're going on a tour around the island, and tomorrow we'll have a look around Bridgetown, then go swimming. What beach do you recommend?"

"There's a lot to choose from," said Ginger. "The Hilton Hotel has one that's very nice but quite windy, or you could go in the other direction to Sandy Lane. Don't forget though, if you do take a taxi, bargain them down. You shouldn't accept the first price they offer you. I'm sure wherever you go, you'll enjoy the beach. You can't go wrong around here."

As soon as the passenger had gone, Ginger dived into his room and began stripping the beds. He was still thinking about Peter. He had gone over it a thousand times in his head, he was certain that the lad hadn't thrown himself over the side. The captain had put it down to misadventure at sea, an easy way out for the company.

Ginger was sure that Peter had been murdered.

If he ever found out that he was right, God help the culprit.

Another thought had also struck him. He had forgotten all about Tom and Paddy, discussing something about diamonds at the beginning of the trip. He had been so upset over Peter that he had not given it another thought.

He had better keep his eyes open a bit more.

About noon, Ginger finished all his cabins, bar one. Old Martha said that she would cover the rest of his work that day, if Ginger did the same for her the following day.

He made his way towards the Pig for a quick beer before having his lunch and then popping ashore. Going along the working alleyway, he bumped into Margaret wearing a t-shirt, shorts and carrying a bag with a towel bulging out of the top of it.

"Hello, Miss Margaret, how are you keeping these days?"

Her face looked all aglow. "I'm off to Paradise Beach with Eileen, Chris, and some of the laundry boys. Ricky has to work today, so I thought I would go for a swim."

"Mm, Paradise Beach. You know what, Miss Margaret? I might go there myself today. Maybe I'll see you later."

"I'll look out for you, Ginger," she laughed, as she carried on her way.

So the rumour was right. Margaret was going out with Ricky.

74

---0---

Margaret met the rest of the crowd at the bottom of the gangway. The heat hit her the minute she left the air-conditioned part of the ship. It was like stepping into an oven. The temperature must have been over 90 degrees Fahrenheit. She could feel the sun on her back.

"Come on, Maggie, you old slow coach," laughed Billy, "we've been waiting ages for you." They walked to the end of the quay to get a taxi.

"How are we all going to fit in?" asked Margaret, laughing.

"Offer them enough money and they'll take us," said Johnny.

A taxi pulled up, and after a bit of bargaining, the driver decided to accept the six of them. Eileen and Chris sat by the driver. The three boys sat in the back, with Margaret on Johnny's knee. They all began laughing and joking amongst themselves.

"You been drinking rum?" asked the driver laughing along with them. "We have lots of rum, man, in Barbados. You must try it."

"We might try some when we get to the beach," answered Joe.

"Is there water-skiing there?" enquired Margaret.

"Sure is, lady, we have everything on this island, including some good women for you men."

That remark made everyone laugh all the more, all the way to Paradise Beach.

Margaret looked out of the window. It all seemed out of this world – beautiful white sands and gorgeous, turquoise water. There were quite a few people on the beach, many of them swimming, and also one or two water-skiing. Some local women in colourful dresses, vivid against their skin, were selling their wares.

"Come on, girls, we'll sit over here," said Johnny, taking the lead.

They laid out their towels, and began rubbing suntan lotion over their bodies.

"This is the life," said Billy, lying on his back with the sun beating down on his white body.

Eileen looked at the rest of them. "I don't know about you lot, but I could do with a bloody drink."

"Don't fret, don't frown, Joe won't let you down." Joe then produced a bottle of rum from his bag, and a few cans of cola.

"Now you're talking," said Chris, sitting up.

"Where did you get that from?" asked Johnny.

"Oh, I bought it on the quayside before you lot turned up, and I remembered to bring some plastic cups, which I whipped from the crew mess."

"And I got the pantry man to make us some sarnies," butted in Eileen.

"Well, Joe, what are you waiting for? Start pouring out the drink," demanded Chris, as she looked in her bag for a cigarette.

"I think I'll go for a swim first," said Margaret, standing up. "Also I want to see how much the water-skiing is. I've always wanted to have a go."

"You must be bloody mad, Maggie," said Eileen. "You wouldn't catch me on one of them, and anyway it's shark-infested water."

"They don't usually come up near the water's edge," said Johnny, holding out his cup to Joe, who began pouring out the rum. "Anyhow I'll be going in for a swim myself."

Margaret stood up and ran towards the water. She put her foot in to test the temperature; to her surprise it was lovely and warm. She dived in and began swimming. It was simply heaven. The sea was crystal clear; she could even see the white sand reflected through the water. After a while Johnny, Joe and Billy joined her, and they all splashed around in the shallows.

A few minutes later, Margaret decided to go for a swim and struck out into deeper water.

She was just getting into her stride, when there was a sudden tug on her leg, together with a sharp pain.

Margaret screamed and thrashed in the water.

Then there was raucous laughter from behind, and she turned round. Johnny was treading water behind her, holding his hands up, crooked like claws and grinning from ear to ear. "That scream was priceless!" he said.

"You stupid thing," she laughed, "I thought a shark had got me."

"Screaming like that it would." He became more serious. "You do know if you do come across a shark, stay still; if you start splashing it only attracts them more."

"Also," added Joe, swimming up beside Johnny, "if ever one does come near you, just punch him on the nose."

"And how many rums have you had, Joe?" asked Margaret. "I know what I would do, swim for my life."

"Seriously," said Johnny as they headed back to the shallows, "you should keep still. Then the shark might get bored and bugger off."

After fifteen minutes of splashing around, they all decided to go and do some more sunbathing.

"I'm going to find out about water-skiing," said Margaret. "I'll be back later."

There were quite a few people waiting for speedboats, pedal boats and water-skiing. It was ten Barbados dollars for half an hour. Margaret booked her turn, and was told that she would have to wait about thirty minutes.

"I'll go back and get some money," she told the man who was running the water sports.

When she returned to the others they had already gone through half a bottle of rum.

"Here you are, Maggie," said Johnny handing her a cup. "Some rum and Coke left for you."

Margaret took it. "I think I'll need this for Dutch courage." She drank it all, and then about twenty minutes later, returned to the place where they had the water sports. Some more crew had come to the beach.

"Lean forward when you feel you're being pulled by the rope," said one of the men steadying her as she sat in the water with a ski on each foot. A young boy grinned at her from the driving seat.

A minute later the boat set off and Margaret went flying forward, splashing into the sea.

After about three attempts she finally got her balance, and off they went. Even though they were going slowly, Margaret's legs were bent and her body with it.

As they headed out to sea, Margaret began to enjoy the air rushing past, and the sun on her back.

I can do this!

She stood taller, and the boy driver turned and grinned. He waved, then Margaret felt a pull on the rope as the boat sped up. Now there was a real wake flowing out from the engine.

After a minute or so, Margaret felt even more confident. She tried a little weave from one side of the wake to the other. With a lean into the turn, she went back again. And again.

That was fun! Now let's try a wider turn…

But this was too much, too soon.

Margaret lost her balance and cartwheeled shrieking into the sea, losing both skis as she fell.

Once she got her head above the waves and had her breath back, she trod water, looking around for the boat.

It was heading away, back towards the beach.

She frowned. Surely it would turn back? Had the boy not realised she had fallen?

She raised her hand and shouted, but instead of turning, the boat kept heading away.

Leaving her in the water.

Alone in the open sea.

In shark-infested water.

Margaret took stock of her situation. She could hardly see the beach. There was nobody around, no boats, nothing but sea.

Her only chance was to try to swim back to the mainland, but would she ever make it?

One of the skis bobbed up close by and she swam over and grabbed it.

If I use it as a float, maybe I can make it to the shore.

But it was not long before her legs started to feel like they were made of lead, and she could hardly get her breath.

A wave broke in her face, leaving her coughing and spluttering.

For some reason this brought her back to swimming lessons when she was a girl. Mr. Andrews, the swimming instructor, leaning over the side as she floundered with tiredness after a long lesson.

"Whatever situation you're in, never panic. Once you panic, you're as good as finished. Just lie on your back and catch your breath." So, still clinging at the ski, that is exactly what she did.

Maybe after a rest, she could swim some more?

Or perhaps if she kept still, the current would wash her to shore?

Unless it was going the other way – out to sea?

So which direction was she going?

Margaret looked up, trying to see if the shoreline was getting closer or further away.

That was when her heart nearly stopped.

There was a grey, triangular fin circling a few yards away.

Fighting the urge to scream and thrash in the water, she watched in horror as it moved lazily around her.

CHAPTER 12

The beach had filled up with more people and other crew members had arrived. Ginger and Lola got out of the taxi and paid the driver.

"I suggest that we make for the nearest bar, Ginger," said Lola, straightening his hair. "There's one over there."

They managed to find a couple of seats, and ordered two rum and Cokes.

"Are you going to be in the Drag Extravaganza this year, Ginger? I think Delores is going to write *Cinderfella*. I want to be Cinderfella." He threw back his head in a theatrical way.

"Personally, I think one of the ugly sisters would suit you."

"Thank you, DEAR!" retorted Lola with a pout." Speak for yourself."

"Anyway," said Ginger, "I haven't decided yet."

"You're not still moping about Peter, are you? I think if you dressed up and joined in the spirit of things, it would help to take your mind off him."

Ginger looked towards the sea. "I suppose you're right, maybe I will." He watched Margaret setting off on her water skis.

"She looks like she's having a good time."

"Who?" asked Lola, sipping his drink.

"Miss Margaret, you know she's boxed off with Ricky, the bosun."

"Oh him."

"What do you mean, oh him?"

"Well dear, I suppose he's rather dishy, but I wouldn't trust him as far as I could spit."

"What do you mean by that?" demanded Ginger.

"Oh nothing really," said Lola, shrugging his shoulders.

"Don't tell me you fancy him," said Ginger with a laugh.

They both ordered another drink, then Ginger frowned, staring across the beach.

"What is it?" asked Lola.

"Isn't that boat that was tugging Margaret?" Ginger said. "I recognise the colour, and the boy driving. It's come back without her. There's some old bloke talking to the boy, and now there's some other person sitting in the water with his skis on ready to take off."

Ginger stood up. "My God! He's left the girl out there on her own!" He immediately jumped up from the bar with Lola following behind, and went running over to the older man.

"What's happened to that red-headed girl the young lad took out earlier? He's never brought her back. She's still stuck out there."

"Oh, Sammy said that an older man was going to pick her up in his own boat. Something about being his niece and he was doing it for a joke."

The owner of the boats started laughing. "I bet she got a shock when Sammy didn't turn back for her."

"Joke!" shouted Ginger. "You call that a joke?"

"Sammy, come over here," ordered the older man.

The young lad jumped out of the boat, and waded ashore.

"Tell this man what you told me."

The young boy looked up at Ginger with big brown eyes.

"A big fat Englishman came up to me and told me to take the lady out as far as I could, go fast then she would fall. He said it was a big joke, and he had his own speedboat. He said he would pick her up himself. It was his niece." I said, 'What a about the water skis, man, Don't lose them.' He said, 'Don't worry I'll get them back safely to you.' Look! He gave me ten-pound English." The boy gave a wide grin and held up the note.

"You didn't mention money to me," said the owner, and snatched it from the boy's hand.

The young boy burst out crying.

"Never mind the money," cried Ginger, "get that fucking boat out at once and pick the girl up. And we're coming with you this time."

Ginger and Lola took off their shoes, and waded out to the boat and climbed in. This time it was the older man who did the driving. The boat started up with a roar, and sped off in the direction of where it had left Margaret.

"Shit!" screamed Ginger, "there's a shark closing in on her! Go faster, man!"

The boat circled Margaret, causing a wave as the driver throttled back. The shark fin turned and headed out to sea, before disappearing under the waves.

Margaret was floating on her back clutching a water ski, with her eyes closed and her lips blue.

"My God!" Lola gasped with his hands over his mouth. "She's dead!"

CHAPTER 13

"Dead!" repeated Ginger. *Oh no! We're too late!*

They all peered down at Margaret.

She floated, white has a ghost, her red hair spread out around her head.

"What are we going to do now?" asked Lola. "I suppose we will have to take her body back to the ship."

"She seemed such a nice girl," said Ginger. "Poor Margaret. What a way to go."

He turned towards the owner of the boat. "You had better give us a hand getting her body out of the water."

The man made his way to the aft of the vessel and began leaning over the side to lift Margaret out. Suddenly, she let out a piercing scream, and began swimming frantically; her arms and legs flying in all directions. "Ahhhh! Shark!" she screamed. "Shark! Help!"

"She's alive!" cried Lola.

"There's no shark," shouted the driver, "we scared it away."

"She must have thought we were one," said Ginger, in a relieved voice. "Don't worry, Miss Margaret," he said leaning over the side of the boat. "There's no more sharks, you're safe now, and we're here." He grabbed her arm and helped to lift her on board. She was shaking and groaning, and fell into Ginger's arms. He took off his t-shirt and pulled it over her head. "Come on, Miss Margaret, there's nothing more to worry about. You're safe with us now."

Margaret looked up at him, her face still white, and in a shaky voice, said, "Thanks, Ginger, thanks a million. I thought I was going to die."

Then another voice came from the sea; one with an American accent. "Hey, what about me?"

They all turned to look, and to Ginger's amazement there was a man's head in the water with two ski tips in front of him. He must have been skiing behind them all this time.

"It's sure was the best ski ride I've ever had," said the man, as they helped him into the boat with his skis. "That was the fastest I've ever been."

---0---

The motorboat's engine stopped as it neared the edge of the shore and a local boy held the bow steady while the four passengers climbed out. Ginger lifted Margaret from the boat. He could feel her still shaking.

"I think the best thing for you, young lady, is to have a stiff brandy."

"But… but… I don't really drink the stuff."

"No buts," said Ginger in a firm voice, "you're having one." He turned to Lola, "Go and get her gear, and by the way don't say a word to the others, just tell them she fell off the skis and decided to have a drink with us. Okay?"

"Okay," nodded Lola, "But honestly, dear, the whole ship will know about it within a few hours."

"That's why I don't want you to say anything," snapped Ginger.

"Don't be a crosspatch. I won't do if you feel so strongly about it," answered Lola. "Anyway, where are they sitting?"

"Over there," pointed Margaret. "You can see Eileen talking to Chris."

Ginger led Margaret over to the bar and sat her in a basket chair by an empty table. He called over the waiter and ordered a double brandy and two rum and Cokes with plenty of ice.

Margaret looked at Ginger. "I thought I was going to die. When I saw that shark's fin, I just froze. I think I might have had a blackout. I just kept my eyes closed and I suppose when the boat pulled up alongside me I thought the shark was coming for me."

The waiter came with the drinks and Ginger handed Margaret her brandy. "Take a good sip of this and I'm sure it will make you feel better." He then began telling her the story of what the young local boy had told him. "Now, Miss Margaret, do you have friends that live here, or somebody that would play a trick on you like that?"

"I don't know anyone, it's the first time in my life I've ever been to Barbados."

"Do you have any real enemies on the ship, maybe somebody that wants to get rid of you?"

"No," she said, taking another sip of her brandy. "I'll admit I don't get on with everyone. The women are nasty to me sometimes, but I'm sure they wouldn't go that far. Maybe the boy was right and that man got me muddled up with his niece."

"Well, if he did," said Ginger, "surely another boat would have come out for you."

Margaret looked at him in horror. "You're not saying that somebody's trying to murder me?"

Ginger could see that she was getting all het up again. He was about to change the subject when Lola returned.

"Here are your things, Maggie. I told the others that you would be staying with us."

"What did they say?" asked Ginger.

"Chris got a cob on, saying you went with them and should go back with them, and Eileen said that she told her she was stupid to try water-skiing and the boys just laughed. They thought it was funny."

"I wonder what Ricky will say?" said Margaret who was looking a little more relaxed from the brandy. "I hope I get more sympathy from him."

"Margaret," Ginger turned to her. "Don't mention a thing to Ricky. Just tell him what Lola told the others, that you just fell off the skis and maybe that you thought you saw a shark, and that's what made you feel upset."

"But I did see a shark," protested Margaret.

"I know, but not a word about that fellow, or us coming out to rescue you. Please, Miss Margaret, promise me."

"Alright, I promise," she said reluctantly. "Maybe I'd better go back to the others, or they'll think I'm making a fuss over nothing."

"Will you be alright? asked Ginger. "Lola and I don't mind taking you back to the ship."

"You know something, I feel much better now," she said finishing the last drop of brandy in her glass. "I'll go and lie in the sun for a while, it seems such a shame to waste such a sunny day. I'm sure a kip will do me good."

"Well, don't you back go into the water again today, and be careful with your drink," he warned her.

Margaret stood up and picked up her belongings. "Thanks for all your help, Ginger, I do appreciate everything you've done for me, and I promise you I won't mention anything about that man, or you and Lola picking me up. See you later."

When she was out of earshot, Lola turned to Ginger. "Why all the fuss about her not mentioning what had happened to her?"

"I don't like what happened, Lola," said Ginger in a low voice. "That was no joke. I'm sure somebody was out to get her."

"Who would want to do a laundry maid in? For heaven's sake, Ginger, you're just being imaginative."

"Oh yes, and who would want to do a bellboy in?"

"How do you know Peter was done in?" asked Lola, taking a cigarette out of his packet. "It could have been suicide. After all he was always feeling depressed."

"I don't care what anybody says," persisted Ginger, "I still think he was murdered. And the same person could be trying to murder Margaret as well.

"What has Maggie got to do with a bellboy, Ginger? She hardly knew him."

Ginger finished his drink. Maybe Margaret knew something that he didn't.

---0---

Margaret found her way back to the laundry crowd. They were rather high-spirited, after all the rum they had drunk.

"I've changed my mind and decided to stay with you lot," she said, placing her towel on the sand.

"We thought we weren't good enough for you," said Eileen, in an aggressive voice. "Anyway, what happened to you? Lola said something about you seeing a shark. I told you not to go fucking water skiing."

"Okay, Eileen, shut up and let the girl speak," said Johnny.

"Well," carried on Margaret, "they took me way out to sea, and then I fell off." She stopped herself saying that the boat left her alone in the water. "When I suddenly saw a shark. I remembered your words, Johnny, not to splash around because it would attract the shark."

"Maggie must be the only person who has ever bothered to listen to you, Johnny," said Billy, rolling over on the sand with laughter. "I know what I would have done, swum for my life."

They all joined in with the laughter, including Margaret.

"Anyhow, she's here to tell the story," said Johnny. "I'll admit though that if it had been me, I'd actually have done the same as you, Billy."

They all laughed louder.

"And did it get you?" asked Chris, looking concerned.

"Well, they're the best false arms and legs I've seen yet if it did," giggled Billy.

Margaret knew she wasn't going to get much sense out of them. "The boat came back and picked me up before the shark got me."

"The fuss Lola made," said Chris, brushing the sand off her legs, "we thought you were bloody dying. Anyhow, are we all going for another drink, or what?"

"I think I'll just lie down here and sunbathe a bit," said Margaret, feeling quite light-headed after the double brandy.

"We might not be back," warned Eileen. "I'm hoping my feller will take me out tonight, so I don't want to be late. Is Ricky taking you ashore?"

"No," answered Margaret. "He's on duty, but he's going to take me to the Hilton tomorrow night."

"The Hilton?" mimicked Eileen. "We are posh now." They all got up to leave.

"I'll stay with her," said Johnny. "I want to try and get a good tan."

They both lay on the beach for about an hour. Margaret fell asleep while Johnny kept jumping up for a swim.

A little while later more crew members joined them. They were waiters who had finished the second lunch sitting, and had the rest of the day to themselves.

"Coming for a swim, Maggie?" asked one of them when she had just woken up.

She was going to explain about the shark, and how she had been in a state of shock, when one of them grabbed hold of her and carried her towards the sea. She screamed, but it was too late. He threw her in.

When she looked around, there were more crew. They were on each other's backs trying to throw each other in the water. The person who stayed on the longest without being thrown off was the winner.

"Come on, Maggie, get on my shoulders," cried Johnny, "we'll see how many we can knock off."

Here was an opportunity to forget about the shark for a while. Margaret, jumped onto Johnny's shoulders and gave a hearty shove to one of the stewardesses.

CHAPTER 14

Time seemed to fly by, and before long the sun was setting. It was one of the loveliest things Margaret had ever seen. The deep pink from the sky reflected onto the water, and the dark silhouette of the palm trees gave the island a peaceful look.

"Do you want to come with us for a drink, Maggie?" asked Charlie, one of the five waiters who were still left. "We'll go to a bar near the town."

"I'd like to see what it's like around Bridgetown," she answered.

"I won't be going," said Johnny, "I want to get back to the ship now."

"Oh," exclaimed Margaret. "Maybe I shouldn't go either. It has been quite a day. I think I ought to go back with you."

"Don't bother about me," said Johnny. "You'll be alright with Charlie and the boys."

"Yeah, we'll look after you, Maggie, you'll be okay with us."

It was agreed that they would find a place to get a drink, and Charlie hailed a taxi.

"We want a bar, driver," he said, dragging Margaret into the cab. The others piled in after them. "And make it a good one."

A few minutes later it pulled into Nelson Street, Bridgetown, and stopped by a bar displaying red fluorescent lighting. They all got out of the taxi and Charlie paid the driver.

It was an old wooden building that had stairs leading to the top floor. As she entered the dimly lit room, she also noticed an older plump woman with a scarf tied around her hair sitting on a chair by another door.

In the corner, on the far side of the room, stood a jukebox, and a few young local girls were dancing around it.

"What are you drinking?" shouted Charlie over to Margaret.

"A beer, please," she called back.

"Find a seat and I'll be with you all in a minute."

He joined them at the table and handed out the drinks. The beer she ordered turned out to be a rum and Coke. She did not like to say anything and just took it from him.

"Want a dance?" asked another waiter.

They walked over to the small dance floor, and the two of them began to jive. Margaret could see the young girls glaring at her. She soon forgot about them and danced to the music. She knew she was good at jiving, and so was her partner. Once the music had stopped, the waiters started clapping them, and then another one asked her up.

After leaving the floor exhausted, she managed to sit down and finish her drink, only to be presented with another rum and Coke.

More crew members had come to the bar and the room was getting fuller. They would chat up one of the young girls, then go on the floor for a smoochy dance, and after a while take their partner to the older woman sitting by the door. Then they would pay her some money, take the girl's hand and lead them up the stairs.

Margaret was about to ask Charlie what was going on, when there were raised voices at the table.

"I'm telling you," said one, an Irish waiter called Patrick, "that horse did win the race."

"And I'm telling you he didn't," shouted the other, an older waiter called Dick.

"I bet you what you want, I'm right. You're wrong."

A second later Dick punched the Irishman in the jaw. Patrick stood up and upturned the table, sending all the glasses and bottles crashing to the floor.

A chair was thrown into the air, just missing Margaret.

A space cleared, leaving Patrick and Dick punching away at each other until they both ended up rolling over the floor together. Margaret ran over to them.

"Stop it! The pair of you."

"Hey whack, are you fucking stupid or something?" cried Charlie, dragging her away from the two men.

A couple of enormous bouncers came on the scene and split the two men up.

"Out of here! Do you hear?" shouted one of the bouncers, picking Dick and Patrick up by the scruffs of their necks, as if they were no heavier than a pair of cats. "You lot as well," he said, nodding over to Margaret, Charlie and the other waiters. "Out!"

The six of them were pushed through the door, leading to the outside stair.

When they were back on the street again, the argument was soon forgotten and they all started laughing.

"You're pissed as a fart, Maggie," joked Charlie.

"Fancy you trying to split up old Paddy and Dick," laughed one of the waiters.

"We'll have to call you the karate girl."

"Where do we go now?" someone asked.

"I know, whack, let's try Harry's Bar."

"Where 'ith 'at?" asked Margaret, then felt she needed try and clarify. Concentrating hard, she said, "I meansh, where – is – that?

"Just follow old Charlie. He'll know the way."

Harry's Bar turned out to be a bigger dive than the earlier one, and filled with more people. The women were of various age groups, and they were the ones who seemed to be chatting up the men. One woman seated in a dark corner was fondling a man's trousers. Another couple were on the floor dancing, their tongues practically down each other's throats.

Margaret wondered why the room kept spinning round, and dropped heavily into a chair.

"Here you are, whack," said Charlie passing a drink over to her.

"Now this is what I call a good bar," said Patrick looking around the room. "I might try one of them girls myself."

A little later the floor was cleared, and an announcement was made. A challenge was issued to any man to go on the floor and make love to one of the women. He was not allowed to use his hands in any way. Margaret did not know what the reward was because somebody grabbed her shoulder, and she turned around to see Terry, one of the second stewards.

"Whatever are you doing in a place like this, Maggie? A nice girl like you shouldn't be in here. Who're you with, anyhow?"

"Ch… Charlie." She swallowed hard and really tried to focus. "And… other w… waiters."

"That figures." said Terry. "Come on, you've had way too much to drink. I'm taking you back to the ship."

He linked his arms in with hers, and as they walked out of the bar, she could hear the crowd giving a loud cheer to one of the volunteers. She glanced back, and saw him with his pants around his ankles, and a woman sitting on the top of him.

"Hey, th…that's Tom, Eileen's feller," she gasped, squinting to see him properly. I… I'll b… bet he'll… she'll… be mad when she finds out."

Terry looked over at Tom, and then turned to Margaret. "Maggie, for heaven's sake, don't say a word to Eileen, or to anybody else about this. You understand?"

Margaret carefully put her finger to her lips, and for a moment she understood with absolute clarity that she must not tell what she had seen. "Yes," she whispered. "I… I understand."

"She'll do her nut if she finds out," he was saying, as he struggled down the stairs with her.

Terry waved down the first taxi he saw, and guided Margaret inside.

When they arrived back at the ship he led her up the gangway, then practically carried her all the way back to her cabin.

CHAPTER 15

The next morning, the second day in Barbados, Margaret found herself ironing passengers' shirts.

The temperature seemed hotter than ever with the ship standing in port. Every time she hung her head down she thought she was going to be sick.

At least her shift finished at two o'clock, so she could lie down for a few hours.

Her mind kept going over the day before, especially the shark encounter, and how it looked as if somebody was trying to kill her.

She knew she had ended up at some bar, but could not think how she had got back to the ship. All these people making her promise not to say anything, they must think that she was a secret agent or something. Ricky had made her promise not to say anything about Peter, also not to tell about his marriage breaking up. Then there was Ginger, making her promise not to say anything about being left in the water, and them picking her up. And on top of all that, hearing somebody saying they mustn't tell anybody about something else. She was trying to work it out all morning what that something else was.

She finished the shirts she had been ironing, and was about to take them into Freddie's office when she heard Eileen talking to some of the other women.

"I came back to the ship early, and I thought I was going ashore, and guess what? He wasn't on board. Wait till I see him, he'll fucking get it from me. And you," she turned around to Margaret, "you were like a bloody baby elephant coming in last night, you woke me and Chris up."

"I'm sorry," said Margaret, "I'm afraid I don't remember much about last night."

"Yeah, we did notice that you were bombed out of your mind," said Chris, backing up Eileen. "Where did you get to after we left you, anyway?"

"Some bar in town. I went with some of the waiters. I'm afraid they got me drunk."

"Nobody gets anybody drunk," butted in Betty, "we've all got a free mind, so don't go blaming the poor waiters."

"Did you see my feller around?" asked Eileen. Her eyes were red and she looked as if she had been crying.

Margaret was just about to say no, when she suddenly stopped. Some of last night's events came back to her. Of course, Tom, he was on the floor with that woman. That was the other thing she was supposed not to tell.

"Lost your bloody voice or something?" snapped Eileen, bringing Margaret back to the present. "I bet he was with you and the other waiters."

"No, he wasn't, in fact I didn't see him at all," she lied.

"If I thought for one minute he was with you lot, I'd kill him."

And if you knew who he had been with, thought Margaret, *he would be a dead man by now.*

At two o'clock Margaret made her way back to her cabin by the working alleyway. She bumped into Ricky. She had dreaded meeting him all morning in case he had found out about her being in those bars with the waiters.

"And what happened to you last night?" were his first words to her. "Whatever possessed you to go into the shanty town, and the bars there? You do realize you're the talk of the ship?" He was furious with her.

Strange, thought Margaret, *I'm told not to say anything, but, by God, they all know how to tell on me.*

"I didn't really mean to, Ricky, it was just that I went water-skiing and I saw a shark. I was so shocked that Ginger bought me a brandy, and then I met the waiters who said they were going for a drink and asked if I wanted to go with them. I'm afraid I got drunk."

"Bloody shark! Come on, Margaret; stop your imagination getting the better of you. I've heard some excuses for getting drunk but that takes the cake. I've been swimming in these waters for years, and I haven't seen a shark yet."

She looked up at him, not knowing what to say next. He was so angry with her.

"I suppose that means you won't be taking me ashore tonight," she said, in a very low voice.

"Oh, don't worry, I'll take you ashore, but don't ever let me hear about you going to those types of places again, because, if I do, it's goodbye to us." He then stormed off in the other direction, leaving Margaret close to tears.

---0---

The waiters had just finished 'beer carry', their first job of the day, and were about to start serving breakfast.

Tom was suffering from a bad hangover, and the crashing of crockery coming from the plate house made his head feel even worse. But none of that stopped his memories of the night before; and how all the lads had egged him on. Whatever possessed him to go with that prostitute, and in front of everybody? How the hell was he going to face Eileen? He must have a good excuse ready for her. He took a swig of his beer, which he had left in the silver locker, before going into the Pacific restaurant to serve his passengers.

He went into the kitchens, where Paddy was laying out the silver milk jugs and teapots, ready for the waiters to pick up.

"Had a good time and a blinking good screw with that woman last night?" Paddy hissed, smiling broadly.

"Shut up, Paddy!" Tom replied. "If Eileen gets the wind of this, she'll kill me!" He paused a moment as another dreadful thought occurred. "And knowing her she's bound to tell the missus, to get her own back on me."

Tom collected a few plates of food from the hot press and made his way through the swing doors into the dining room.

The dining room was nice and cool and he could hear passengers talking amongst themselves.

He had a table of sixteen but only ten had turned up. The others must have gone ashore for lunch. He took away their soup dishes and placed three plates of poached supreme of brill with hollandaise sauce in front of the passengers who had ordered it. The smell of the fish made his stomach turn over.

"How are you today, Tom?" asked one of his passengers politely. "We sure love Barbados; the people are really friendly here. Did you manage to get ashore last night?"

"Yes," answered Tom, in a civil voice.

"Did you go anywhere nice?" asked one of the women. She was about seventy years of age, and still drinking her soup.

The woman was named Miss Pike and she annoyed Tom; she was always the last person to finish at his table.

"Just a drink in one of the bars."

"Was it any good?" inquired another passenger.

"Not bad," said Tom, feeling more irritated.

"Can you give us the name of it?" asked one of the men. Then turning to his wife he said, "Maybe we could go there tonight, Barbara."

"Sorry, I've forgotten the name of the place, but I can tell you the name of another one."

Why couldn't these bloody people shut up and eat their bloody meal, he thought to himself.

The only thing left for him to do was to face Eileen; he knew she would have a massive cob on. Tell her half the truth? Nip ashore and buy her a bottle of her favourite perfume from the duty-free shop on the quayside? That would help to sweeten her up. He couldn't take her ashore that evening as it was his turn to cover for one of the other waiters, but he would promise to take her out in San Juan. Hopefully nobody would split on him over that woman.

Shipmates usually stuck together over these kinds of things.

When Tom returned to his cabin, Eileen was sitting on his bunk waiting for him. He had just managed to get ashore for her perfume. His other three cabin mates and the steward whose job was to clean the crew quarters, were sitting smoking and drinking with her. As soon as she saw him she jumped up from the bunk and rushed towards him.

"You bastard!" she screamed. "What happened to you last night? I thought you were going to take me ashore."

The other four men stood up and made their way towards the door.

"See you two later," said one of them, "we're just nipping up the bar for a quick pint."

"I'll bring your clean towels later," added the steward, as he was going through the door.

As soon as they left, Eileen slapped him across the face and was about to take another aim at it, when he grabbed both of her arms.

"Now listen to me!" he shouted at her. "I can explain everything."

"It had better be a damn good explanation," she replied.

He sat her next to him on the bunk, and poured her out a drink. "You see, Eileen, I had just nipped ashore to get you something from the shop, a little surprise for you. Then I bumped into Paddy and a couple of the boys. They said, "Come across the road for a quick drink." I said, "I can't, I'm taking out my bird."

He then put his arms around her shoulders and began stroking her neck. "They said, 'Oh, just have one drink. It won't hurt you', and I'm afraid, Eileen, I did mean to get back on time. You know what it's like, when you've had a couple of drinks, you

103

forget the time. But believe me you were in my thoughts all the time." He then took out a small, wrapped parcel from his pocket and handed it to Eileen. "For you, luv. Do you forgive me?"

Eileen unwrapped the package and took out the perfume. He could see that she was beginning to melt a bit. "Now I can't take you out tonight," he continued, "but I promise I'll take you ashore in San Juan."

"My favourite perfume, Tom." She began to open the top of the bottle and smell it.

"Do you forgive me now, luv?" he asked, in a pathetic voice.

"Well, now you've explained everything, I suppose so."

He took her in his arms and began to kiss her.

Whew! That was a close one.

CHAPTER 16

That evening Margaret paced up and down the cabin, waiting for Ricky. She wasn't sure what time he was supposed to pick her up. She had got ready for seven o'clock, and now it was approaching eight. There was only Kitty in the cabin with her; the other two girls had gone up to the Pig for a drink.

"Where's Ricky taking you tonight?" asked Kitty, as she was trying to draw an even line around her eye with a pencil.

"Hopefully the Hilton, but I'm not sure what time he's picking me up. He was awfully angry with me this morning, over me getting drunk last night." She looked up at Kitty's reflection in the mirror. "I suppose you've heard all about it?"

"Yes I did, but don't worry, we all get pissed now and again." Margaret nodded at her reassuring words.

There was a knock on the door. She opened it, and Ricky stood there dressed in a black suit. Her heart missed a beat. He did look nice. He always did.

"You ready then?" His manner seemed to have changed from earlier on.

"Yes, I'll just get my cardigan," she said, as she rooted in her locker.

They said goodbye to Kitty, and made their way to the gangway.

The evening was warm, and Ricky hailed a taxi. They both jumped in, and he directed the driver to the Hilton Hotel.

To Margaret's relief, he reached out to hold her hand, though he said little on the way.

When they arrived, a doorman opened the cab and escorted them through the big glass doors of the hotel. Inside the building, Margaret was breathless. *What a beautiful place*, she thought. This was the first time she had been to such a grand hotel. Inside there were shops displaying expensive jewellery, and even a garden right in the centre of the building.

Ricky led her to the lounge and ordered drinks. The lighting was very low and soft romantic music was playing in the background. The turquoise water of an illuminated swimming pool shimmered through the window. She felt like she had landed in heaven.

"Sorry about this morning, Margaret," he said. "I felt so angry. You see I know you're a nice person and I don't want to think my girl would go to places like that. I respect you Margaret."

My girl! What lovely words, and he respected her. She felt her heart swelling with joy.

"You won't find me in places like that anymore Ricky, I promise you."

He squeezed her hand. "Fancy a dance?"

They both made their way onto the floor, and Ricky put his arms around her. They danced in a close embrace to 'Strangers in the Night'.

"Would you like to take a walk outside?" he asked, when the music had stopped.

She nodded, letting him lead her off the floor. They walked beside the swimming pool, arms around each other. She could hear the crickets in the background. The silvery moon shone brightly over the sea.

"Oh, I've got a little present for you," he said, putting his hands in his pocket. "Open it up when you get back on board. It's just a little something to say I'm sorry for shouting at you this morning."

"Ricky! You shouldn't have bought me anything, but thank you, thank you very much. I must be the happiest woman on the whole of this island."

He kissed her again.

The evening just flew by; before long it was time to go back to the ship. The doorman hailed one of the many taxis that were lined up outside the entrance to the hotel.

Ricky tipped the man, and they both climbed into the taxi. It drove through Bridgetown and at last they arrived at the ship's terminal.

Entering the docks, Margaret thought what a dream the *Ocean Star* looked, all lit up at night. It was exciting to think that she was actually living it!

When they reached the top of the gangway, Ricky turned to Margaret. "I've got to get changed now, then go to the aft-end and help take the ship out. I'll see you there later." He gave her a quick kiss, and left in the direction of the crew quarters.

Margaret lingered a moment. The deck was full of crew members, most of them drinking cans of beer, some leaning over the side of the ship, still bargaining with a few locals, who seemed keen to make a last-minute sale.

The captain made an announcement over the Tannoy, informing passengers and crew that the ship was about to be put to sea, and would all those people not sailing leave the ship immediately.

The sounds of the engines starting up resounded through the still air, and a few minutes later another announcement was made. "Hands to station, for'd and aft."

Ricky seemed to appear from nowhere, advising the crew to stay away from the ropes and keep to the other end of the deck.

The anchor rattled up into the bow. Another order came through from the bridge. "Let go for'd and aft."

A docker standing on the shore-side released one of the ropes from around a bollard, then a deckhand hauled it on board as it twined around a moving capstan. Finally the rest of the ropes were released and the ship began to move away from the quayside; the tugs in the water at the other end pulling the boat towards the sea. The pilot was on the bridge using the bow thrusters, as the ship gently sailed out of Barbados harbour.

Owd Rosie came over to where Margaret was standing. "Did you have a nice evening, kid? I had a walk on the quay with Betty and Eve."

Margaret gave a non-committal grunt, her head too full of the lovely evening she had spent with Ricky.

"Well, Maggie," Owd Rosie looked at her watch, "It's well past me bed time. I'm going down to me cabin. See ya in the morning, kid."

As she walked away another person came up to Margaret.

"How are you feeling this evening? You look more sober than last night."

Margaret turned around to see Terry, the second steward, standing beside her.

"Fine, thanks," she replied cautiously.

"Don't you remember me from last night?"

"No. No, I can't say I do," she said, trying to think where she had seen him before.

"I was the one who saw you home safely. Surprising how drink can make one lose one's memory."

"Oh! I'm sorry." Then Margaret vaguely remembered him guiding her up the gangway. To her relief Ricky came to her side, changing the subject.

"Well, one more port, then Rio here we come," he said jokingly.

"See you both later," said Terry, leaving the pair of them together.

"Was he trying to chat you up?" asked Ricky laughingly. "Hope you told him that you're boxed off with me. You're my girl." He then looked at her and said in a soft voice. "Want to come to my cabin for a quick nightcap?"

Margaret looked at him. "Well, it's turned twelve. I ought to go to bed."

"Come on, one for the road."

It did not take much persuasion for Margaret to accept his invitation.

He put his arms around her waist and led her towards the crew quarters.

Margaret still felt nervous entering the male accommodation, even though she was with Ricky. She could still remember that awful man's words, the night she had been in the officers' quarters, and how he would see that she got instant dismissal if she were caught up there again.

They crept quietly up to Ricky's room. He slowly opened the cabin door, which he usually kept unlocked, and switched on the small light hanging from the bulkhead.

Margaret sat down on his daybed while he reached for a couple of glasses from a nearby shelf. He poured them both a gin and tonic and handed one to Margaret. The ship began to roll a bit, and she could hear the waves hitting the side of the ship.

"We must be out in the open water," he said, taking a sip from his glass. "By the way, aren't you going to open up your present?"

"Oh, yes. I've been dying to open it all night." She took the small parcel from her handbag and began tearing the neatly wrapped paper off the package. When she at last saw what it contained, she gasped with pleasure. "Oh, Ricky! Chanel No. 5. My favourite perfume!"

The last time she had been given perfume was from Jim on her twenty-first birthday, and that had been Chanel No. 5.

Funny – since meeting Ricky, Jim had gone quite out of her mind.

"Well, don't I deserve a kiss?"

She looked up at Ricky and smiled. "You certainly do," and put her arm around his neck and kissed him.

He pulled her towards him, and his hands slipped down to her breast.

109

This time she did not push his hand away…

A while later, she lay on her back, gazing into his eyes.

"I love you, Margaret," he whispered in her ear.

"I love you too, Ricky. But, but…"

"But what?" he inquired.

"Well," she began" I just hope you don't think I'm cheap. You know, letting you make love to me."

He sat up and rested on his arm. "Now look here, Margaret, don't ever think that. We love each other, and that's all that matters. In fact, I love you even more."

She looked up into his face. She loved everything about him, every inch of his body, even that little scar beneath his chin.

He lay back down again, and they rested in each other's arms. As the ship sailed on.

CHAPTER 17

George Bowder sat in his armchair drinking a straight whisky with his legs stretched out on the coffee table.

The last few weeks had been very trying. The passengers were getting him down. He had to sit at the dining table with them every evening, and answer all the damn silly questions they kept asking about the ship. If he'd said it once, he'd said it a hundred times; that it had steam turbines geared to twin screws, and a service speed of twenty knots. And the capacity of 160 first class and 898 tourist passengers.

How could he be polite to these people when he felt like telling the lot of them to shut up and leave him alone?

There was always the option to get away from them by going to one of the twice-nightly shows in the Dolphin Lounge, but all the prancing about and inane songs pissed him off as well.

Sometimes, to relieve the boredom, he would go to the wardroom after dinner for a nightcap, and a chat with the other officers. Some of them would bring young passenger girls back for a drink. That's when he would make an excuse and retire to his cabin for the night. The sight of those men fondling women made him sick.

He sighed and knocked back his whisky. It was the same old thing, trip after trip; the same boring types of people, even if the faces were different.

George Bowder tapped his glass in annoyance.

And of course, there was that thing with Peter, the bellboy.

If only the stupid kid hadn't panicked, he wouldn't have ended up dead.

And to put the tin hat on it all, that damn girl from the laundry had come into his room, just as he had pushed the body through the porthole.

According to Ricky, the stupid woman hadn't put two and two together and realised exactly what she had seen. Ricky assured him that he had kept her quiet about it, and that she had never mentioned another word about the incident. But he still didn't trust her. Women were all the same. Big mouths. They could never keep anything to themselves.

For instance, what had she said to that bloody redheaded queer he had seen her ashore with? He wouldn't trust that fellow either. What if she said something, and the queer realised that it was the bellboy's departure that she'd seen?

George Bowder swung his legs off the table and poured himself another whisky.

His plan to get rid of the bloody woman had been a good one. And it had all gone so well; even down to a shark coming up while she was abandoned in the sea.

But, damn it, she'd had the devil's own luck to get out of it alive. Why hadn't she drowned, or become shark food? Being left out there alone should have made her panic, so the shark would have had her. That would have been the end of the problem.

And to cap it all, only a few minutes later, she'd been seen sunbathing, cool as you like, as if nothing had happened! And according to Ricky, she then went off and got pissed in some seedy nightspot, only hours later.

Bloody woman.

Well, he wasn't going to give up on his plan. He would get rid of her somehow.

A knock came on the door.

"Come in," he called out. It was Ricky, as expected.

George reached over to the ice bucket for a beer. "Busy?" he asked, as Ricky sat. "You look tired." He pushed a glass across the table.

"Yes, I suppose so. I've told the men I want them to start painting the lifeboats today. When we're in San Juan tomorrow

112

we can lower them down and test them. Mind you, knowing that lot they'll be off to a bar and spending all night there.

"You look like you've had a night on the tiles yourself," observed George, unable to keep the slight tone of accusation from his voice. It was not fair that Ricky should be having fun while he was so bored.

"Margaret didn't leave my cabin till about three this morning. I'm glad it's her and not me, having to face the heat of the laundry." Ricky opened the beer and took a big gulp from the can.

"Has she mentioned any more about that bellboy?" asked George, eyeing the unused glass with a small frown.

"I've told you before, you've got nothing to worry about," Ricky said. "I'm sure she's forgotten all about it. She's succumbed to my charms." He flashed his uncle a toothpaste-advert smile. "Anyhow, it's about time you stopped messing about with young boys. If Aunt Jane found out, she'd kill you. I think you're a bloody fool, and it's only because I'm your nephew that I'm standing by you."

"And if I told Babs about the steam queen you're with, you'd be as good as dead yourself."

"Whose idea was it to chat her up, to keep her quiet?" snapped Ricky.

"Okay, okay, let's drop it. Call it quits. Like you said before, we stand by each other." George managed a thin smile. "Anyhow I want to get down to other matters. The diamonds.

He went over to the curtains and pulled them tightly closed, then moved to his bunk and dropped heavily to his knees with a grunt. He unlocked one of the drawers beneath the bed and rummaged a moment, then removed a sock and shook something out.

Heaving his bulk up, he put the object in Ricky's hand. It was a woman's hair comb, made of dark brown plastic, about four inches long and three inches deep, decorated with different size diamonds on both sides.

"I told you I would think of something. This is how you'll get the diamonds I bought in Freetown off the ship. This comb. They sell them in the shop, with glass diamonds for decoration. Apparently women like that sort of thing. Anyway, I took out the glass stones, and put in the diamonds. It's mostly real ones now, but I left a few of the glass ones in, so it's not so obvious."

Ricky turned it over in his hand, then looked up. "You prised out the fake stones and glued in the real ones?" he asked.

George nodded. "The glass ones were surprisingly realistic." He paused, with a satisfied smile. "Tell me which are real, and which are fake."

Ricky studied the stones carefully, then shook his head.

"Exactly," said George. "Only a trained eye could tell the difference – but it's such cheap plastic that no-one would suspect these are real stones." He took the comb back. "I won't give it to you just yet; not till after Rio. When we get back to Liverpool, and should the customs stop you, remember, you bought it from the ship's shop as a present for the wife. There are dozens of them in there, so they won't be at all suspicious."

"What if they do spot that some of them are real diamonds?"

"Keep your eyes on the prize, Ricky. You were as keen as I was in England to use this trip to make some real money, so don't back out on me now. Remember you said you didn't mind taking the risk? I could have got somebody else."

"Yes I did." Ricky hesitated a moment, tapping the comb thoughtfully. "I won't skin out, Uncle George, but now I've seen them and I know that they're real, I suppose it's a bit scary."

"When we get them off at the other end, think of the money we'll make." George took the comb back and dropped it in the sock.

"You mean, when I get them off," Ricky said, as George locked the draw again.

"You going ashore tomorrow?" asked George, ignoring his comment.

"Not during the day; too busy keeping an eye on my men," Ricky replied. "I'll take Margaret ashore tomorrow night. That should keep her happy. I guess she'll be having a look around San Juan on her own in the afternoon."

"Got her in bed yet?" asked his uncle suddenly.

"Not that it's any of your business," said Ricky, with a smirk. "But yes, last night." He paused. "She's so naive, though," he added. "At times she reminds me a bit of a puppy. Always looking up at me with her big brown eyes."

"A bit different from Babs," George observed with a dry laugh.

"I'll admit, it does irritate me at times. In fact I think I should get an Oscar for my acting." Ricky stood up and put the empty can on the table. "Well, I'd better go and get some splicing done."

"Yes I'll have to go myself, I have inspection to do," said George, also standing up. "See you again soon."

---0---

The heat was unbearable as Margaret and Billy folded the scalding sheets sliding out of the calender.

"Go anywhere nice last night?" asked Billy, taking a half-folded sheet from her, finishing the fold and placing it on top of the others.

Margaret felt herself blushing, and hoped Billy would think it was from the heat.

Ricky's hands on her. His body pressed against her.

It had been nearly perfect. Nearly, but somewhat painful. She'd never expected it would hurt so much the first time. Maybe it would get better.

115

"Yes, I went to the Hilton with Ricky," she gushed. "It was beautiful; it even had a garden growing inside the hotel. If I was ever on honeymoon, that's the place I would go."

It did sound forced, but Billy seemed not to notice.

"We went to the beach again, but I didn't find any sharks," he laughed.

Margaret shot him a frown. "Stop taking the mickey out of me," she said. "I was scared out there."

His eyes widened. "Sorry, Maggie," he muttered. "Didn't mean any offence."

She gave him a forgiving smile. "No matter. None taken."

They were interrupted by Freddy, coming down from his office.

"Don't forget," he shouted to everyone, "it's laundry inspection today." He looked at Billy. "When you've finished putting that batch of sheets through, start on the napkins." He turned to Johnny. "You tidy the place around a bit. You can also scrub part of the deck by the machines where Billy and Margaret are working."

Betty was at the press, swilling down a beer. "Make sure you get rid of that can, Betty," Freddy shouted. "And yours as well, Lil and Eve."

The three women nodded. Lil took the cans and hid them in the bottom of the bin.

About twenty minutes later, the captain and a few officers entered the laundry. They looked very official in their spotless white uniforms and gold braids. The captain had a torch, and was inspecting every nook and cranny.

The captain was a small man, with a peaked cap that looked bigger than his head, and brown skinny legs beneath his baggy shorts.

To think I hoped to fall in love with him, Margaret thought. *What a drippy little fellow!*

One of the other officers was the opposite of the captain; a big lump of pasty white flesh. Margaret's glance travelled up his bulging uniform to his name badge, which said, 'George Bowder, Second Engineer'.

Then she looked at his face. Her blood ran cold.

It was him! That awful man! The one she had seen the night when she had walked into the wrong cabin.

For a couple of seconds their eyes met.

She found herself unable to breathe.

If looks could kill, she would now be dead.

CHAPTER 18

The warm glow of the rising sun spread across the harbour at San Juan, Puerto Rico, as Ginger came up on deck. He had just finished his scrub outs, and had decided to go up for some air before starting on his cabins. He leaned on the upper deck railing as the anchor rattled and splashed into the water at the bow.

There was also plenty of activity going on at the aft-end. The deckhands were scurrying about with various ropes, taking orders from the bosun, Ricky. He was certainly a handsome man; tall, tanned and with a good physique. Ginger could understand how Margaret was besotted with him.

He had heard that Ricky was married, but apart from that he didn't know much about the man. How would it end up between him and Margaret when the ship got back to Liverpool? It was very rare that men left their wives for another woman. Seafarers were renowned for having a woman in every port, or affairs at sea, particularly with a stewardess or the odd passenger.

Whatever the outcome, it would be Margaret that would end up with a broken heart.

He was still gazing down at Ricky when he noticed the second engineer had joined him. Big and ugly, he was thinking to himself, when something made him think of Peter. The bellboy was always going on about the man. Something about giving the poor kid a hard time.

Maybe the second engineer fancied the boy? A closet queer? A cold shiver ran down Ginger's back. There was something about the man he didn't like. It didn't seem to bother Ricky though; they were having a good laugh together.

The upper deck was beginning to fill with early rising passengers. Mick, the head barman, was leaning over the ship's rail talking to a woman. He had seen him a few times talking to

119

Tom. Ginger could still recall a bit of the conversation between Tom and Paddy, about diamonds. He hadn't heard any more and had completely forgotten all about the incident up until now. Maybe it was drink talking.

Ginger gave a sigh and stood up from the rail. Time to get down below and see to his passengers.

A short while later he was just finishing vacuuming a middle-aged couple's cabin, when they came back from breakfast.

"Thank you so much," said the man, who Ginger considered a real gentleman. "Where do you suggest we visit today?" The man put his arms around his wife's shoulders and gave him an expectant smile.

"Why don't you go to Old San Juan, and visit Castillo De San Felipe Del Morro? It's a great fortress and tourist attraction, built by the Spanish at the northwest end of the city. It covers more than two hundred acres and rises one hundred and forty-five feet above the ocean. The castle was continuously improved until 1787. It is now a National Historic Site."

"My word, Ginger," laughed the man, "you're better than any tour operator I know."

Ginger smiled to himself; if only the couple knew how long it had taken him to memorise it from a travel brochure. "Then afterwards, you could go to Luquillo beach," he added. "It's a few miles east of San Juan. It ranks among the most beautiful beaches in the world."

"Well thanks, Ginger, we might just do that. It sounds very interesting." The man turned to his wife. "You fancy that, Dorothy?"

She nodded, "But don't forget, dear, that I want to do some shopping."

"Women," laughed her husband. "Thanks for the advice, Ginger, we'll tell you how we got on when we get back."

"Enjoy your day now," said Ginger, as he saw himself out.

The laundry finished early that afternoon, so Margaret arranged to go ashore with Owd Rosie. To her surprise Lil decided to join them. The others all had different plans.

Margaret knocked on the door and Lil opened it. "Nearly ready, girl," she said, swaying slightly as she held on to the door frame. "Had a couple of drinks already," she said with a wink at Margaret. Then she called back over her shoulder, "Come on, Rosie, we're waiting for you."

Owd Rosie appeared, checking in her handbag. "Ready, kid," she said, and marched past. She was wearing a bright yellow dress and red shoes. With hair to match, she resembled a fairground beauty.

They made their way towards the crew gangway, situated by the working alleyway.

They did not get a taxi because the shops were within walking distance. When they arrived Margaret noticed the street was rather narrow, with all sorts of shops selling mainly clothes – t-shirts, jeans, dresses, the lot, and they all seemed to be at a reasonable price. She couldn't resist looking in the jewellers' windows. Displayed on shelves were beautiful precious stones, and a huge selection of 14-carat gold chains. Compared with prices in Britain, they were very cheap.

The first shop they entered, Margaret saw a pair of jeans and a cute pair of boots to match. She tried them on, and found they fitted perfectly. She was just going to pay, when she saw a pretty white dress. She couldn't stop herself from trying that one on as well. It was as if it had been made for her. It looked lovely. Margaret decided to wear it that night for Ricky.

She had only seen him once since the night at the Hilton, and that was the day before, when she had bumped into him as she came up from the laundry. Her mind had been on that awful officer at the time, so she was pleasantly surprised to see Ricky standing there. As ever, her heart missed a beat when he gave her one of his charming smiles.

Ricky suggested that they had an early night that evening, so they wouldn't be too tired going ashore in San Juan. Margaret felt a bit hurt that he hadn't asked to see her for a few minutes before going to bed. At least she was going to meet him tonight and would be wearing this beautiful dress. She handed over her American dollars to the Puerto Rican sales lady, then looked around the shop for the other women.

There was no sign of them. Margaret shrugged. No doubt they would be in one of the other shops.

When she got outside the store, she looked up and down the street. It was packed with local people, all talking in Spanish. No sign of Lil, or Owd Rosie. Margaret decided to carry on up the street looking at the shops.

She saw a man's jumper in one of the windows and thought it would be a suitable Christmas present for Ricky, so went in to buy it.

Afterwards Margaret walked up the cobbled road, pushing through the crowd. If she'd had the money she would have treated herself to the beautiful diamond brooch she saw while gazing at the enormous display of jewellery in a shop window. It was of a poodle dog, all covered in tiny diamonds with two sapphire stones for its eye.

Margaret loved window-shopping in jewellery stores. Diamonds were her favourite. The only diamond she nearly had would have been the one from Jim. It was pretty but a tiny stone.

And unlikely that she would ever get another one.

Unless of course, Ricky bought her one. When his divorce came through.

Whatever was she thinking about? He hadn't even proposed to her.

She walked on until she came to the last line of shops. The crowd of people had dwindled by now, so she turned to walk down one of the side streets. It was almost empty.

She saw a little café, with a couple of tables outside on the pavement. She decided to sit down and have a coffee. The waiter, a plump little man who looked in his late fifties, came out to her. He spoke to her in Spanish. She shook her head to show she didn't understand. He went back inside the cafe and a minute later came out with a menu.

"In English," he said, placing it on the table.

She looked at the menu and pointed to coffee.

"Con leche?" he asked.

Margaret just nodded her head; she was not sure what that meant.

"No problema, un momento," he said, taking the menu with him.

He returned a while later with a coffee and a small jug of milk.

She smiled to herself. *Ricky*. What a special night it had been when they slept together. She did love him, and wanted to please him in every way.

Then her smile became a frown, as the image of that awful second engineer elbowed Ricky out of her mind. What a dreadful look of hatred in his eyes!

Okay, she went into his cabin by mistake, but surely there was no need to look at her the way he did? It was a mistake after all, and she had apologized to him at the time.

Suddenly, another thought struck her. Could it have been he who tried to murder her in Barbados? She felt her imagination running away with her. She must stop it immediately. If Ricky ever found out what she was thinking, he'd go mad. After all, what motive would the officer have to get rid of her? She had only walked into the cabin by mistake.

The waiter came out again, and pointed to the coffee.

"Otro café?" he asked.

"Um, no thank you," she answered. "Just the bill."

He did not seem to understand, so she handed him a dollar bill.

"Gracias, Senorita," he said, taking away her cup.

Margaret decided to make her way back to the shops to see if she could find the other women. If not, she would go back to the ship and have a sleep before going out again that evening with Ricky.

Clutching her shopping bags, she kept walking; fairly sure that she'd taken enough turns, so that she was now heading back to the ship.

The street was narrow, with very dilapidated houses and no shops. Several washing lines stretched over her head, with threadbare-looking clothes flapping lazily in the sun.

Then Margaret gave a shocked gasp as she realised the street ended abruptly in a dilapidated fence.

It was a dead end.

She took a deep breath to calm herself. Probably best to retrace her steps back to the café. She could ask if someone there spoke English and could direct her back to the port.

As she turned, there were heavy footsteps behind her.

A large figure was standing in the street, blocking her only way out.

There was no mistaking the shape of the man, nor the distinctive white uniform.

It was the second engineer.

He gave a sneering grin, and flexed his hands, as if ready to put them round her neck.

Margaret glanced at the dead end. How quickly could she pull herself over the fence? But the thought of him grabbing her ankles and yanking her down meant that was not an option.

The second engineer's grin widened into a victorious smile.

Margaret tightened her grip on her shopping bags.

Then she ran straight at him.

As she came up to him, she gave a feint to her left. He leaned his bulk in that direction, his hands reaching for her. Then she dodged to the right, moving much faster than he could respond with all his weight. As she went past, she swung her shopping bags round in a wide arc.

The bags caught him on the back of his head. There was a thud and he gave a grunt – presumably as the boots inside made contact. He over-balanced and fell to his knees.

Now Margaret was clear, she ran as fast as she could along the street. She passed the café, then saw a shop on a corner she recognised.

Skidding to a halt, she ran into the side-street by the shop. There was another one she recognised, and another.

With her breath coming in gasps, she continued to run, until there were more and more people around her.

She slowed to a halt, and looked back over her shoulder.

There was no sign of him.

She came to a halt and put her hands on her knees as she struggled to get her breath back. She couldn't stop shaking.

There was a tap on her shoulder.

Margaret gave a small scream and froze.

"Where 'ave you been to, kid?" said a woman's voice. "We've been looking everywhere for you."

Margaret had never been so pleased in all her life to see Owd Rosie and Lil.

CHAPTER 19

It was warm and sticky that evening in San Juan. Mick stood on the observation deck leaning over the ship's rail, watching the passengers and crew going ashore.

Margaret and Ricky walked down the gangway. Margaret looked quite attractive with her long, red hair hanging over her shoulders. She was in a white, sleeveless dress that showed off her neat little figure.

A few minutes later Tom and Eileen appeared. Tom was struggling to support Eileen as she tried to totter along in extremely high-heeled shoes.

Mick grunted in annoyance. *What a bloody moron. Why on earth did I leave him with the diamonds?*

And what an idiot going with that prostitute in Barbados in front of all the ship's crew? Apparently he didn't even have the sense to use a condom. No doubt he'd be up to the doctor's in a couple of weeks with a dose.

And another thing. *How was Tom going to get the diamonds ashore*?

Would he and Paddy be stupid enough to get caught?

Oh God, I hope not!

Last time Mick talked to him, Tom said that he had a something up his sleeve. Paddy had also reassured him that they would get the diamonds off in Liverpool without any problems.

He wished he shared their confidence.

If anything went wrong, there was a lot of money at stake. He told Tom, at the time of handing the diamonds over, that the rest was up to him. At this stage he could only sit back and wait, just hoping that everything would turn out all right.

---0---

127

Tom helped Eileen off the gangway and happened to look up at the top deck.

Mick was standing there.

Tom didn't know who was the biggest problem, Mick or Eileen.

The former of the two had kept pestering him about what he was going to do with the diamonds.

What with such a hectic time in Barbados, and trying to smooth his bird over, he hadn't had much time to think about them. What made him mad was that Mick said he would leave it all to him how he would get them off the ship – and then hadn't given him a moment's peace about it.

He felt like telling the stupid bastard to take the wretched things back. But he knew the consequences of doing that would be very unpleasant.

Tom had told Mick that he had something planned, and would discuss it at a later date. That seemed to pacify him for a while, and especially with Paddy backing him up. The thing was, he didn't have a clue at this stage how he was going to get them off. The only thing he could do would be either to put them in Eileen's handbag, or to take them himself.

Knowing the silly bitch, not only would she lose her handbag, but he didn't particularly want to see her again once they were shore-side.

He could take them off himself, of course. He already had them hidden in the false heel of a shoe, down in his locker. That was all right while he was on board ship, but the customs in England knew it was an old trick. He was also under suspicion with them. He had been caught in the past for smuggling a few watches ashore. It wasn't as big an offence as diamonds, but still, they would always search him to make sure he never took anything else ashore.

"You got a cob on, or something?" snapped Eileen, making Tom jump out of his skin.

"No luv, just thinking what a lovely evening it is, just the two of us together." He gave her a quick peck on the cheek. He always knew how to get round her.

They walked out of the terminal, heading towards the nearest bar.

"Aren't we going to take a taxi?" grumbled Eileen with a frown.

"I thought maybe we could go for a drink over at one of the bars, then go for a meal."

"Okay," she answered reluctantly. "I was hoping we could go to a show, like Maggie and Ricky's going to do."

"Yes luv, I know a show's nice, but I thought it would be more romantic sitting in a quiet, little restaurant having a nice meal and a bottle of wine. Just the two of us." And also much cheaper, he thought to himself.

The first bar they went into was full of the ship's crew. Paddy and Alfie, the greaser, were sitting with a couple of bathroom stewardesses. Nearby was some of the galley staff.

"There's Paddy and Alfie," said Tom, "We'll go over and join them and the two khazi queens."

Eileen squeezed herself next to the girls.

"What are you all having to drink?" asked Tom, dipping his hands into his pocket.

"Here, I'll come and help ye to carry them," offered Paddy.

They both walked over to the bar together, leaving the three women and Alfie talking amongst themselves.

"I saw old Mick standing on the gangway," said Tom, when he was out of earshot. "He keeps going on about the diamonds. Have you thought of any good ideas, Paddy?"

"By Jaysus Tom, stop yer worrying, we've got weeks to go before we're back in Liverpool. Forget them for now. Just enjoy yerself. We'll think of something, nearer the time."

"I suppose you're right, Paddy."

They both walked back to the table with a handful of drinks.

"Here," said Tom, putting the drinks on the table, "get this down you."

They all clinked their glasses together. "Cheers, and Rio here we come."

---0---

Ginger went ashore with Lola; they were aiming for a gay bar at the top of a steep street in Old San Juan. They popped into the first bar on the way for a first drink. Ginger spotted Tom and Eileen sitting amongst a crowd of crew members.

"We'll have a quick one here, dear, then make our way to our usual gaff," Lola said, taking out a cigarette and perching on the nearest bar stool. "Now we're going to put on a Drag Extravaganza for the run down to Rio, then we'll do the pantomime after we sail from there. I bought some lovely material for my dress, and I hope that you're going to go in drag as well."

"I'll have to think about it," said Ginger, who was trying to attract the barman's attention.

"What's wrong with you this cruise?" snapped Lola. "I remember the time you used to be the life and soul of the party, and look at you now, a bloody recluse."

"Yeah, I suppose you're right, I think it must have been the shock of Peter dying at the beginning of the trip that's done it."

"If I hear another word about that Peter, you can go ashore on your own. I've had enough of you going on about him." Lola took a heavy drag on his cigarette, then gave a pout and spun round on the stool with his back to Ginger. A large waft of smoke billowed over his head.

"Okay, don't get a cob on. I won't mention his name again."

Ginger managed to get the barman's attention, and ordered a couple of gins.

When the barman finally served their drinks, Ginger looked at Lola. "We'll drink these, then get on our way."

They both enjoyed the evening in San Juan. Lola managed to get off with a young gay Puerto Rican and Ginger spent the rest of the evening with a queen called Pepe.

At about two o'clock the following morning, they started back to the ship. Ginger caught a glimpse of George Bowder coming out of one of the nightclubs, with a face like thunder. He hadn't seen them and was crossing the road, heading towards the ship. For some reason he kept rubbing at the back of his head.

The sight of him made Ginger start thinking again about Peter. Could it have been Bowder that murdered the lad? He wasn't going to let sleeping dogs lie. He was going to try and find out more information about the man.

Eventually, they arrived at the ship, which looked very impressive all lit up at night.

"Shall we nip down to the galley and get a bacon and egg sarnie?" asked Lola, who still seemed to be on cloud nine.

"Okay, I feel a bit hungry as well."

They went to the galley to see if old Bert, the night pantry man, would make them a sandwich. They would give him half-a-crown each. That was his little perk. Then they saw Tom and Eileen standing there arguing away.

"So, you bastard!" she was saying. "A quiet little restaurant just for the two of us. Romantic, eh? And what do we do, spend the whole evening in that low down bar, pissing it up with that stupid khazi queen Maureen, who kept going on about spewing passengers in her loos, and then we end up here for a fucking cheese sarnie."

"Maybe we won't bother after all," said Ginger, grabbing Lola's arm, and turning slowly away.

CHAPTER 20

The day after leaving San Juan, Margaret was working hard in the laundry. Dirty linen had built up during the days in port. The heat was unbearable, especially after the ship had been standing in dock. She mopped the sweat from her brow as boiling damp sheets kept coming from the calender. There seemed to be no end to them. The ship had also begun to roll, which made it difficult to stand.

But hot sheets and rolling ships were nothing compared to her much more pressing problem; that the second engineer was now openly trying to kill her. How were you supposed to react if you knew that somebody was trying to murder you? Especially if you've hit them over the head with a pair of boots?

And have no clue as to when they would strike again?

And worse still, what if the man you loved, the man you relied on, seemed no help when you needed him?

The evening with Ricky had started so well. Margaret had tried, really tried, to put the second engineer out of her mind and concentrate on having a good time.

Ricky had taken her to the El San Juan Hotel. It was such a beautiful place, with the most breath-takingly gorgeous chandelier Margaret had ever seen hanging in the entrance hall.

They had gone to see a show there, starring none other than the great Sammy Davis Jr. How amazing, to be in the presence of such Hollywood royalty! And his voice! Absolutely sublime.

But good though Sammy Davis was, she simply could not get away from the frightening experience in that dead-end street. It hung over her head like a permanent rain cloud following her on a sunny day.

George Bowder had tried to kill her in San Juan.

And presumably at sea off Barbados when she was abandoned with that shark.

So maybe this all came back to that night in his cabin. What if she had been right all along, and Bowder had just been putting Peter's body through the porthole?

Which meant he was now trying to silence her?

So she turned to the one person she thought she could trust; Ricky.

"Do you think that Peter was murdered?" she asked softly, in a break between songs.

What happened next took her completely by surprise.

Ricky had never looked so mad, or acted so angrily.

"For God's sake," he snarled, leaning forward like an angry tomcat. "Will you shut up about Peter?"

Margaret had never heard him speak like that to her before.

"We're supposed to be watching a show and all you can do is go on about Peter," he hissed. "I'm telling you now, Margaret, if I ever hear you mention his name again, we might as well call it a day."

Her heart sunk to the pit of her stomach.

"Do you understand," he carried on, "that if anyone hears you talk like that, they'll think you've gone barmy. And let me warn you, my girl, if any of the bosses ever finds out it was you spreading such rumours, you'd be in serious trouble. You know what?" She shook her head. "If the chief steward knew, he'd have you flown home immediately." He sat back. "Now do not let me hear that boy's name mentioned again."

It was a good thing she hadn't told him about the second engineer in town today. That would have really put the tin hat on their affair.

Margaret excused herself, telling him she had to go to the toilet. She only hoped he hadn't seen the tears welling up in her eyes.

When she reached the ladies' room, she burst out crying. Thank goodness nobody was around to see her. After a few minutes she knew she would have to get back to Ricky, or he might think that she had walked out. So she grabbed a tissue from the box that was on the dresser, ran it under the cold-water tap and dabbed at her swollen eyes. She then tried to disguise the redness with some eyeliner and make-up.

From that moment on, she would never talk to Ricky about Peter again.

She went back to the table where she found Ricky ordering another couple of drinks. For the next hour they did not exchange conversation, but just sat watching the show. Now it seemed that Sammy Davis Jr was no longer a superstar, but just some lounge singer, going on and on with a set that never seemed to end.

One thing she found out about Ricky was that, as soon as he blew up, he would just as quickly calm down. No more was mentioned over the incident, and after the show he took her for a meal. He was back to his charming self.

However, when they arrived back at the ship, he did not take her back to his cabin. Instead, he escorted her to her own, gave her a quick kiss goodbye and said that he would see her the following day. She wasn't sure whether to be relieved or disappointed.

Anyhow they were back to normal again, and that was all that mattered.

---0---

Margaret looked at her watch. Thank goodness it was nearly break-time.

"Can you go up to the galley and get some tea, Maggie?" asked Lil, putting a big, empty teapot in her hand. "Freddy says he feels like a cup."

Margaret grabbed the pot with enthusiasm. Anything to get away from the heat of the laundry.

She made her way up the spiral staircase of the laundry and went along the working alleyway. Then she came to another flight of narrow iron stairs that led to the galley. She went past the plate house and on to the pantry where there was a big urn of hot water.

She was greeted with wolf whistles from some of the men as she walked by. She thought she heard somebody shout out, "Here comes iron drawers."

"Give me that, tatty 'ead," said one of the pantry men, taking the teapot from Margaret and sticking it underneath the urn. He was wearing pale blue, tiny chequered trousers and a white jacket, covered with an apron, like all the galley staff. He kept winking at her as he was filling the pot with hot water.

"Going to the boat race tomorrow night in the Pig, kid?" he asked.

She looked at him, puzzled. "Boat race?"

"Yeah, we always 'ave one, at least a couple of times a trip. They're good fun."

"I've never been to one," said Margaret. "What's it all about?"

"Never been to one?" laughed the pantry man, still winking at her. "What 'appens is that you 'ave teams of eight people standing at a table, four at one side and four at the other. You 'ave a pint of beer in front of you, also a boiled egg. The first two start with eating their egg, then drinking the pint of beer. When they've finished the beer they turn the glass upside down on their 'eads, and the next person begins the same thing." He finished filling the teapot with water and handed it over to Margaret. "Then," he continued, "the first side to finish is the winner of that team, then there's a knockout contest with the winners of the other teams, until the last one wins. You should see them; it's a right laugh. They all end up pissed as farts!" He was roaring with laughter.

"Mm, could go to that," said Margaret.

"Make sure you don't miss it. I might see you there tomorrow night," he said giving her a last wink, as she walked away.

Just as Margaret was about to descend the stairs to the working alleyway, she had to stop to allow Ginger to come up.

"How's Miss Margaret today?" he inquired when he had reached the top.

"Oh, fine thanks, Ginger," she replied.

"Enjoy yourself in San Juan?"

Margaret hesitated. Even with Ginger she was cautious. Best to play safe.

"Yes," she murmured. "And you?"

"Never had a bad time there yet," he said walking away laughing.

It was only when Margaret had reached the bottom of the stairs that the thought struck her. Ginger! Had she been mistaken, being so cautious?

Maybe of the whole crew, he was the one she could actually confide in! Ginger and Lola were the only men who knew that somebody was trying to murder her! And now she could even tell him who the killer was.

Margaret glanced back up the stairs. Ginger was gone. Should she run after him? Or wait and get him on his own – somewhere private where they could really talk?

The only snag was, though, that she rarely saw him and she wasn't allowed on the passenger decks, except when the ship was in port and only if the gangway was situated on C deck so one had to go that way to disembark.

Or maybe she could see him in the Pig? But no, there were always too many people hanging around.

Margaret bit her lip. Whatever happened, she must talk to Ginger.

Before Bowder tried again, and it was too late.

Something knocked her arm, and she looked up. It was Ricky.

"Steady girl," he laughed, "you're spilling all the tea there."

"Hello, Ricky," she said.

"I'm in a bit of a hurry," he replied, giving her a peck on the cheek, "so I can't stop to talk. I'll see you on the aft-end at eight o'clock tonight."

Margaret felt her spirits lifting. At least she and Ricky were back to normal. Almost as if she hadn't said anything at the El San Juan Hotel.

With a lighter step, she went into Freddy Brown's office and placed the teapot on his table. He smiled at her and she carried on down into the bowels of the laundry, feeling the heat hitting her like she was walking into an oven.

Eileen was talking to Betty and Eve. She could hear her swearing and saying something about her feller, Tom, and that she wouldn't be seeing him again.

Chris was sitting over with the laundry boys and Kitty was in her usual position, sitting on the ironing board, half asleep, wearing her dark glasses. The break was soon over and everybody went back to their duties.

Margaret was still trying to think of a way to see Ginger alone. The thing was – it was possible to go for weeks on a big ship without seeing the same person twice.

At ten to twelve, the noise of the calender stopped. Betty and Eve turned off their presses. The laundry staff walked up the iron stairs, all looking worn out and tired with the heat.

Margaret was just passing Freddy Brown's office, when he called out to her.

"Maggie, will you come here a minute?"

She felt rather startled, and went over to him.

"Could you do me a favour, please? I have a dress shirt for a passenger and it's quite urgent. It wasn't ready when the steward

138

came down for it, so would you mind taking it up to C deck for me? Just give it to one of the bedroom stewards. If you can't see anyone around, there should be somebody in the pantry. Tell them it's for cabin C227.

Margaret took the shirt from him, thinking that her luck was in. That was Ginger's deck.

She cut up the spiral stairs from the working alleyway and opened a heavy fire door, leading into the passengers' accommodation. She then went past an aisle of passengers' cabins, until she came to some stairs leading to C deck. Margaret knew which was Ginger's pantry and made her way towards it. She could hear talking and, as she entered, she saw four bedroom stewards standing around and Ginger sitting on the chair.

One of them was waving his hands in the air saying, "And do you know, there was shit all over the deck-head. Well, I ask you! Then the woman turned to me and said. "Steward, I'll give you five pounds if you'll clean it up." I turned to her and said, "Madam, I will give you ten pounds, if you tell me how you did it."

The bedroom stewards roared with laughter. Then one of them noticed Margaret standing there.

"What do you want, luv?"

"I've got a shirt here for C227, I was told to bring it up to this deck," murmured Margaret, giving Ginger a significant stare, trying to show him she needed desperately to talk.

But this was not to be. Ginger gave a vague smile, and simply took the shirt from her.

"I'm going that way in a minute," he said. Then he carried on talking to the others.

Margaret had no option but to walk out.

When would she ever be able to tell him what she knew?

CHAPTER 21

As the sun was rising, George Bowder finished his 4am to 8am shift. He had been working on one of the engines down below. The heat was so unbearable, he was more than pleased to see the next shift turn up.

The smell of salt on the freshly hosed decks was strong as he came out. It was going to be another hot day.

The deck steward was setting out the chairs, while one of the girl passengers jogged past him in the direction of the swimming pool.

He idly watched the girl's bottom as she went past. He couldn't help being reminded of that bloody laundry girl running away, after clouting him with her shopping. He rubbed his head again. It still hurt.

The worst thing was that could so easily have had her. In an empty dead-end street. If he'd got his hands round her neck she wouldn't have stood a chance. He could have hidden the body in the scrub by the fence and been away with no-one any the wiser. It would have been put down to a street robbery by some local. Must happen all the time in that dreadful place.

But now she was still alive. And the worst thing was that she had actually seen him.

And recognised him.

Would the bloody girl put two and two together and realise that it was he who had tried to murder her in Barbados, and why?

Ricky said she had mentioned Peter again, and had been warned off in no uncertain terms. Strangely enough, though, the girl hadn't said anything to Ricky about the episode in the street.

George frowned. Why had she kept that quiet? It's not the kind of thing you forget to mention... 'Oh, by the way, one of the crew tried to murder me today...'

What was she playing at?

George was so deep in thought that he ended up outside the nursery. He could go no further because it was all caged off. He watched one of the nursery stewardesses using a hosepipe to fill the children's paddling pool, while another one was placing toys around the deck. He turned and went towards the aft-end.

Maybe it would be better for him to keep out of the girl's way for the time being, and next time make sure that she didn't see him at all. After about eight days at sea, and with the excitement of Rio, she might put the incident out of her mind.

According to Ricky, she was besotted with him, so that would help. As long as he got rid of her before they got back to England, that was the most important thing.

He stood on the passengers' deck and gazed out to sea.

Somebody from the galley had thrown a bucket of slops through the hatch. Suddenly a flock of seagulls swarmed upon the food, fighting and screeching over each morsel. George gave a hollow chuckle. The seagulls were like the bloody women in the crew; always screaming and flapping around.

Pests, the lot of them.

Looking down at the crew deck, underneath him, he could see some bedroom stewards leaning over the ship's rail, chatting. One of them was that redheaded queer that he had seen Margaret talking to a few times. He wondered how much the fellow knew. He looked at his watch and decided to go back to his cabin for a quick whisky before breakfast.

---0---

Ginger finished off his last drop of tea, and turned to the rest of the bedroom stewards. "I think I'll go down and see if anybody's made a move, and also give Martha a hand with some of the trays. See you all in the Pig later."

He went down to his section, and stood with his hands on his hips as he looked down the corridor. Too many trays had not been collected by Martha, and were still outside the rooms. Ginger knocked on one of the doors, and when there was no answer, unlocked it and went in.

It was a three-berth cabin; the untidiest of all the ones he looked after. Clothes were scattered around the beds and chair, with toys everywhere.

This was a cabin he dreaded cleaning. The kid wet the bed, so the sheets on the top bunk had to be changed every day. He made a start, but was too late; a child's voice came from the alleyway. Ginger stood back, as the mother and son came in.

"Sorry, Ginger," apologised the woman, "but little Jeffery doesn't feel very well, so I think he'd be better lying down for a while."

"I'll just change his sheet first," said Ginger smiling, but feeling annoyed that he had not managed to get the cabin done before they came back. It meant that he would have to start all over again when they eventually left, and probably change the top bunk a second time.

The next cabin looked as if nobody had used it; everything was so neatly in place. The only giveaway was that the beds were crumpled, with the sheets untucked.

It belonged to that nice couple who complimented him on his tour guide suggestions in San Juan. They had already tipped him well and promised him more.

Ginger laughed to himself. It was always the nice, pleasant passengers that were the least trouble who tipped best. The ones that gave you a work up; the ones who wanted everything they could get; they were usually the bums who either under-tipped, or even did a walkout job.

He started on the bunk, but his mind was still elsewhere.

Margaret. Had she wanted to speak to him the other day? She'd given him such a significant look when handing over the shirt for C227, yet it was only after he'd taken it and she'd gone that it clicked; she was trying to tell him something.

She seemed such a nice girl; a bit shy, but hardly the type to make enemies. So why did he feel sure that somebody was trying to do her in? That episode in the sea off Barbados had all the hallmarks of a murder attempt.

It was only natural that she wouldn't always get on with the other women; they were such a raucous bunch. But that was hardly a reason for murder.

At least she had Ricky – for all he would inevitably break her heart at the end of the trip. Poor kid.

Ginger finished the beds and stood back. "That Ricky," he muttered to himself, "I need to find out more about him, for Margaret's sake. Then get a word with her alone." A sudden thought occurred. "And Ricky seems very thick with that second engineer, Bowder. More than you'd expect from a working relationship. What if there's a connection with Peter's death?" he nodded. "I think I'll have a look into that as well."

He looked around the cabin. There was nothing left to do, so he let himself out.

At about midday, Ginger was left with the three-birther cabin still to service. There was a 'do not disturb' sign on the door. The kid must still be in bed. He went into the pantry, where Martha was quietly sipping at her gin and tonic.

"I'm just nipping up the Pig, Martha," he said. "I won't be long, then I'll relieve you for your lunch. That cabin with the young kid still needs doing."

"Don't worry, Ginger luv, if they come out I'll nip in and get it done."

"Thanks, Martha," said Ginger with a gratified smile.

He made his way up to the Pig and got a beer, then sat with some of the other bedroom stewards.

"I didn't see you at the boat race the other night, Ginger," said one of them, taking a big gulp of his beer. "It was a right

144

laugh. The last team could hardly stand up. It was the deckhands that won it in the end. They always seem to win everything," he added. "Last night they won at darts."

"Isn't one of your brothers a deckhand, Rob?" enquired Ginger.

"Yes. In fact, sometimes I wished I'd been one myself. They have a blooming good life, you know, always drunk."

"You don't do too badly yourself," observed Ginger.

"Well, you know what I mean. They're out working in the fresh air, and don't always have the chief steward running around after them."

"They have the chief officer though," pointed out Ginger.

"Yeah, I suppose you're right. Also, I hear Ricky the bosun keeps bossing them around, I think if I was a deckhand, I'd feel like punching him on the ruddy nose."

"Talking about the bosun, does your brother mention him much?"

"Not a lot. I've heard him say he's a pain in the ass, and fancies himself too much."

"Know anything about him?" asked Ginger, trying to keep his tone casual.

"Don't tell me you fancy him?" laughed Rob.

Ginger felt himself go red, then lowered his voice, so as not to let the others hear him, "No, to be honest with you," he said, crossing his fingers under the table, "Margaret, the laundry maid, is going out with him, and she, er, asked me to ask about him."

"Oh, that young red-headed steam queen? Yes, I know who you're talking about. Not a bad kid. Too good for him."

"Why do you say that?"

"Well, he's married, and has a couple of young children. In fact, I've met his wife. She's a right looker…" He paused, then added, "But also very hard, if you know what I mean."

Ginger nodded and sat back. A couple of children, eh? Margaret had never mentioned anything about them. Ricky had probably kept that little fact quiet.

"Yes, I've heard that his uncle's on this ship as well. Typical seafarer, they always have somebody related to them."

Ginger's ears pricked up.

"Did you say his uncle? Who's that?"

Before Rob could answer, Lola rushed up to the table.

"Can't stop Ginger," he burst out. "I've got a full table, and I don't trust the commis waiter when we're busy. He hasn't a clue what he's doing. It's about the Drag Extravaganza tonight. Teresa's not well and she's dropping out. She wants you to take her place. I said you would."

Rob had got up and was now over at the bar. Ginger dragged his attention to Lola.

"I told you before Lola, I don't want to do it."

"Come on, Ginger, don't be an old spoilsport. I'll lend you one of my costumes. You'll enjoy yourself, it'll be fun."

Reluctantly, Ginger agreed, and Lola, thanking him profusely, scurried away.

To Ginger's relief, Rob came back, carrying a tray full of beer.

"So you said that Ricky's uncle worked on this ship?" Ginger asked, as Rob sat and handed out the beers.

"Yeah," answered Rob, taking a swig.

"Do you know who the uncle is?" persisted Ginger.

"Yes, he's an engineer."

"An engineer?" asked Ginger in surprise.

"Yes, the second engineer. George Bowder."

CHAPTER 22

Margaret put the finishing touches to her makeup. Tonight was the Drag Extravaganza and she had never been to one before. Ricky had explained to her that it was a concert where all the gays dressed up as women. She wondered if Ginger would be amongst them.

The last time she had seen him was up in the pantry. She could have kicked herself that she hadn't taken the chance to speak to him. She did not expect him just to take the shirt and stay there talking.

She needed to get hold of him. Meanwhile she must never wander ashore again on her own. Even on board she automatically felt cautious when there were no other people around.

"'Ave you finished with that bloody mirror yet?" snapped Eileen. "If you stand there long enough you'll see the blooming devil through it."

"I just have," replied Margaret, looking at Eileen's reflection.

"Fucking sarcasm will get you nowhere."

"The sooner you make it up with Tom the better," butted in Kitty. "You've been nothing but a nark, ever since we left San Juan."

"Do you think you'll make it up with him tonight?" asked Chris.

"If anybody had asked me that question a day after San Juan, I would 'ave told them, definitely no. But now I've got over my anger, I suppose I'm beginning to change my mind a bit. I do miss him." Eileen started to cry. "All I wanted was for him to take me for a meal so we could be together," she snivelled. "And what 'appened? We ended up in the nearest bar sitting with the rest of the crew. And Maureen, the khazi queen, all she could talk about was somebody spewing up in her toilets."

Kitty came over to her and put her arms around Eileen's shoulders.

"Come on luv, I bet when you go up to the Pig, you'll make it up with him."

That made Eileen cry even more.

"Here, have a beer," said Chris, opening up a can. "It'll do you good."

Eileen took the beer, and then began dabbing her eyes dry.

There was a knock at the door and Margaret opened it. It was Owd Rosie, Betty, Eve and Lil.

"Are you ready, girls?" asked Lil.

"We'll be up in a minute," said Chris, "Eileen's just got to finish her makeup."

"Okay kid, we'll save you all a place." She looked over at Margaret, "I suppose you'll be sitting with Ricky?"

"Yes, don't worry about me, Lil."

"Come on," said Lil, turning to the other women. "We'd better get up there."

Margaret waited for the other girls, and they all left together.

The Pig was packed out. Margaret saw Ricky sitting over with the deckhands. He had saved her a place next to him. Eileen, Chris and Kitty went to sit with the other laundry women.

The stage was all decked out in tinsel, and looked quite impressive.

Margaret settled herself next to Ricky; he already had a can of beer waiting for her.

She looked around the room for Ginger, but could not see him; however, she noticed Tom with Paddy and the waiters. Tom was looking over in Eileen's direction. Margaret hoped that they would make it up. Living with Eileen these past few days was murder. She felt quite sorry for the girl, especially when she

148

had burst into tears tonight. She could understand how upset she must be feeling.

If it was her and Ricky, Margaret would feel the same.

A few minutes later a woman with long blonde hair, in a beautiful evening dress full of sequins, got hold of the microphone and made an announcement.

"Good evening, ladies and gentlemen, may I welcome you all to tonight's Drag Extravaganza. I hope you all enjoy the show and a big round of applause for all of us beautiful women taking part."

There was lots of whistling, clapping and stamping of feet.

"That's Lola," whispered Ricky in Margaret's ear.

"For real, Ricky?" Margaret whispered back. "I thought it was an actual woman."

There was a musical introduction, then two other drag queens entered. They began singing 'Sisters'.

The whistles from the audience grew louder, and the two singers played up to the crowd. One of them came up to a waiter, sat on his knee and started fondling his hair. "And Lord help the sister," he carried on singing, "Who comes between me and my man."

The audience clapped, whistled and banged their beer cans on the table. The waiter's face turned scarlet.

The two singers left to thunderous applause, and another woman came out. She had long red hair, an unnaturally big bust, and was beckoning the audience to join in with her. 'Old Shanty Town' was her first song, followed by 'Bare Foot Days'. The whole crowd sang along. "She's got a lovely voice," said Margaret, in Ricky's ear.

"You know who that is?" he said, trying to make himself heard over the noise of the singing.

"Who?" she asked.

"Your mate, Ginger."

"Ginger? No!" Margaret studied the singer carefully. Now Ricky said it, there was a slight resemblance, but she would never have recognised him in a thousand years.

The Drag Extravaganza lasted about two hours. It was one of the best shows Margaret had ever seen.

An hour later, the Pig was still quite full, with raucous chatter, drunken shouts and occasional singing.

Margaret glanced around. Tom was leaning over at the laundry women's table, talking to Eileen. Then there was a big cheer from the women as Eileen stood up and went over to Tom. They held hands as he led her over to his table.

She's made it up at last, thought Margaret.

A deckhand came over to her table holding a guitar. "Come on, Ricky, give us a song."

Ricky took the guitar, strummed a few chords, then launched into song with 'In My Liverpool Home'. He had quite a good voice, although it was soon drowned out by the rest of the crowd joining in.

Margaret waited until the song was finished, then whispered in Ricky's ear, "I really have to nip to the loo."

She made her way to the bottom of the stairs as fast as she could. Just as she was going through the door, she spotted Ginger, still in drag. He had his back to her, talking to another of the performers. They looked deep in conversation and unlikely to leave anytime soon. So Margaret decided that answering nature's call took precedence and ducked into the toilets.

She was as quick as she could be, and ran out to grab Ginger. But to her dismay she found that he had gone.

She ran round the corner, but there was no sign of him.

Maybe he'd gone to the Pig? But when she pushed her way back inside, there was no sign of his busty figure.

Ricky was now singing another song. He saw Margaret, gave a smile and pretended to serenade her.

150

She grinned as he finished the song and put down the guitar.

"I won't have any voice left to give you lot orders tomorrow," he said, laughing at the deckhands.

"Well, at least have another drink," said one of them.

"Okay, one more for the road, and then I want time with my girl."

Those last few words made Margaret quite forget her mission to find Ginger.

When they had finished their drinks, Ricky and Margaret made their way back to his cabin. He said something as they walked, but it was slurred, and she didn't catch it. Although there was no doubt she had had a few too many herself.

He led her into his cabin and switched on the bulkhead light, then locked the door behind them.

Ricky took her in his arms, then she felt his hand pulling down the zip of her dress…

A short while later, they were lying together on his bunk.

"That was beautiful, darling," he said, and then turned on his side.

She put her arms around him, hoping that he would face her again and give her a kiss.

But he just lay there and after a moment, started snoring.

Margaret stared at the back of his head and sighed. Clearly he wasn't going to walk her to her cabin as usual, and she would have to go alone.

She got up and dressed, and was just about to let herself out of the door when she noticed that there was something lying on the deck. It was a small photograph. It must have fallen out of his locker. She walked over to the light and looked at it more closely.

It was a photo of Ricky, standing proudly with his arm round a beautiful woman. In front of them were two lovely children, a boy and a girl.

Margaret's hands began to shake. He had never mentioned anything about children to her. She put it back where she had found it and ran out of the cabin on the brink of tears.

Why had he not mentioned his children? She would never have allowed herself to get so involved with him if she had known.

How were they going to be affected by the divorce?

Margaret made her way through the passageways, tears now flowing freely.

That photograph burned in her mind. If only life wasn't so complicated! She loved Ricky with all her heart. But he'd lied to her – or at least, concealed the truth. Could she give him up now? Not if she loved him so much.

She stopped to get her bearings, and wiped her eyes with a hankie from her bag. Ricky would usually take her back through the passengers'accommodation. but with being on her own she did not like facing the master-at-arms. So she took a turn instead into the working alleyway.

It was very quiet at this early hour of the morning, and with living quarters at far end, Margaret had quite a way to walk. She made her way as quickly as she could. There was not a person in sight, which made her uneasy. She was used to walking through when it was busy with other crew members.

An iron door opened just up ahead; one that led up from the engine room.

Margaret stopped sharply, gripping the side rail for support.

A foot in a white shoe emerged.

As she stood frozen, a man stepped out; his bulk filling the alleyway.

The second engineer.

For a dreadful few seconds they stood facing eachother in silence. Then Bowder hissed, "You. The steam queen."

Margaret's legs felt like jelly as she clung to the rail.

Bowder took a step forward. "No bags to swing at me now, you little bitch."

Margaret found herself staring at the man as he advanced, transfixed like a deer in headlights.

Run! Now! Run for your life!

She pushed off the rail. Turned and ran.

The alleyway seemed to stretch forever, and she could hear the thud of his feet behind her.

Where was the turning to the passengers' accommodation?

With the welcome chance to bump into the master-at-arms?

Then suddenly the thudding behind her stopped.

Margaret slowed and glanced back. Bowder was stopped in the middle of the alleyway, his face red and his hands on his knees. He seemed to be fighting for breath.

Margaret backed away, then turned and ran again, before he could recover.

She reached her cabin and slipped inside, locking the door.

As the ship sailed on.

CHAPTER 23

The restaurant was busy the next evening, as Tom came out of the revolving doors leading from the galley.

He was still thinking about the night before; how he had made it up with Eileen. He was getting fed up with men's company all the time, and besides, she wasn't really a bad bird. Oh, she had her faults, but he could have a laugh with her.

It had been an eventful morning in the restaurant. Lola had not shown up at the start of the shift, and poor young Paul the commis waiter, had to take over from him. The headwaiter was doing his nut, promising that he was going to log Lola for failing to be on duty. When lunchtime came, Lola finally appeared, still with some make-up on. Tom overheard one of his passengers saying, "I'm sure that waiter's wearing lipstick."

"Yes, he is," agreed man's companion. "Maybe too much kissing with his girlfriend."

But it seemed that Lola had overheard this as well. He marched over to the table and started shouting at them.

Tom was quick to wade in and try to calm down both his passengers and Lola, but it was the headwaiter who soon appeared.

Lola was ordered back to his cabin until he had sobered up.

To everyone's amazement, Lola flung down his tray cloth, burst into tears, and stormed out of the Pacific restaurant.

And now it was dinner, and Lola was back on duty. He was a very subdued queen, apologising to everyone.

Tom had taken the orders for dinner from all his passengers, apart from one. The stupid old woman who was always last to finish was going through the whole menu.

"I'll have the jellied consommé en tasse," she said, as Tom wrote it down. "No, no. The pear fritters sound nice. I'll have those instead." Tom scratched it out, and wrote 'pears'.

"Now shall I have the fish, the baked silver smelts, St Germaine?" Tom paused with his pen poised. "Or maybe the roast leg and shoulder of Welsh lamb?" She looked up at Tom. "What do you recommend?"

Fighting back the urge to recommend she just order something, he said, "the lamb is good."

She smiled. "Maybe so, but I'll have the fish." Tom kept his pen poised. "No, maybe the lamb, if you say it's good."

"Are you sure?" he asked.

"Oh!" she looked confused. "No, I'm not sure. Maybe the fish."

Tom wrote it down, and said, "Fish it is," then quickly left before she could change her mind again. As he walked away he heard her saying to the passenger sitting next to her, "He's such a nice young man our waiter. Very patient."

The galley was busy as usual, and noisy too, with plenty of banging and clattering of pans, plates and cutlery. The chef was running around the kitchen like a scalded cat, losing his temper with some of his staff.

Tom took another quick swig of beer, in its usual place at the back of the silver locker.

"Another few days and then we'll be in Rio," said Paddy, grinning back at him. "I can't wait. It's certainly a man's paradise. I think the women there are the most beautiful in the world. I'm certainly going to pick one up. In fact," he leaned closer to Tom, "I'm going for one, for full time. More expensive, ye know, but by Jaysus, it's worth it. In fact I bet more than half the ship's crew will fall through there. It's worth a logging."

Tom nodded. Paddy was right, the women were beautiful, and they had that lovely brown eggshell-coloured complexion.

Maybe he would have been better making it up with Eileen after Rio? Well, he would decide what to do when they reached it.

---0---

Margaret had spent the whole day down in the laundry thinking about her two massive problems; Ricky's photo, and the murderous second engineer.

First Ricky.

If only he had told her he had two children. She didn't want to break up a family. According to the way Ricky talked, it sounded as if there was only him and his wife, and in addition he made her out to be a proper bitch. In fact, Margaret had ended up feeling sorry for poor Ricky.

She must try and get hold of him sometime today and speak to him. Last time she had confronted him over his wife, he had explained how wrong she was thinking that they were happily married. What was going to be his excuse this time?

And the second engineer.

She had put two and two together ever since the ship had left San Juan. It must have been Peter's feet that she had seen on the night she had walked into Bowder's cabin. Otherwise why was the man out to get her? A cold shiver ran down her spine. He'd murdered Peter, and now he was out to kill her. That was why she had to see Ginger. He was the only person that she could talk to. He would understand. He would know what to do.

At last the long day came to an end. She climbed the stairs leading to the working alleyway.

"Coming for a quick drink?" asked Billy. "We're having a few down in the cabin."

"Not now Billy, if you don't mind. Some other time. I've got to wash my hair."

"Wash your hair," he laughed, "you women are all the same."

Margaret left him at the top of the steps as he went off in another direction. The truth was, she was hoping to bump into Ricky. Sometimes he would be sitting in the Petty Officers' mess room, which was situated off the working alleyway.

She popped her head around the corner. He wasn't there.

Maybe he was at the aft-end. At times she would find him doing some splicing.

She hurried along and couldn't help shuddering when she passed the iron door. Another chance meeting with Bowder last night – and no-one else there to help. Thank goodness she'd found the ability to run, and he'd been so out of condition he couldn't keep up.

At last she reached the stairs leading to the after-end. She went through the doors leading to the open deck.

She looked around for Ricky and was pleased to see him standing there, cutting away at some rope.

"Hello Ricky," she said, walking over to him.

"Hi, Margaret, and how's my girl today?"

He had only to say the words 'my girl', and it made her heart do a somersault.

Ricky took her in his arms and gave her a quick kiss.

"You fell asleep on me last night," she said, feeling her voice trembling.

"Sorry about that, Margaret, I guess I had too much to drink."

"Ricky, I…"

"What is it, love?" He had such an open, honest look that her nerve failed her.

"Nothing."

"Okay. Are you coming down for a drink later?" He gave her a broad smile.

Margaret heard herself saying. "Yes, Ricky, I'll look forward to seeing you."

"Right then," he said, dismissing her, "I've got a lot of work to do. I'll see you tonight."

158

She left him to continue with his work.

When she arrived back at her cabin, she climbed onto her bunk and sat staring at the far wall, clasping her knees to her chest.

What kind of girl can run away from a murderer, but can't even have a difficult conversation with her boyfriend?

At eight-thirty that evening Margaret knocked on Ricky's door. It was usually unlocked and tonight was no exception, but she always felt that it was good manners to knock first.

He opened the door with a big smile.

"Come on in, Margaret."

She went over to the day bed and sat down. He poured her a beer.

"You're looking very serious tonight, love. Something up?"

"Well yes, Ricky, there is." She could feel herself trembling. She did not want it to end with him, but she could not take him away from his children either.

He sat next to her, and his eyes looked grave.

"You see, Ricky," she began, "when you fell asleep on me last night, I had to get up and see myself home. I was just about to go through the door when I saw something on the floor and picked it up. It turned out to be a photo of you, your wife and children." She frowned. "I can't go out with a man if I think he's going to walk out on his kids." She was about to carry on now that she had found her words, when he interrupted her.

"Has anybody ever mentioned to you that I have kids?" he asked.

"No. Nobody at all."

"Then," he continued, "how do you know I have any?"

"Well, by the photograph."

"And do you know what my wife looks like?"

"No, no idea at all."

"So how do you know then that it is my wife and my children?"

"I suppose I don't," admitted Margaret, feeling a bit foolish.

"That photo happens to be of me, with my cousin and her two children. She was widowed a couple of years ago. Does that answer your question?"

"You mean, Ricky, that they are not your children?" She downed her beer in one go.

"Exactly. If I'd had had any, I would have told you long ago. I hope you're not going to cross-examine me anymore, Margaret," he said laughingly.

She felt so relieved that she put her arms around his neck and gave him a big hug.

"Hey, steady on," he said, giving her a kiss. "Here, I'll pour you another drink."

She looked at him affectionately. How could she have ever doubted him?

CHAPTER 24

The *Ocean Star* sailed slowly into Rio harbour. Margaret was drinking in the breath-taking view, when Billy tapped her on the shoulder.

"That's Sugarloaf Mountain," he said, pointing across the bay.

"I can't wait to get ashore," said Margaret, on her toes with excitement. "It's just what I imagine paradise to be like."

"A lot of blokes on here think like that too," laughed Joe, the other laundry boy.

"We'd better get down and get some work done, kid," said Owd Rosie, "The quicker we get finished, the quicker Freddy will let us go."

"Off ashore with Ricky tonight, Maggie?" asked Johnny.

"No," answered Margaret, "but he's going to take me out tomorrow night."

"Where're you going today then?"

"Well, this afternoon Rosie and I are taking a taxi to Christ's Statue," said Margaret. Rosie nodded.

Johnny paused a while, and then said, "Seeing Old Freddy's giving us the day off tomorrow, why don't you come to the beach with us? We'll be back early, because we want to go out as well later. You'll have time to get ready for Ricky."

"Thank you, Johnny, I'd love to," answered Margaret with enthusiasm. "That's if you don't mind me tagging along with you all."

"Oh, you won't be with us in the evening," he laughed back.

The laundry staff finished at eleven o'clock that morning. Margaret and Owd Rosie had some lunch in the mess room, then disembarked by twelve-thirty.

They both entered the terminal, and Margaret stopped to look through the windows of Stern's, the famous jewellers. She was thinking what a fantastic display of precious stones. The settings were beautiful; very unusual.

"I've never seen jewellery like it," she gasped. "I wish I was a millionaire, I'd buy the lot. Could you picture the look on the faces of that crowd in the laundry if I came down wearing all this?"

"I don't think you'd be working in a laundry, kid, if you were that rich," said Owd Rosie dryly. They decided to have a quick look inside the shop.

"Can I help you?" asked one of the assistants, who spoke in a half-American and half-Portuguese accent."

Margaret stared at the girl. She was very pretty, with an olive complexion. The kind Margaret had always longed for.

"No, thanks, kid," said Owd Rosie. "We're just looking."

"Could I have a look at that ring, please?" asked Margaret, pointing to one with a pale blue stone.

"That one?" asked the girl, reaching for the ring.

Margaret nodded.

"You've picked Rio's most famous stone, an aquamarine." A smile came over the girl's lovely face. "An exquisite stone."

Rosie asked the price, and when told, both women pulled a face at each other.

"It would be very expensive in England," continued the assistant.

"We'll look around the shops, kid, I bet they'll be cheaper there."

"Maybe cheaper," repeated the girl, still smiling, "but beware, they have many shops in Rio selling stones. They might not cost as much, but sometimes they are made of glass. Here, all our stones are of a very good quality. We are a reputable company."

"How can you tell the difference between a real stone and a glass one?" asked Margaret, out of curiosity.

The girl looked at her again, and said, "Rub the stone quite fast against your skin, then feel it. If it is warm, then it is glass. Stone will not heat up."

"Thank you, that's very interesting. I'll have another look at it when we come back," said Margaret, handing the ring to the assistant.

"Have a nice time in Rio," said the girl, returning it to the showcase.

The two women made their way out of the terminal and headed towards a row of Volkswagens, that turned out to be the taxis. Ricky had told Margaret to check the price first at the terminal, which she had already done, then make a deal with the taxi driver.

The driver was a pleasant man who spoke good English. He explained to them that they would have to take a two-to-three mile train journey on the Corcovado Railroad, to get to the Christ the Redeemer statue. He would drive them to the station in Cosme Velho.

They thanked him and jumped into the taxi.

Rio was a very busy city. Margaret felt slightly dazed by the mayhem of the city's streets, avenues and sidewalks. The driver kept switching lanes, cutting in and out, tailgating, and provoking a din of shrieking brakes and blaring horns. He drove on, casually smiling and flapping his hand, from one near-disaster to the next.

At last they reached the quaint little station in Cosme Velho. Both Margaret and Owd Rosie were relieved to get out of the taxi.

"Come on, kid," said Owd Rosie, grabbing her arm. "I think the train's in."

Margaret paid the taxi driver, and they both headed for the station.

The journey was thoroughly pleasant; so different from the scary taxi ride. They saw tunnels of lush foliage and the scenery was splendid. When at last they reached the summit, the two of them were greeted by a dizzying view of Sugarloaf Mountain, the southern beaches, swanky residential districts and the shimmering Rodrigo de Freitas lagoon.

"Look!" shouted Margaret to Owd Rosie. "The Christ Statue!"

Margaret started reading out loud, from an English plaque near the monument. "The Christ Statue presiding over the scene is 99 feet (30 meters) tall. The work of a team of artisans headed by French sculptor Paul Landowsky, it was completed in 1931. Behind Corcovado is a network of sub-tropical jungles known as Tijuca National Park. It includes 60 miles (100km) of narrow, two-lane roads featuring a number of spectacular look-out points." Her words trailed off when she looked around and noticed Owd Rosie had walked away, not listening to a single thing she had been saying.

---0---

Ginger went round to Lola's cabin and found him putting the finishing touches to his make-up. Two of the other queens, Delores and Ruby, were sitting on the bunk drinking beer.

"Off to Copacabana, dear?" Delores asked Ginger, when he entered the cabin.

"A Queen's paradise," he laughed back at him, helping himself to a beer from the icebox.

"We might see you around there later on," said Ruby." We thought we'd go for a meal, then on to a nightclub. The talent in Rio is unbelievable, some of them look more like women than the real ones, and more glamorous. I can't wait, my dear, to get there."

"I like a man to look manly, a hunk," said Delores.

"Remember last time we were here?" interrupted Lola, "The Carnival was on." He added a little more lipstick, then pouted at his reflection. "I thought I looked one of the nicest. Certainly better than any of those at the Mangueira Samba School. What fun following in the procession!

"Don't fall through tomorrow," said Ginger, "like you did the other morning after the Drag Extravaganza.

"Oh stuff the head waiter," said Lola, turning angry, "he needn't have had me up in front of the captain for a logging. Other wingers have fallen through and he's turned a blind eye to them."

Ginger and Lola got out of the taxi in the homosexual area of Copacabana, situated at the western end of the beach. It was full of bars and clubs.

The night was warm, and Ginger could hear the music sounding through the red-light district of the streets of Rio.

"Well, we've got several places to choose from," said Ginger, "the Pussy Cat, Erptoka, Swing, Don Juan, or Frank's Bar."

They chose the latter.

As the pair of them were about to enter the bar, George Bowder, the second engineer, came out. Ginger nudged Lola.

"That's George Bowder. He's Ricky's uncle. I must tell Margaret."

But Lola wasn't listening. He was staring at one of the prostitutes; a glamorous redhead in a short skirt, leaning against a wall.

"I swear that one's a bloke," he said. "Great legs, though."

CHAPTER 25

Margaret had her swimming gear packed and was ready to go ashore. She looked over at Eileen who was turning over to sleep off the night before. Tom had taken her for a meal, so at the moment she was at peace with the world. Kitty was also in bed. It was hard trying to get things together, with only a small bunk light to see by. Margaret was frightened of making too much noise. She knew what the result would be if they woke up.

She crept quietly out of the cabin, closing the door gently behind her. She was to meet Johnny, Billy and Joe at the bottom of the gangway.

What a lovely time she had had the day before! Rio was a beautiful place. The only thing to spoil it was that she hadn't seen anything of Ricky. He had told her that he would be busy in port. Anyway tonight he was going to take her out for a meal, then they were going up the Sugarloaf Mountain.

The boys were already waiting on the quayside, and waved Margaret over as soon as they saw her.

"Come on, Maggie," shouted Johnny, "We haven't got all day."

They walked past the jewellers that she and Owd Rosie had looked in the day before. Margaret was still in two minds as to whether to splash out and buy the ring. Then a thought came to her mind, wouldn't it be nice if Ricky bought her one?

The four of them went over to the taxi rank and struck a deal with the driver. Again the journey was nerve-racking, but with the excitement of going to the famous Copacabana beach, and seeing Rio again, it didn't seem too bad.

At last they reached their destination, jumped from the taxi, and made their way towards the crowded beach. Thousands of people were sunbathing and playing near the water's edge; a melting pot of class and colour. Some people were flying kites that resembled eagles, and every few yards there were vendors selling iced tea.

"Copacabana welcomes everyone, whatever their class or colour," said Johnny, standing beside her. "Unlike its wealthy neighbour, Ipanema."

They found a spare bit of sand and laid out their towels to secure their places.

Margaret couldn't wait to get into the sea. As soon as she had changed, she picked her way through the bodies to get to the water. Johnny followed closely behind.

Everybody seemed to be lovely and tanned. The women were so beautiful and the men really handsome. Most of them were in couples, embracing and kissing each other.

She was just putting her toe into the water to test it, when Johnny picked her up and threw her into the sea. Margaret screamed, half-laughing. It wasn't as warm as the Caribbean, and the surf was strong, swelling and ebbing.

Later she lay on the beach to sunbathe, then slept. She didn't want to be too tired for the evening.

When Margaret woke up, the others had disappeared.

With panic rising she searched across the beach.

Then she let out a relieved breath. They were playing some kind of ball game with the locals. She decided to go and join them.

Even though none of the locals could speak English, they all laughed away together, the others chattering in Portuguese. They seemed friendly people.

"I think it's time we had a bite to eat," said Johnny, after playing for about half an hour.

They left the party with a friendly wave, and went to collect their belongings.

The four of them walked along the sidewalks, mingling with the people, as they made their way through street markets and beachfront bars.

Margaret thought the atmosphere was incredible.

At last they found a little bar, where they could sit outside. They ordered a cool draught beer each and a plate of Sandwiches Americana.

Margaret gazed across the hills rising above the beach. Rich and poor seemed to be equally represented in Rio. There were the luxury high-rise apartment buildings for the wealthy, as well as the shantytowns hanging like tarnished ornaments from the forested granite mountains.

When they had finished eating, Johnny decided that they had better make their way back to the ship.

Though Margaret was enjoying every minute of the day, she did want to arrive back in time to get ready for Ricky. She felt rather sorry for him having to work the two days in Rio.

---0---

Tom was sitting in a club watching a strip show. Though it was early afternoon, they still had entertainment on. He was drinking an ice-cold beer while a young girl on the stage danced naked around a pole, manoeuvring her body in a sensual way.

But his mind was only partly on the girl. The night before he had taken Eileen for a cheap meal at one of the open bars in Copacabana. Would that pacify her for a while? Probably. She could hardly accuse him of not taking her out, and for all she knew, this afternoon he was putting his head down in his bunk.

Across the floor, he noticed Ricky, the bosun, sitting with a couple of deckhands. They seemed to be enjoying the dancer's gyrations immensely.

The dancer gave him a 'come-on' look, and slowly licked her lips. The low lights, sexy music and the dancer looking him in the eye – all these began to excite him. He could feel a familiar stirring in his crotch.

It was no good; he couldn't stand it any longer.

After the show, he had to have her away, or any woman who was available.

To his relief he saw Ricky and the deckhands getting up to go. The less they knew about his business, the better.

A short time later Tom did the same, but he went in a different direction.

---0---

Margaret arrived back at her cabin in time to get showered and changed; tired but happy after her lovely day in Rio with the laundry boys. Although she did feel a twinge of guilt that poor Ricky had been working.

Eileen was chattering away about the night before; how her fella had taken her for a great meal and what a fabulous evening they'd had together.

Chris had been away all night and still hadn't returned, but the other two didn't seem too bothered about it.

"Do you think she'll be alright?" inquired Margaret, who had a feeling that Eileen and Kitty were sharing some secret joke.

"Don't worry about her, luv," replied Eileen, "I think she has some cousins living here."

"What a long way from Liverpool to come and live," said Margaret, "Fancy choosing Rio."

They both laughed out loud.

Margaret decided to laugh back and go along with the joke. Let them have their fun.

There was a knock and Ricky popped his head through the open cabin door. Margaret felt very proud of him. Tall and tanned, he was wearing white trousers, with a black shirt to match.

"Ready then?" he asked, with a broad smile.

As usual, looking at him, her heart started beating faster.

"See you later, girls," she said, as she slipped her arm around his.

They went through the passengers' accommodation to reach the gangway. On the way they passed Ginger's section. Old Martha was sitting in the pantry, but there was no sign of Ginger. Martha was knocking back a drink and talking fifty to the dozen to another bedroom steward. She nodded as they walked past, while a strong smell of gin wafted their way.

It was early evening and the air still felt warm. They walked through the terminal to the taxi rank. Stern's the jewellers was still open.

"I saw a beautiful aquamarine ring yesterday, when I was with Owd Rosie," she said to Ricky, "it was in that jewellers. In fact I'm in two minds whether to get it or not."

"If you feel like buying one, go ahead," replied Ricky. "Treat yourself."

So he hadn't got the hint. Maybe if it hadn't have been a ring, he might have done.

"You know something, Ricky, I think I will," she said, on impulse. "I've subbed enough money."

They both walked into the shop, and the same assistant came over to serve them.

"You changed your mind?" she said sweetly, as she took the ring from the showcase, and then slipped it onto Margaret's wedding finger. It fitted perfectly, and the stone shone beautifully.

She noticed Ricky eyeing the girl up and down, and felt a tinge of jealousy, especially when the assistant smiled back at him, gazing up into his eyes. Clearly the girl fancied him.

"I'll take it," said Margaret almost immediately, twisting her finger around, admiring the colour of the stone.

The assistant took the ring and placed it in a little square black velvet box. She looked surprised when Margaret began fiddling in her bag, looking for her purse.

"Isn't your boyfriend going to buy it for you?"

"No," Ricky laughed, with a wink at the shop girl, "I've got another little gift for her."

"A present for me, Ricky?" asked Margaret, looking pleasantly surprised.

"I shouldn't have told you yet, so forget all about it for now. I'll give it to you when we've sailed."

Margaret walked out of the shop with Ricky, feeling that she was on cloud nine.

"We'll take a taxi to Copacabana and have a nice meal there," Ricky said as they made their way towards the rank.

Margaret was still feeling overjoyed about him mentioning a little gift.

As soon as they got into the cab, he put his arms around her shoulders. "I think this is going to be a good evening, one I think we'll always remember."

She snuggled closer to him; of all the people she would wish to be with, in this wonderful city, it was the man beside her.

The sun was beginning to set on the bay as they sat down at an outside restaurant on the Copacabana. She could hear samba music playing in the background.

Ricky ordered a couple of drinks called caipirinhas. A national drink made with crushed lime, peel and all, sugar, ice and cachaca, a strong liquor distilled from sugar cane, with a good measure of vodka.

"When we've finished our meal," Ricky said after they had ordered, "we'll make our way to Praia Vermelho, and catch the cable car to Sugarloaf Mountain. It goes in two stages, you know." He raised his voice above the music coming from the beach, "The first stage is to the 705-foot Morro da Urca. That's the low mountain in front of Sugarloaf. Then the final leg is from there to Sugarloaf."

"How high is Sugarloaf?" asked Margaret, trying to show interest in the technical side of the conversation.

"About one thousand three hundred feet," replied Ricky. "I have been up there before. It was in the daytime and the view was out of this world. You could see all over Rio; the beaches of Leme, Copacabana, Ipanema, Leblon and the mountains in the background." He paused and looked up. "Of course, it's getting dark, so instead you'll see all the lights of Rio. It's magical; you'll love it."

The waiter came with the drinks, and Ricky lifted the glass towards Margaret, smiling, "To us."

She lifted hers, and they clinked glasses.

"Cheers," they said together.

The cable car was an experience in itself. According to the little plaque by the door it held twenty-four passengers. It was certainly full to capacity that evening, with locals chattering away in Brazilian Portuguese.

They reached Morro da Urca and got out to wait for the second car. Ricky was right. The city below looked absolutely fabulous in the dark; as if lit up by a million twinkling fairy lights.

The next cable car arrived and all those going to the top piled in. It rose smoothly away from the platform and ascended towards the summit.

Margaret left Ricky's side and squeezed through the crowd to the window so she could get a better look at the view. It was open and a cool breeze was blowing in. She held onto the frame and peered out.

The lights below looked amazing; even better than at Morro da Urca. She leaned a little further out to see more, but then had a wave of dizziness as she realised just how high up they were. She retreated inside, shuddering as an awful thought occurred.

What an ideal place to commit a murder! Just tip someone over the side!

At that very instant the car juddered to a stop, swinging in mid-air. Then the lights went out.

A voice close by said, "Hello steam queen."

Margaret knew it only too well.

It was the second engineer.

With a scream, she started pushing her way through the crowd, desperate to get away from the open window and back to Ricky.

But a large body blocked her way, and she looked up; straight into the second engineer's eyes.

With another scream, she turned away.

There was a set of gleaming white teeth in the dark.

It was Ricky, smiling at her.

CHAPTER 26

Lightning flashed and thunder rumbled as Mick stood by the lounge bar window, watching the *Ocean Star* pulling away from the quayside.

There was a rumour going around that three crew members had missed the ship. Not unusual for Rio, it had happened many a time in the past. They would get a DBS in their discharge book, which meant Displaced British Seaman, and be flown home.

The day before, he had taken his girl Jill to Ipanema. The property values were said to be the highest in Brazil. They spent the afternoon at the beautiful beach, and in the evening he took her for a meal and a show. Being a barman he knew how to tip well, so they ended up with one of the best seats in the house.

Jill had seemed overwhelmed with the extravagant costumes of the performers, and also enjoyed dancing to Latin American music. She whispered in his ear that she would remember that evening as long as she lived. Mick told himself that he always knew how to make a woman feel happy. In fact when they had got back to the ship, and ended up in his cabin, she proved it. Their lovemaking was fantastic.

"I see that the cable car up Sugarloaf Mountain broke down last night," said one of the lounge stewards, busy emptying and cleaning out the ashtrays. "If it had been me up there," he added, "I'd have shat myself."

Yes, I'd heard they'd had an electrical fault," answered Mick. "I'm glad I wasn't on it." He turned away from the window, preparing to get on with some book work.

At least the DBS crew didn't include Tom and Paddy, who were back on board safely. He had heard that Paddy would be going up on the bridge for a logging; he hadn't turned up for duty in the two days in Rio. *The dirty little bastard*, Mick thought, *he'll be up to the doctors' in a week or two.*

A couple of entertainers came up asking for the keys to the piano. They were Mildred and Vince, a husband-and-wife team, who told Mick they wanted to rehearse their act while the lounge was quiet.

Mick passed the keys over to them, wondering how they ever managed to get the job. The singer Mildred was tall and scrawny, while Vince, the pianist, was small, bald, and had a tiny moustache over thin lips. Mick was fed up with their incessant middle-aged music.

What a pity it hadn't been them that had missed the ship.

---0---

Tom was serving lunch. His passengers seemed to want everything on the menu. Had they starved themselves in Rio? All except for that old bitch, who was going through the menu again, changing her mind with every item.

To make matters worse, the commis waiter had fallen through, and wasn't there to help.

How would the passengers feel if he threw soup in their laps, and clocked that old woman round the head with a tray?

At least it would make him feel better.

The truth was, he was feeling decidedly unwell. It hurt like hell to have a pee, and there was also pus coming out.

He must have caught a dose.

He would have to go up and see the doctor for an injection. Hopefully that would clear it up before he got home, and back to the wife.

"I say, whack, you must be the most miserable-looking man after Rio," said Charlie, who was standing by the hot press, as Tom joined him in the queue.

Tom just nodded at him. The sooner lunch was over the better. He'd be putting his head down right away. He went over to the silver locker, and took a big gulp of his beer.

Paddy came over to him with a big grin on his face.

"I sure had a raring good time in Rio. Ye should have seen the tart I was with. She was bloody beautiful. By Jaysus, I hope we come to this port again." He wiped his nose with the back of his hand and continued. "I've got to see the captain later today for a logging. Mind ye," he said, leaning closer to Tom, "it was worth every minute, so it was."

---0---

Ginger finished his last cabin and put his vacuum down with a sigh.

He'd had a great time in Rio. And now to think that it would be Christmas Day just before they reached Dakar.

There had been decorations up in Rio, but with the weather being so hot and sunny, he hadn't really taken much notice. But today the weather had changed. He'd been upstairs early, standing in the doorway, watching the torrential rain beat down on the decks.

Ginger also had to get his costume ready for the pantomime, using some material he'd found in a shop in Rio. He had finally agreed to take part.

Lola had been excited because she was going to play Cinderfella. Originally Delores was going to play the part, the excuse being that she was smaller.

It had taken a fair bit of persuasion by Ginger – and some outright bribery – before Dolores agreed to let Lola be the star.

Ginger put the vacuum away, then decided to go up to the Pig for a quick drink. He was on afternoon watch that day, so a beer would go down well. He could always grab lunch in the crew galley later.

There weren't many people in the Pig, and none of the girls were there. Lola would still be serving lunch, and so would Teresa and Delores.

He got a beer and went over to sit with Rob, who was on his own, nursing a can of beer.

"I believe you're going to be in the pantomime," said Rob, half-smiling. "I bet it'll be a bloody good show, especially if it's anything like the other one you queers put on. I certainly enjoyed myself."

"Thanks, Rob," answered Ginger. It was nice to hear someone praising the queens for a change. "This should be even better, a bigger laugh. In fact I think all us girls will be in it this time."

Another bedroom steward came over to their table. He put a couple of cans in front of them.

"Thanks, Sid," said Rob, "but I was just going for my lunch."

"Oh, come on, Rob," the other man said with a laugh. "Get it down. It'll do you good."

Without much persuasion Rob took the can from Sid, and brought out an opener from his pocket and punctured two triangular holes in the top. He then did the same for Ginger, and poured them out.

The three men carried on drinking.

After a while, the Pig started filling up, and one of the deckhands went over to the piano to bash out a song. That started the ball rolling, and a few minutes later everyone was joining in, singing along.

Rob offered to get another round in. "Just one more," shouted Ginger, "I'm on duty this afternoon, and I've got to go down and relieve old Martha."

"When I've had this one," Rob yelled back, "I'm going down to my cabin and crash out!"

Just as Rob came back with the drinks, Ginger noticed Eileen and Chris come into the bar.

178

"By the way," said Rob, looking over in their direction, then leaning in so he could be heard. "Did you ever say anything to that redhead steam queen, over that fellow she's boxed off with?"

"You mean the bosun Ricky?"

"Yes, him," replied Rob. "I heard a rumour it was him, the steam queen and some officer who missed the ship and got a DBS."

Sid shook his head. "No it was three wingers from the Atlantic restaurant. And I saw the bosun and the redhead coming back on board myself." He drank some beer. "She looked all done in, poor chit. The bosun was practically carrying her."

Rob added, "Well, I saw her going ashore with him yesterday. I can't stomach the man. Doesn't half fancy himself."

"No, I haven't seen anything of her," said Ginger, going back to Rob's original question. "We always seem to keep missing each other." He paused. "In fact I thought Margaret might have been up with the girls for a quick drink. Maybe she's gone down to her cabin for a kip, before going back down to the laundry."

"How they stick that heat down there," said Sid, "I'll never know. In fact I went down there the other day, before Rio, to collect a shirt for one of my passengers. Freddy told me to get it from one of the women, but she hadn't finished ironing it. I had to get out of that place fast, what with all that boiling hot steam hitting you the minute you entered. And," he added, "there was hardly any air coming out of the vents. Yeah, I hold my hand up to them steam queens. If anybody deserves a gold medal, they bloody do."

Ginger laughed. "That shirt for C227?" Sid nodded. "I ended up taking it."

"Cheers mate," Sid said.

Ginger put down his empty glass and stood up. "See you all later," he said, and left the Pig.

Ten minutes later Margaret and Kitty came in.

179

CHAPTER 27

Earlier in the laundry, Owd Rosie had been in a very talkative mood, much to Margaret's annoyance.

"Yes, kid," she said. "I believe it was three wingers from the Atlantic restaurant that missed the ship. I wouldn't like to be in their shoes."

If only the woman would stop rabbiting on. Margaret had too much on her mind to worry about three stupid waiters.

The horror of finding George Bowder in the cable car, just as she'd been thinking how easily she could be pushed through the open window, made her almost faint every time she thought of it.

Would he have risked it in such a small, crowded space – even with the lights out?

She could easily believe he would have tried, then claimed he was attempting to stop her stumbling in the dark, or something.

At least Ricky had been there to gather her into his arms. Although she dared not tell him her fears of what Bowder might have done, so she'd said it was all about being scared the cable car would plunge to the ground when it stopped and the lights went out.

He'd seemed almost angry about that – as if this had spoiled something he'd been planning.

Then after a few minutes, the car started moving again to cheers from everyone inside, only this time they were going down the mountain.

When they reached Morro da Urca, shock had set in, and Margaret was feeling so faint she could hardly stand.

Ricky was helping her into the next cable car, when the second engineer came over.

"I see you are taking the same trip as me," he said.

Margaret shuddered at how close the man was to her; his sweaty odour had sickened her.

The sooner she could get to Ginger, the better.

The temperature in the laundry seemed to be getting higher. Margaret kept mopping her brow as the sweat poured down her face. Even her white cotton uniform was soaking wet.

As soon as the shift was over, Chris and Eileen went straight to the Pig, but she and Kitty decided to get changed first, then meet the other two up there.

They got back to the cabin and started to get changed.

"It's a right shame it's pissing with rain," Kitty observed. "Or it would be nice to cool off on deck."

"Hmm," Margaret agreed.

"I've seen you at the rail on the lifeboat deck a few times," Kitty said. She gave Margaret a hard look. "You do know you aren't supposed to be there? You could get in right trouble if you're caught."

"I like it up there," Margaret replied. "I can see flying fish, or dolphins diving in and out of the water. And the lifeboat gives me shade if the sun gets too hot." She smiled. "Anyway, Ricky knows it's my favourite spot. He even says they should put a plaque there with my name on."

They set off for the Pig.

Just as she was passing through the crew alleyway, Margaret happened to see Ginger, walking up the stairs to the galley.

She bolted up the stairs after him, but it was too late; he had disappeared through the door. She would have carried on after him, but knew the slagging she would get from the galley crew, so decided against it and went back to join her friend.

"Where the hell do you think you're running off to, like a scalded rabbit?" asked Kitty, looking wide-eyed at Margaret.

"I just wanted to see Ginger about something," she said, knowing it sounded a feeble excuse.

Kitty shrugged, and they carried on.

When they arrived in the Pig, Billy came over and shoved an envelope in her hand.

"From Ricky," he said. "He gave it to me when I was passing the crew galley."

"Thanks, Billy," she said, tearing it open and unfolding a short letter.

'Dear Margaret,' it read, 'Couldn't find you around, so just to let you know, I'll see you down in my cabin at eight thirty, instead of nine. Will give this note to the first person I see. Love Ricky.'

She smiled to herself. This wasn't the first time she had got a little message from him. It would always be typed, as he had only got a typewriter at the beginning of the trip, and wanted to practise his typing skills.

"Everything okay, Maggie?" asked Billy, looking over her shoulder, trying to read the letter.

"Yes," she smiled back at him. "It's only Ricky telling me to see him half an hour earlier. Thanks for giving it to me, Billy."

He walked away, looking slightly disappointed that it hadn't been something more exciting.

Margaret tucked the letter back in the envelope. Seeing Ricky half an hour earlier would mean getting his gift even sooner.

Later in the mess room, Margaret was having her dinner, while Owd Rosie was trying to chew through a tough piece of steak with teeth that kept slipping around her mouth. Margaret had to look away. It made her feel sick.

Tony, the crew mess man, came over and placed a fresh jug of water on their table. "What's this I hear, Maggie, about you being stranded up Sugarloaf Mountain?"

"Yes," she said, glad of an excuse to turn away from Owd Rosie. "It was awful, I thought the cable car was going to plunge to the ground. I nearly had kittens."

Tony burst out laughing. "I'd have more than bloody kittens if that was me. Anyhow," he continued, "how did the other people react, did they panic?"

"Well," answered Margaret, "there were only about a dozen of us in the car, and that included Ricky, and the second engineer…"

"You mean that old George Bowder fellow, and Ricky the bosun?" interrupted Tony, before she had time to finish her sentence.

"Yes," answered Margaret.

"God help you being stuck with them two, I think I would have preferred to take the plunge." He turned from the table, and headed towards one of the stewardesses, who were shouting over to him about her cup being dirty.

Margaret couldn't help wondering what he'd meant by that last remark.

Dead on eight-thirty, Ricky let her into his dimly lit cabin.

She sat down on his day bed. There was a bottle of champagne standing in a bucket of ice, half covered with a white napkin, with two upturned glasses.

Ricky unlocked his cupboard and took out a small wrapped parcel. He said with a boyish smile, "It's just a little something from me. I saw it in the ship's shop, and immediately thought that's definitely Margaret." He handed it over.

Margaret's hands were shaking as she unwrapped the paper, pausing at one point to look up expectantly at Ricky.

Would it be a brooch, or maybe a necklace? A pair of earrings? Something to show his love?

But all she found inside was a dark brown plastic hair comb, covered with diamante stones.

A comb?

Was that what all the fuss had been about? The way he'd been going on, anyone would have thought they were real diamonds.

All that gorgeous jewellery in Rio and this was his surprise?

184

"It's lovely, Ricky, thank you," she said, putting on a brave face.

"I know that it's only a small gift, to fit in your beautiful red hair when you have it up." He smiled. "You might be wondering why I didn't give it you on Christmas Day." He put his hand on her knee. "I have got you a Christmas present as well."

That was nice, but Margaret was still puzzled as to what all the fuss was about.

"Let's have some champagne." Ricky popped the cork and poured them both a glass. Although as he put the bottle back in the bucket, she noticed it was actually only sparkling wine.

"Cheers," he said, as he clinked his glass against hers.

They both sat there, quietly drinking the fizz.

Ricky took the glass from Margaret's hand and put it on the table. He looked seriously into her eyes and gave her a little kiss on the lips.

"You see, Margaret, I know that it is only a small gift, but I want you to guard it with your life."

Guard a plastic hair comb with my life? Filled with fake diamonds? How cheap does he think I am?

His next words began to change things.

"When we get back to England, I will be coming to your house after a few days. But first I shall have to go home with Babs. As you know, she will be meeting me on docking day. Now Margaret, even though I don't really want to go back with her, because I've explained before it's all over with the two of us, I will need to go with her initially." He kissed her again. "For me it's going to be very hard work, because I will be thinking of you all the time."

Her heart began to melt again, as she looked deep into his eyes.

"I am going to tell Babs," said Ricky, looking as though he could be in tears at any moment, "that I want a divorce, and that I have met you."

185

"I don't want to break anybody's marriage up," said Margaret, "I don't want that on my conscience."

"Darling, I have already told you, that it was over before I ever met you. In fact, I think she has another man."

"Well, I suppose in that case, it's not my fault," replied Margaret.

"No, it's got nothing to do with you."

Ricky then stood up and poured the remainder of the drink into the glasses, then handed hers back to Margaret.

"You see," he said, "the reason I want you to take care of this comb, is that when I come to see you, I want you to give it back to me."

"Give it back!" squeaked Margaret.

"Yes. I know it's only a cheap little gift, but if you have it when we meet again, I will know that you have taken care of it, and you must really love me. Then that's when I will be swapping it for a real diamond ring."

"An engagement ring?" Margaret could hardly keep the joy in her voice.

"Yes, and then it will be me that keeps the comb safely, until I swap it back again, along with a gold band."

"Oh Ricky," cried Margaret with joy. "You old romantic thing, you!" She put down her glass and flung her arms around his neck.

"Will you promise me now, that you will look after it for my sake?"

"Is it alright if I wear it?" asked Margaret, "I will take care of it."

"Well, only wear it on a special occasion when you're with me. Maybe when we're in Madeira, on New Year's Eve. Don't forget I want to give it back to you with that other ring. Oh, and Margaret," said Ricky, the grin going from his face, "don't mention anything to anyone; what I've said about Babs and me.

186

Keep that a little secret between us. You know what people are like – they talk, and I want to be the one to tell her first."

"Ricky," said Margaret, trembling with excitement, "I won't say a thing about you and Babs to anybody, I promise. And as for the comb, now I know what the motive behind it is, I'll look after it as if it were filled with real diamonds."

CHAPTER 28

It was two o'clock in the morning. Tom was drinking beer with Eileen on her bunk. Chris was sprawled on a bunk with her beer. Kitty was fast asleep on the top bunk.

Margaret peered round the door, then slid in, looking rather sheepish. She was clutching a small package.

"I thought you'd all be in bed," she said, rather apologetically.

Eileen said, "You look flushed, Maggie. She winked at Chris. "Been on yer back a bit, eh?"

"Would you like a drink, Maggie?" asked Tom, bringing a beer out of a cardboard box.

"Well," she hesitated, "okay then."

She twisted the little parcel in her hand, as though she was trying to hide it.

Eileen leaned forward.

"What the fuck is that you're fumbling with?" she demanded, pointing at it.

"A little present from Ricky," Margaret answered.

"Well come on then, show it us all," cried Eileen, who looked as if she was about to snatch it from her.

Margaret reluctantly unwrapped the package and showed them what it held.

"Mm, not bad," said Chris, taking it from her hand. "It'll look nice in your hair."

"Here, let me 'ave a look," said Eileen, grabbing it from Chris. "Don't tell me they're real diamonds set in cheap plastic," she said sarcastically.

Tom looked at the comb closely. They did look real. It was surprising how realistic they could make things, in this day and age. He tapped it thoughtfully against his hand. *Now there's an idea…*

"Where did you get it from?" asked Chris.

"Ricky gave it to me. It's only a cheap comb. He bought it for me from the ship's shop, I think it's a lovely thought though."

"Is it your Christmas present?" Eileen asked, trying to stop the laughter in her voice.

"No," answered Margaret, frowning at her. "Ricky has already got me my present, this is just a little gift to let me know that he is thinking of me."

"Bloody shit!" retorted Eileen. "I've heard of everything now! And what about his wife?"

"What about Tom's wife?" snapped Margaret.

"What about her?" asked Eileen, standing up and beginning to stab her fingers in Margaret's chest.

"Stop it! The pair of you," said Tom, pulling Eileen away from Margaret. "Leave my wife out of this. Sit down and behave yourselves."

Eileen flopped down again and took a gulp of her beer.

"Is anyone meeting you when the ship gets back to Liverpool?" asked Tom, sounding as if he was trying to change the subject.

"No," answered Margaret, putting the present away in her bottom drawer. "I had a letter in Rio from my mum, and she says that my sister and brother-in-law will be away the day the ship gets back to Liverpool. Mum hasn't been too well lately; so I've written her back to tell her not to bother travelling all the way down to meet me. I'll get the train home."

"What station will you be leaving from?" asked Tom, wanting Eileen to see that he could be politely interested in someone other than her.

"Exchange Street station. I'll get a taxi there, and then get another at the other end to take me to my house. Luckily enough, I don't live too far from the station."

"Why do you want to know?" asked Eileen, turning to Tom. "You going to hold her fucking hand to make sure she gets home alright?"

"Okay Eileen, stop the sarcasm," said Tom standing up and finishing his beer. "Anyhow I'm going now, see you tomorrow."

He gave Eileen a quick kiss on the lips and left before she could reply.

Outside the door, he paused a moment.

That comb!

Margaret said that Ricky had bought it from the ship's shop.

Tom grinned as he set off down the corridor. He had the answer at last, on how to get his diamonds ashore in Liverpool!

All he had to do was get another comb exactly like Margaret's. Give it to Paddy, along with the stones. Paddy was a mechanically minded person, so he would be the one to set the jewels.

Then swap it with Margaret's when she was out of her cabin, and hey presto, she would be taking the diamonds ashore for him.

When Tom crept into the cabin, his other shipmates were fast asleep. They had automatically left his bunk light on, so he quietly slipped off his clothes and jumped up on the top bed.

Now he had the answer to smuggling the diamonds off the ship, Tom couldn't sleep. He lay on his back with his hands behind his head, working out the details, until eventually the night steward knocked on the door with his wake-up call.

---0---

Tom found Paddy on the poop deck with a morning pint, and explained his idea.

"Once we've swapped the combs and she's taken ours through customs, how are we going to get ours back?" asked Paddy.

191

"Easy, Paddy," Tom replied, "All you have to do is take the same train as Maggie, sit next to her, ask to see her comb, and when she's not looking switch it over."

"Yeah, but I don't live anywhere near where she lives," protested Paddy.

"I know that, you know that – but she doesn't. All you have to do is pretend that your sister, or someone close to you, lives near her part of town."

"I don't have a sister."

"Well, for fuck's sake," said Tom, finding Paddy's stupidity starting to get on his nerves, "just make up any old story. Don't forget we have a lot of money at stake here."

"By Jaysus, Tom, trust ye to give me the dirty work to do."

"Look Paddy," Tom snapped. "I haven't got time to argue with you. Trust me, this plan is good. It'll work, okay?" He turned away. "I need to get back to the restaurant, and help put the Christmas trimmings up. I'll pop round to the shop before I start dinner, and should be able to get a comb similar to Maggie's. Once I get it, we'll make arrangements when and where to meet."

The ship's shop was open for crew between five and six.

"Can you tell me where the combs are?" Tom asked. "The ones covered in dia..." he stopped himself. "The ones covered in stones."

"You mean the ones behind you, on that stand?" asked the shop assistant, pointing over his shoulder.

Tom turned around. To his relief, there were at least half a dozen on display.

"Yes, they're the ones." He selected a comb, catching sight of Ginger at another rack looking at some eyebrow pencils.

He examined the comb closely. Although it looked the same as Maggie's, it did seem to sparkle more. Probably because of the brighter lights in the shop.

He handed it over to the young woman, who put it in a small paper bag.

"It's a little gift for the wife," Tom said. "It will look really nice in her thick hair."

The assistant smiled back as she took his money. "Yes," she said, handing it over, "they are pretty. I've had a few men coming in and buying them for their wives." She laughed. "Wish I had a man who would buy one for me."

"A good-looking girl like you should be able to pick a man up any time," said Tom, giving her his most charming smile, and a wink to go with it.

As he left the shop he noticed a bemused look on Ginger's face.

Tom slipped the comb in his jacket pocket and went straight to the restaurant. He passed the silver locker on the way, but could not see Paddy to make arrangements when to meet. He carried on into the dining room. The room looked nice now with all the Christmas trimmings up.

When at last Tom did get to see Paddy, he was so busy with his passengers that he didn't get a chance to arrange anything. Old Miss Pike had spilled her soup all over her dress, and was demanding that the company replace it with a new one.

Tom had to use all his charm to persuade her to let the bedroom steward take it down to the ship's laundry.

At one point he had to pop to the loo, and the pain when he urinated was getting worse. He still hadn't seen the doctor, but things had got too far now. He would see the doctor first thing in the morning at the crew surgery.

When Tom finally finished his last sitting, he managed to get hold of Paddy alone.

"I've got the comb," he said. "Maybe, we can make arrangements to meet tomorrow night at the aft-end."

"Ye look knackered, Tom," said Paddy, who didn't exactly look the picture of health himself. "I think tomorrow would be a

good idea. I'm going to have an early night meself tonight."
Paddy paused. "I've been giving your plan some thought," he
said slowly. "And I think it's a good one. Mick will be pleased.
Well done." He grinned. "We'll get them stones off the ship after
all."

CHAPTER 29

Ginger was sitting in his pantry talking to Martha, when a woman passenger popped her head around the corner. "Excuse me, steward," she said, "but the waiter told me to give you my dress to take to the laundry."

The woman pointed to a large soup stain on the dress she was wearing.

"Ah, good evening, Miss Pike," said Ginger politely. She was a first sitting passenger, and always managed to forget to turn her *Please Do Not Disturb* sign, around to *Please Make Up Our Room*. The woman had done the same thing this evening, so Ginger had just left the cabin.

"Well madam," continued Ginger, "you'll have to take the dress off first, unless you want to go down with it."

The woman gave a little childish giggle.

"You are funny. I'll go and take it off and give it to you straightaway. Do you think they will have it done by tonight?"

"Not tonight, the laundry is closed. I will send it down first thing tomorrow morning."

"Oh, they're closed, are they?" asked the woman, looking surprised. "Do they sleep on board ship?"

You silly old fool, thought Ginger, *what do you think the laundry staff do, get a lifeboat down and row ashore every night?*

"Just give me the dress and I will take it to be cleaned," said Ginger, trying not to show impatience in his voice.

The gong had just sounded for the second sitting passengers, so Ginger started diving into each room, as they left to go to dinner.

He was just in the middle of turning down a bed when Miss Pike appeared at the door with her stained dress.

"Here you are, steward," she said walking into the cabin, and passing the dress over.

"This is a nice room," she commented, looking around the cabin.

"Not much different than your own," answered Ginger, "The only difference is that this is a three-berther, and yours is a single.

"Yes, but it's much bigger than my cabin," insisted the woman. "Oh, and by the way," she went on," you haven't serviced my cabin this evening."

"The reason is, madam," said Ginger carefully, "you still had *Do Not Disturb* on your door."

"How silly of me," she giggled again. "I forgot to turn it around."

Ginger took the dress from her, and went back to his pantry. He put it into a plastic bag, then went back to finish off the cabins.

The following day at breakfast, Ginger noticed that Miss Pike had turned her sign around to make up the room, so he decided to get that serviced and out of the way.

It was a small cabin, and he had to admit to himself that the woman did keep it tidy, apart from the dressing table, which was full of different bottles of perfume. It stank of the stuff.

Ginger remembered about her dress. When he finished the cabin he went back to the pantry, to make sure Martha had taken down the woman's laundry. He grimaced as he spotted the bag still where'd left it. Martha had done one of her usual disappearing acts, so he'd have to take it himself.

Halfway down the spiral staircase to Freddy Brown's office, he had to wait for a girl coming up with a big teapot in her hands. There was no mistaking that red hair; it was Margaret.

Her face lit up as she saw him.

"Ginger!" she exclaimed. "At last! I've been wanting to see you for ages, but could never find you!" She took a step up, so

196

they were closer. "Can I meet you somewhere quiet?" she whispered, her eyes burning into his. "Somewhere where we can be alone? I must talk to you." She glanced around, as if making sure they were truly alone. "It's very important."

Important? She was normally so bubbly. What had spooked her? Ginger nodded slowly. "What time do you finish during the day?"

"Between twelve and two."

"Can you get down to my cabin for quarter past twelve? There shouldn't be anybody around at that time, they're usually in the Pig having a drink."

"I don't know where your cabin is," Margaret whispered, biting her lip.

"I'll hang around just at the top of the stairs about twelve, and then I can take you down to my cabin."

She squeezed past him, giving him a little kiss on the cheek. "Thanks, Ginger, thanks a lot. You don't know how much this means to me."

He left her to carry on up the stairs, while he made his way towards Freddy Brown's office.

After dropping off Miss Pike's dress, he went back to his section, almost immediately bumping into Lola.

"Ginger, darling, do you mind if I go down to your cabin at lunchtime and have a quick drink with you, because we've got to discuss the pantomime?"

"Shouldn't you be working in the restaurant at that time?" asked Ginger.

"Oh, it'll only be for a few minutes, I can get Paul to cover for me."

"Lola, can you make it tonight? I've got something important on."

"You've got something important on? Tell me, what is more important than the pantomime?"

"Listen, Lola," said Ginger, lowering his voice to a whisper. "I bumped into Margaret earlier on, and she wants to see me on my own. She sounded rather upset, frightened, even. So I told her that I would pick her up at twelve and take her to my cabin. If it doesn't take too long, I'll pop up to the Pig and let you know, but in between time, I must find out what is troubling the girl."

"Okay," said Lola, reluctantly. "But we do need to start rehearsing this pantomime. We have only a few days left."

"I won't let you down, Lola. Do let me see Margaret first, though. And another thing, promise me not to say a word to anybody. Let's just keep it a secret amongst ourselves."

"Are you going to tell me what she says then?" enquired Lola.

"I'll tell you, but by God, it is only between us, and absolutely nobody else."

Lola nodded in an understanding way, and headed back to the restaurant. Ginger watched Lola leaving the section then turned to finish off his last cabin.

At twelve o'clock Ginger stood by the stairs at the top of the laundry. The first person he saw was Eileen, followed by Owd Rosie, then Lil and Betty, chattering away like magpies.

A few minutes later Margaret arrived. She was alone.

"Thanks for coming, Ginger," said Margaret. She was still looking around her, as if checking that nobody was about.

Ginger walked with her along the working alleyway, and then turned off down another pair of spiral staircases, which led to the bedroom stewards' accommodation.

"I hope I won't be in trouble being down in the men's quarters," said Margaret, sounding a little nervous.

"Don't worry, Miss Margaret, you're with me now. I'll see that you don't get into any trouble."

They passed by a few cabins, until they reached Ginger's.

"Funny smell down here," remarked Margaret. "It smells a little like dirty socks."

"It's the cabin across the way," said Ginger, "they're smoking weed. Keep that to yourself though. Don't go spreading the word around the ship."

Ginger tried his door. It was locked.

"That's good," he said, taking his bunch of keys hanging on a chain from his pocket. "We've got the cabin to ourselves."

"Gosh," said Margaret, when Ginger had opened the door to let her in. "There're six beds in here. I thought it was bad enough having four in ours."

"Yes, it does get a bit crowded at times, but if you don't feel like socialising, you'll notice that each bunk, much like your own, has a little curtain you can pull across. I do that many a time when I want to read, or have an early night, while the others are up drinking. Anyhow, Miss Margaret, sit over there, that's my bed, and I'll get you a drink."

He then went over to his locker and opening it pulled out a beer from a box that was jammed tight at the bottom of the cupboard.

"Now, what is it that you want to tell me?"

"I know who the murderer is. The one that killed Peter." She paused. "And he's trying to kill me too."

"You do?" said Ginger, his ears pricking up at the name of Peter being mentioned. "Who is it then?"

"It's the..."

Before Margaret could finish her sentence, a loud blast of sound came over the Tannoy.

"That's the emergency signal," said Ginger standing up quickly. "We have to go immediately. You can tell me who it is later." He went over to his locker and grabbed a couple of life jackets. "Come on. We have to get out of here right now."

CHAPTER 30

As soon as Ginger and Margaret reached the top of the stairs and went through a doorway, she could smell smoke.

"Oh god!" she yelped "The ship's on fire!"

There was a mechanical sound and the watertight door ahead slid shut.

Margaret spun round, but the door they had just come through was closing as well.

Ginger grabbed her hand. The smoke was getting thicker.

"We're stuck!" she gasped. "We're going to die."

"Don't panic. There's a flight of stairs, over there. Come on, we'll go up them."

They ran towards the stairs, when suddenly the door leading down into the engine room opened. Out came George Bowder, staring at the pair of them. Before Margaret could say anything, Ginger had dragged her up the stairs.

They reached the galley, and carried on going up the next flight of stairs. The smoke was getting worse.

At last they came to another door leading to the passenger accommodation.

"Just keep going up those stairs over there, Margaret," instructed Ginger. "You'll come out on the open deck. I must go to my section and make sure my passengers are alright."

He left Margaret by the bottom step.

There were people coming from every direction, some pushing past her, all trying to get to the outside deck first.

A message came over the Tannoy: "Ladies and Gentlemen, this is your captain speaking. I have an important announcement to make. We have a small fire in the crew quarters, which we are getting under control. This is not a fire drill exercise. It is for real. Please do not panic, but go quickly and quietly to your muster stations, wearing your life jackets and some warm clothing. If you do not have a life jacket with you, there will be members of the ship's company who will be issuing them on the boat deck, and also instructing you how to wear them. Again, I repeat, do not panic, and go immediately to your boat stations. I will keep you informed on any further developments. Thank you."

Margaret pushed her way towards the outer deck, along with many of the passengers.

There was much barging and shoving as everyone spilled onto the deck, and a smartly dressed elderly lady in front of her tripped and fell with a frightened shriek.

Margaret immediately pulled the woman away from the danger of being trampled by the other passengers. She was small and slim, which made it easier. Once they were safely to one side, Margaret helped the woman stand up, supporting her for a moment while she found her feet.

The woman looked up at her, Her bun had dropped out of place, making her long grey hair fall across her face. She then pushed her hair away and said, "Thank you, my dear. What is your name?"

"Margaret Hargreaves."

"And are you a passenger?"

"No, crew. I work in the laundry."

"Well, Margaret Hargreaves, you really are most kind. I won't forget what you've done."

---0---

Tom had been in the middle of serving soup to Miss Pike when he heard the seven short blasts, followed by one long one on the ship's whistle. He put down the ladle.

"That's the emergency signal," he said, as calmly as he could. "You must go up to your muster stations immediately."

"But I haven't had my soup yet," complained Miss Pike.

Forget your bleeding soup, or you'll end up in it!

"It's an emergency, madam. I must ask you to go on deck immediately."

The woman raised an eyebrow at Tom's authoritative tone. But then she must have seen the other passengers leaving their tables fast. So she decided to follow suit.

Suddenly Tom remembered the diamonds.

He should be instructing his passengers on how to get to their muster stations. *Fuck them*, he thought to himself, *the diamonds are more important*. He made a rush to the galley where most of the crew had left, and ran down the spiral staircase to his cabin.

The air was thick with smoke in the first corridor he came to, and a quick glance each way showed that the watertight doors were shut.

He kept going down the spiral staircase until he reached the crew quarters. The watertight doors were closed here as well.

He pulled the lever to open the first one, setting off an alarm bell. Ignoring the sound, he squeezed through. It closed immediately after him, still ringing.

He went through another and set off that alarm also.

He got to his cabin and let himself in. Unlocking his locker, he grabbed the shoe with the diamonds hidden in the heel and swapped it for the one he was wearing.

He went back through the watertight doors with their alarms still ringing, until he was back in the passengers' accommodation, where there was thick smoke.

Breathing through his handkerchief, he made it to the outer deck.

The boat deck was crowded with passengers and crew members, standing by their lifeboats. He went over to boat number five, and saw Paddy standing there with some other members of the crew, along with some passengers. As Tom went over to join them, the captain made another announcement.

203

"Ladies and gentleman, this is your captain speaking. I am pleased to announce that the fire is now under control, and I advise all passengers to return their life jackets to their cabins. Those passengers who were issued with life jackets from the boat deck, please return them to the crew members who will be collecting them as you leave the deck. I am very sorry for any inconvenience caused, and would like to advise all passengers that between 3pm and 5pm this afternoon, there will be complimentary drinks in the Dolphin Lounge. Again, I apologise for any inconvenience. Thank you."

"By Jaysus, that was a fucking waste of time," said Paddy, looking annoyed, "I was in the middle of me beer as well."

"You'd think that they could offer us crew members free drinks," said one of the crew, looking at Tom.

"I was hoping we'd go down in the boats," said another. "It would have been exciting."

"By the way, Tom," said Paddy with a grin. "Do ye realise that ye 'ave one brown and one black shoe on? Don't tell me ye were that pissed?"

To Tom's annoyance, everybody looked down at his feet, and started laughing.

---0---

That evening Ginger went on duty to do his turndowns, but his mind was elsewhere. He desperately needed to finish the conversation with Margaret, and frustratingly, hadn't managed to find her since the fire.

He'd heard somebody say that it had started in the cross alleyway, by the passenger corridor. Apparently someone had piled up garbage against the wall, then some other idiot had thrown away a cigarette end on it, not checking that it was still alight.

204

The smoke lingered in the passengers' accommodation for a while, finally clearing away by the evening.

There was the sound of raucous laughter coming from one of the cabins. The free drinks must have done them some good.

Ginger went into the pantry. Martha was clutching her usual gin and tonic, swaying on her stool with eyes that were glazed over.

"Have you had many calls?" he asked her.

"I've never stopped," she replied, "they've been ringing for ice, drinks, the lot. One woman, she…" Martha paused, and Ginger feared she was about to fall off her stool. "She insisted… that I got the doctor; she said she couldn't breathe, like. The smoke or something." She took a gulp of her gin. "I've had enough, Ginger."

You've had more than enough, love.

"Listen, Martha," he said, "finish your drink and get off now. I'll take over."

"Well," she hesitated, "I'll just have another one before I go down, if you don't mind answering the bells."

"I'll keep my eye on them."

"By the way, Ginger, one of the engineers seemed to be lingering around this deck. You don't often see them around here. Maybe it was because of the fire."

"More than likely," said Ginger absently, not really listening. Martha finally staggered off.

Ginger tutted – there were lots of dirty cups and plates in the sink that Martha should have washed up. Now he'd have to do it.

She'd left a pair of her thick rubber gloves lying on the side, so Ginger decided to use them. They were such a tight fit that he struggled to get them on, then once they were on, he realised they weren't going to come off again without a fight.

He washed up anyway, then, after a few tries to get the gloves off, remembered he had some hand cream in his locker across the alleyway, which might help.

He unlocked his locker door, and switched on the light.

There was a big flash, a loud bang and all the lights in the alleyway went out.

Ginger leapt back in shock, tripped and fell against the far wall.

For a moment he sat in the dark, dazed and confused. Then he clambered to his feet and staggered over to the pantry.

Thankfully the phone there was working, so he called the electrician to report the event, then collapsed into a chair.

A few minutes later, an electrician poked his head round the corner.

"What have you done, Ginger?" he asked with a broad grin. "Trying to set the ship on fire again?"

They went over to the lockers and the electrician examined the switch.

He turned to Ginger with a frown. "Somebody's been tampering with this. See these wires hanging out? Good thing you were wearing rubber gloves, mate, or you would have been toast."

He hummed tunelessly as he worked on the switch and wires for a while, then stood back as all the lights came on again.

"That's fixed it," he said, his grin back in place. "Next time I would advise you to keep your locker door... locked."

Ginger wasn't in the mood to argue. His locker was always locked. The only person who could open it would either be the night steward, or an officer, who would have a pass key.

Ginger went cold.

The murderer, the one that killed Peter, and also tried to drown Margaret in Barbados... was he now trying to kill him too?

CHAPTER 31

It was the following day. Margaret was working on the calender in the heat, the sweat running from every pore. But her mind was elsewhere.

Billy gave her a concerned frown. "What's bothering you, Maggie? You look distracted."

"Nothing, really," she replied.

But that wasn't true, of course. She was bothered, and for good reason. She'd been so close to confiding in Ginger. So close. But had failed because of the fire.

So she still had to find him alone and tell him what she knew.

She could go up to the Pig at lunchtime and see if he was there, but she decided against that. She felt a fool being seen up in the bar on her own. And what if Ricky should see her; he'd want to know why she was there.

Ricky! She had been told by Eileen that when the alarm had gone off, he had rushed down to her cabin to look for her.

"He even wanted me to give him me key, when I told him you weren't there," Eileen had said. "I told him to go and fuck off. Did he think you were that barmy that you'd lock yourself in the cabin during a fire? Anyhow, being a bosun I thought he would be rushing in the other direction, up to the boats."

Margaret smiled as she put the sheet through again.

Ricky had her so much on his mind! When they met in the evening he had even asked if the comb was still safe! What a sentimental old dear he was! He made her feel so safe when she was with him.

If only she could feel safe about Bowder. Which meant finishing the conversation with Ginger.

She decided to slip to Ginger's section, and speak to him this evening.

207

At twelve o'clock the machines stopped, and everybody made their way up the stairs.

When Margaret had reached the top, to her surprise there stood Ginger.

"Ginger!" she exclaimed, "I didn't know when I would see you again. Am I glad to see you!"

"Listen, Miss Margaret, I can't speak to you at the moment; I'm on shift. Can you meet me on the aft-end early this evening after you've finished down in the laundry?"

"Yes, I think we should be finished at about 5pm today."

"Good. Just stand by the rails. Don't make it too obvious that we have arranged to see each other."

Margaret nodded and they went their separate ways.

---0---

Tom came out of the surgery, rubbing his arm where the doctor had given him the injection. His fears were right. He did have a dose.

He went up to the Pig for a consolation drink. Paddy was already there.

"You made me look a fool after the fire, pointing out my odd shoes," he snapped as he sat down. "One had the…" he leaned in and whispered, "the you-know-whats… in the heel."

"More fool you for walking around with them."

"I was rescuing them from the fire, you idiot!" Tom hissed.

"It would take more than a fire to destroy them," Paddy replied. "They're dia…"

"Be quiet!" snapped Tom. "Are you mad?"

"No more than you, walking around in odd shoes."

"Will you just forget that?" Tom drank some beer to calm his jangling nerves. "Listen, we need to put my plan in action. I have the comb. You are good with your hands, so you can set the

208

stones. Then give it to me, and I'll do the switch on Maggie, okay?"

Paddy nodded. "Okay."

"Remember, Paddy," Tom added, "not a word to anyone, not even Mick. This is our secret. If Mick pesters us over the… stones… again, we tell him they're safe, and we'll get them off the ship without any problems."

"I only hope the wee girl doesn't lose them," said Paddy, swilling down the remainder of his beer.

"I don't think there's much chance of that. She's potty over Ricky, and I'm sure anything that he gives her she'll guard with her life."

"Anyhow," Paddy said, "I'll get the job done as soon as possible, I don't like having the things on me."

Tom finished his beer and left. At least on that last point he and Paddy were in full agreement. The diamonds would be out of their hands until Paddy changed the comb over again in England.

He could just picture the scene; Paddy giving him the comb, then he would proudly hand it over to Mick. Who would, of course, be surprised when he learned of Tom's ingenious idea.

"My word, Tom," he would say, "I never realised that you had such a brain. I wish that it was me that thought of such a brilliant idea."

Mick would then arrange to pass the diamonds over to his contacts, and then they would meet again to divide up the money.

The money! What a beautiful thought. Tom had already spent it all in his mind.

---0---

The sun was streaming down as the *Ocean Star* sailed through azure blue waters, warming Margaret as she climbed the stairs to the funnel deck.

On the way she passed the pool deck. It was full of passengers wearing brightly coloured clothes that set off their dark tans; some stretched out sunbathing; others splashing around in the turquoise pool. Topside waiters were weaving in and out of the crowd with trays of drinks.

Margaret reached her destination and breathed a sigh of relief; the funnel deck was empty. She laid down her towel and took her suntan lotion from her bag, then rubbed it all over the parts of her body she could reach. Then she lay face down to have a little doze.

After about half an hour she could feel her back burning, so she sat up and put a t-shirt over her blue one-piece bathing suit.

There was a rumble from her tummy, so she got her sandwiches and orange juice out of her bag, and sat quietly eating her lunch. The deck was still empty, as the stewardesses wouldn't be up until about two o'clock.

The midday sun was now getting unbearably hot, so Margaret decided to go down to her usual spot on the port side of the boat deck and enjoy the shade under one of the many lifeboats that were suspended along the side of the ship.

As she stood at her favourite place by the side rail there wasn't a cloud in the sky.

She laughed at some flying fish that leapt out of the sea just below her, then at a school of dolphins that broke the surface as they swam alongside.

Her laughter disappeared in an instant. That horrible second engineer had seen her and Ginger together as they ran through the alleyway during the fire. What if that put Ginger in danger? What if Bowder was watching her at this very moment? Margaret turned quickly around, but thankfully there was no other person in sight.

210

She leaned on the rail.

She would see Ginger this evening, and he would help make sure George Bowder was stopped.

She had to stop thinking of him. Margaret decided to put the man out of her mind, and leaned over the rails to take a closer look at the dolphins.

The next instant, the rail give way. She plunged from the dizzying height of the ship's side, heading towards the sea. Margaret screamed.

The speed of her falling took her breath away. She could see the sea coming to meet her. The last thing she remembered, before hitting the water, was having the presence of mind to hollow her back, and put her hands straight in front of her head, forming a dive.

She hit the water, sinking what seemed like a mile into the depths of the ocean, before managing to turn and push upwards.

When Margaret eventually came to the surface, she gasped for breath, and could taste the salt from the water.

Then she felt herself being dragged under, as the current pulled her towards the ship. Margaret swam with what bit of strength she had left. Her arms felt tired and her head kept going below the water.

She had to keep swimming away from the ship, or she would be sucked under.

After what seemed like a lifetime, she realised at last that she had reached safety away from the ship. But had she? She knew that she was alone in shark-infested water.

Margaret noticed a small, round object falling from the side of the ship into the sea, landing not too far away. She swam slowly towards it, even though by this time she hardly had any strength left. It was a lifebuoy. She grabbed it with all her might. Suddenly she spotted something out of the corner of her eye. It looked long and slippery, and began to move alongside her.

Margaret's heart beat even faster. She dared to look again, and then to her relief it wasn't a shark, but some dolphins.

Here she was, stuck in the middle of this massive ocean, with nothing but miles and miles of open sea.

Margaret could just see the after-end of the boat in the distance, as the ship sailed on.

CHAPTER 32

A few minutes earlier, Mick was out on the open deck, waiting for his girl, Jill.

He had just closed up and locked the bar, once he had checked it had been properly vacuumed and all the ashtrays had been emptied. There was still some stale smoke and beer smell from the early hours of the morning. It had been a busy night. His men had never stopped – particularly as the captain had offered all the passengers free drinks after the fire.

What a stampede that had caused.

And it was not as if that was a one-off. In a few days and it would be Christmas, and the passengers were getting into the festive spirit to prove it.

He gave the room a last glance over. The Christmas trimmings were glittering, even though the lounge was only partially lit. It would be ready for the afternoon shift, which he had off. He then locked up the bar, and went out on the open deck to wait for Jill.

The bright sunlight made him screw up his eyes, so he fished a pair of sunglasses out of his top pocket and slipped them on.

He leaned over the ship's rail and looked back towards the stern. The white surf churning up from the propellers to become the ship's wake was hypnotising. He could watch it for hours.

The breeze was warm, and he could hear the distant hum of the passengers' voices coming from the lido deck.

He idly took in a school of dolphins following the ship, diving in and out of the water. The next instant he thought he heard a scream, and a vision of a body falling from the upper deck landing in the sea. Before he could think what he was doing, he ran over to the nearest lifebuoy, lifted it off the ship's rail and flung it as hard as he could towards what he could see by now was the head of a person.

There was a man who was standing near him. Mick asked him to keep his eye on the object in the sea.

Mick then went rushing up the steps to the bridge, and entered the wheelhouse, where the helmsman was steering the ship.

"Man overboard," he yelled.

The officer immediately sounded the alarm of three long blasts on the ship's whistle.

The captain and the other officers suddenly appeared.

Mick went to the port side of the bridge wing, and pointed to out what seemed like a head swimming towards lifebuoy.

The next instant the ship started a Williamson Turn, which would take it back along its original course.

An announcement was made over the Tannoy. "Bosun, second engineer and lifeboat crew to launch No. 2 Lifeboat. A doctor is also needed."

Mick went down the steps to make his way back to the Dolphin Lounge deck. He clung onto the railings to stop himself falling. The ship was still turning around. When he eventually got back to where he had left the man by the rails, the man had gone. With the ship turning round he could not see anything from that angle.

A crowd of passengers were leaning over the rails, chattering excitedly.

There was the sound of electric winches as one of the lifeboats was lifted off its stand, ready to be lowered.

When the ship slowed to a stop, the lifeboat was winched down to the sea, with Ricky, the doctor, George Bowder and four deckhands on board.

Mick could now see the person more clearly. It seemed to be a girl with red hair, clinging to the lifebuoy.

One of the crew members nearby shouted, "Shit! It's Maggie! The steam queen!"

The lifeboat powered towards her, and stopped alongside. The deckhands leaned over and pulled her slim white body in its blue swimsuit onboard.

Some other deckhands were barricading the area around where Mick stood. Passengers were pushing and shoving each other, all trying to see what was happening. Mick had to keep a firm hold, as the ship was now listing from the weight of seemingly every person on board standing at the rail to watch the drama.

One of the masters-at-arms shouted at the crowd. "Please, ladies and gentlemen, make space for the crew to get by." Then he added to Mick, "Please move away. Give them room." Mick stepped aside as two deckhands appeared with a stretcher.

The lifeboat returned, and was hoisted up the side of the ship, then pulled onto the boat deck. Margaret was lifted out and laid onto the stretcher. A blanket was wrapped around her, and she was carried away in the direction of the ship's hospital.

Mick had a lump in his throat. As the one who raised the alarm, he felt somehow responsible for her recovery.

Hopefully she would survive this dreadful ordeal.

The crowd began to disperse, as the ship sailed on.

CHAPTER 33

Ginger was alone in the Pig, nursing a beer. He was drumming his fingers on the table, scowling with anger at himself.

Why hadn't he made more effort to see Margaret sooner? She'd been so agitated, saying she knew who'd murdered Peter.

Ginger stopped drumming and took a sip of beer.

He should have got her to say who it was then and there, while they were making their way on deck. Not left it till later.

That was a mistake, because whoever Margaret suspected was now clearly trying to murder him too. The tampering with the light switch had all the hallmarks of just such an attempt.

What was it old Martha had muttered? Something he'd ignored, because she was pissed, as ever. But in the light of the locker switch incident, it might be important.

Ginger frowned. What had she said? Something about someone wandering about? Someone who could have tampered with the wiring?

He groaned. *Listen, next time!*

An alarm sounded. *Man overboard!*

A few deckhands, who had been sitting at the opposite end of the room, jumped up and rushed out. Ginger decided to follow them up on deck to see what was happening.

It took him some time to get to the well deck; it seemed the whole ship – passengers and crew – were all heading in the same direction. When he finally arrived and pushed through to the rail, he found himself beside some stewards, all staring at the drama taking place out at sea.

One had a pair of binoculars, and was giving a full narration of the events at sea. "They're pulling the body into the lifeboat," he announced. "Looks like a woman to me." He paused, then exclaimed, "Oh blimey! She moved! She's alive!" He leaned forward and adjusted the focus. "I'd say from that red hair it's Maggie, the steam queen!"

Ginger grabbed the binoculars and focused them on the lifeboat. The fellow was right; it was Margaret! "Thanks, mate," he said, passing them back.

Had she just survived another murder attempt?

---0---

Tom's first thought when he heard that Margaret was the 'man' overboard was one of despair. How was he going to get the diamonds ashore now?

Then Eileen told him that Maggie was alive, and was recovering in the ship's hospital.

Tom let out a small sigh of relief. Up till that point, the plan had been going well. Tom had given Paddy the diamonds and the comb he had bought from the shop, and Paddy had promised him that it wouldn't take him long to set them. He'd even got hold of some super-strong glue. Apparently Rob, whose brother was a deckhand, knew that Ricky the bosun had some, and had managed to borrow it.

Eileen had invited Tom down to her cabin that evening, as Chris and Kitty were in the Pig and Maggie in the hospital. Eileen had made it clear that as they had the cabin to themselves, she was expecting him to make love to her.

That was another problem; how to keep her at bay without arousing any suspicions? The last thing he wanted was Eileen finding out he'd got a dose. She'd kill him.

Later that night, Tom was sitting on Eileen's bunk, with one arm around her waist and a can of beer in his other hand.

Their conversation had come to a halt. Eileen must have taken this as her cue.

She put down her beer, and his as well. Turning to him, she put one arm around his neck. Then she moved in for the kiss, while stroking his knee.

But it was when her hand started moving upwards, that Tom pushed her away.

"What's the matter?" she exclaimed, sitting back.

"Sorry luv, but I don't feel very well. Maybe it's all the work preparing for Christmas."

Eileen looked him straight in the eyes. "You 'aven't got another woman, 'ave you?" There was real menace in her voice.

"No luv, you know that you're the only one for me," he stammered. "Even though I do have a wife, you know it's really you that I love."

She took a few deep breaths. "Then why don't I excite you anymore?"

"Eileen, you'll always excite me. It's just that I feel knackered. Do try and understand, luv." He gave her a small kiss.

She picked up her beer and finished it, then stood up to get another. When she returned to the bunk, she sat further away with her back to him.

She gave a loud sniff. "It's just that we don't often get time on our own." She turned to face him, her eyes brimming with tears. "And with Maggie being in hospital, I thought that it would 'ave been a golden opportunity for us."

"Listen, luv," began Tom, "do try and understand. I really don't feel very well. Maybe I'm coming down with the 'flu, or something. I'll tell you what; I'll go and see the doctor tomorrow and see if he can give me some tablets."

Eileen stayed where she was and crossed her arms.

Tom moved closer and put his own arm around her waist. He took her chin in his hand and tried to pull her face around towards his, but she turned it in the other direction.

"Come on, luv," he whispered. "Don't get a cob on with me." He tried another tactic. "If you really loved me, you would at least try and understand how I'm feeling." He sat back. "You're nothing but plain selfish."

"I'm selfish!" snapped Eileen. "That's a laugh. All I wanted was to make love to you."

He turned away. "Well if that's the way you feel, Eileen, I can't really say any more."

"Yes, that's the way I fucking feel," she said, with venom in her voice. "I've had enough."

Tom stood up, then went in for the final kill. "I've done everything I can. I keep telling you how much I love you. In fact," he gave a significant pause, "I was planning on a little surprise for you in Madeira."

"A little surprise?" Eileen looked at him in amazement.

"Yes," continued Tom, "but now it's clear you don't really love me anymore – otherwise you would try and understand me. Maybe it would be better if I was off." He put down his can, stood up and began slowly walking towards the door.

"Wait a minute, Tom," said Eileen, jumping to her feet, "I do love you! I suppose I just felt hurt that you didn't want a bit of sex." Her tone softened. "So what was that surprise you 'ad for me in Madeira?"

"Well, am I forgiven before I tell you?"

"Yeah, I suppose," she said.

Shit! What was the surprise?

He did some quick thinking, then turned towards her, making his voice sound sad. "I was going to take you out on New Year's Eve in Madeira for a nice meal. Just the two of us."

He had hardly got the words out of his mouth, when Eileen threw her arms around his neck. "Oh, Tom!" she paused for a few seconds. "Maybe I was in the wrong." She stood back, studying his face. "Come to think of it, I suppose you don't look too well."

Tom put his arms around her waist, and gave her a gentle kiss.

Victory! Oh yes!

"I'll tell you what, luv," he said, pulling away from her, "let's open up another beer."

Eileen burst out laughing. "I'm just nipping to the loo first." She gave him another kiss and left.

Tom took two beers from the cardboard box and opened them, then plonked himself down on the bunk.

His eyes fell on the cabinet that was wedged between the other two bunks. Above it was a smeared mirror, while the top was full of make-up, perfume and empty cans of beer. Underneath there were four drawers, one for each person living in the cabin.

A thought occurred. A few nights earlier Margaret had gone to the bottom one to put away her comb. And there were no locks on the drawers, only on the lockers.

Had Maggie still left it in the same place?

Here was the perfect chance to check, while Eileen was out. With a quick glance at the door, he dropped to his knees, put the beers on the floor, then slowly opened the bottom drawer.

Inside was a bundle of panties, bras, and a few t-shirts.

Tom began to rummage amongst the clothes, trying not to disturb them too much. He felt something hard near the bottom, and gently pulled out a wrapped package. He opened the paper with fumbling fingers, and there it was! The comb!

There was the click of a heel from the corridor.

Tom quickly folded the paper, pushed the package back in the drawer and closed it.

He was still on his knees when the door swung open, and Eileen came in.

"What are you doing on your knees? Praying?" she asked.

221

"No luv, I just opened a couple of beers, when I dropped my can opener," said Tom, slipping it from his pocket and showing her.

He grabbed the cans, then stood up and gave one to her with a smile.

At least he now knew how to swap their comb for Magaret's.

CHAPTER 34

Captain Quinn was having pre-Christmas drinks in his cabin, and had extended an invitation to the wardroom for the officers to join him.

George Bowder was amongst them.

He was eyeing up the personal steward, known as the 'captain's tiger', who was busy pouring drinks and bringing in fresh ice buckets. The young man certainly looked neat and tidy in his well-pressed trousers. A bit like Peter.

"Yes, this seems a bloody unlucky voyage," the captain was saying. "What with the young bellboy going over the side, then the fire, and now that laundry girl, there's going to be a long inquiry when we get back to England."

"Surely, Francis," said George, taking a sip of whisky. "If the young lad had thrown himself over the side, they will just put it down as 'misadventure at sea'?"

"Not that simple, old fellow. There will still have to be a full inquiry when we get back home."

George took a bigger gulp of his whisky.

The conversation ebbed and flowed around him, but although he made the required smiles and nods, he wasn't really listening.

If only he hadn't lost his temper and killed the damn kid, he wouldn't be in the mess he was in now.

And worst of all, it had been stupid of him to panic. He should have stayed calm and simply sent the boy away – after all, who would take the word of a bellboy against his?

Except that bloody laundry maid would still have seen Peter in his cabin, and would no doubt have told everyone.

So she had to go.

This last attempt should have worked – it really should. Ricky had made it clear that she usually leaned over the same railing each day at sea, so it was the perfect opportunity.

Yet she had survived this attempt, just like all the others. How many lives did the bloody girl have?

Too bloody many, as she had proved once again, when she was pulled alive from the water.

And to cap it all, he'd even had to go out as one of the lifeboat crew and pick her up! He would never forget the look on her face, her freckles sticking out from her pasty white complexion, as she stared back at him with hatred in her eyes.

Then on the journey back she was lying right beside him, gibbering on about some bloody dolphin.

At least no-one had questioned his official report that the rail was faulty and her fall was an unfortunate accident.

And she was as thick as thieves with that other redhead, the queer. Who could have known he'd be wearing bloody rubber gloves when he touched the switch?

"Hello George," said a voice, bringing him back to the present. It was the chief steward, a tall, thin, elegant man with swept-back black hair, going grey at the temples. His poise always made George feel like a fat, sweaty oik beside him. "Don't worry, old boy," continued the chief steward. "It might never happen!"

"What? What might never happen?"

The chief steward laughed. "Whatever was bothering you, old boy. You looked like doom when I came up just now."

"Oh, ah, yes. Nothing really. Just, er, concern for that poor laundry girl."

The captain came over with the doctor.

"What's that, George?" the captain asked.

"He was concerned for the girl who went overboard," the chief steward answered. He turned to the doctor. "How's she doing?"

224

"She'll live," replied the doctor, much to George's annoyance. "A nasty shock for the poor girl. I've put her in the hospital and dosed her with some powerful sleeping tablets, so she can recover fully." He gave a small shrug. "Truth be told, she's very lucky to be alive. It's quite a height from the boat deck. It's a wonder she didn't break her neck."

"Actually," the captain observed, "she shouldn't have even been on the boat deck. The women only have special permission to use the funnel deck. However this time I will overlook the situation, though she must be warned not to use it again."

Damn the girl, thought George, *she was nothing but a bloody nuisance.*

Suddenly George felt unable to breathe, and knew he had to get away. He edged away from the group, trying not to make it look too obvious, then left. Taking a gulp of cool night air, he wandered off in the direction of the wheelhouse, still clutching his whisky.

The bridge was dark and quiet. The quartermaster was at the helm, and the chief officer was checking the radar system. George walked towards the windows; he could just see the bow moving gently up and down to the rhythm of the sea.

"All right there, George?" asked the officer-of-the-watch. "Not enjoying the party?"

"It was getting a bit crowded in there. I thought I would just pop in here for some peace and quiet."

"Yes, it is peaceful in here," agreed the officer, "especially when you go out on the wings of the bridge and look up at the sky and see all those stars, millions of them. You feel like you're in another world."

"You know something," said George, "I think I'll go out there for a while. Thanks."

He went out onto the side of the bridge. There was a warm gentle breeze. He looked up. As suggested, there was a mass of stars, twinkling and shimmering. You never got to see a sight like that, except over the darkness of the seas. It had a calming effect – as if it was impossible to feel anger in the face of such magnificence.

A lesson Ricky would do well to learn.

The lad was becoming very tetchy over Margaret's clinginess, and George knew of old how Ricky was quick to sudden rages. That was dangerous, because Ricky knew too many of his secrets. He might say something in anger that he, George, may seriously come to regret.

Which meant that getting rid of the girl would benefit them both. Perhaps when they got to Dakar? That was a place where a girl on her own could come to harm.

On that pleasant thought, George finished his whisky and headed back to the party.

CHAPTER 35

Margaret came groggily awake. Someone was moving a strong light across her face. Then she remembered; she was in the ship's hospital. She lifted her head and squinted upwards. The light was a morning sunbeam coming through the porthole as the ship rocked gently back and forth.

The memory of the day before suddenly came flooding back to her. She could still remember the horrible feeling of knowing that her feet had left the side of the ship, the fall tickling her stomach, taking her breath away, before she hit the water.

Margaret would never forget how she felt when she was left to the mercy of the cruel sea. She still didn't know how she had the strength to swim to the lifebuoy that somebody must have thrown over the side for her.

As she flopped back on the pillow, a hospital attendant popped his head around the corner of the door.

"Ah, good morning, Maggie, I see you've finally woken up." He gave her a quizzical look. "My goodness, you're a lucky girl. It's a wonder you didn't peg it out there." Before Margaret could respond, the doctor walked in.

"Good morning," he said briskly. He turned to the attendant. "Could you bring the young lady a cup of tea, please?" As the attendant left, the doctor said, "And how are you feeling?"

"A bit better now, thank you, doctor." She paused. "I suppose a little hungover though."

"That's only natural," he answered, "I did give you some rather strong tablets, and you've been asleep now for nearly two whole days. It's what your body needed to recover. You were in the sea for quite a while before the boat reached you."

He leaned over her and shone a torch into her eyes. "Good. All good. But I suggest you relax here for a couple more hours, have some tea, then, if all is well, I'll discharge you."

Two hours later, he was back. After checking her again, he said, "Right. You can go now. Just take it easy for the day, and don't do anything strenuous. You can sit on deck and maybe read a book, but I do not advise you to sunbathe. Stick to the shade." He paused, then added with a laugh, "And definitely don't go leaning over any dodgy rails." He became serious again. "To be honest if I were you, I'd stay in your cabin a while." He nodded. "Come and see me tomorrow and all being well I can pass you fit for work again."

Margaret let herself into her empty cabin, then leaned back against the door with a long breath out. It was good to be back. Her mind began to wander again, over the events of the day before. What a relief it had been for her seeing the boat turning around. Somebody must have spotted her fall over the side. By the time the lifeboat came heading over in her direction, she had developed cramp in her right leg. Margaret knew that if she hadn't had the lifebuoy to cling on to, there would have been no way she could have survived. She had felt far too weak.

It was lovely seeing Ricky's face when she was lifted out of the sea, but in the instant she felt that pleasure, the next it was marred by the vision of the second engineer staring down at her. Oh, she was certain now that she had been right about the bellboy being murdered by him.

Now she was back in her cabin, the first thing she did was to check in her drawer for the comb. But as she pulled it open, she stopped with a frown. There was something wrong with the way her clothes were all pushed to the sides of the drawer.

Someone had been in here.

Quickly she felt underneath, then breathed a sigh of relief when she pulled out the packet.

The comb was still there, sparkling reassuringly.

She must put it away in her locker, where it would be safer.

She was still holding it when the door was flung open and Chris stomped in.

"Maggie!" she said. "You're back! We were worried about you. How are you feeling now?"

Margaret put the comb back in the drawer and stood up.

"I suppose I still feel a bit shaky, but apart from that, I'm okay, thanks."

"What happened, love?" asked Chris.

"I fell over the side," answered Margaret.

"Yeah, but how? Did somebody push you, or did you go climbing over the rails? What actually happened?"

Margaret explained how the rail had given way.

"God, that must have been scary," said Chris, "I'm glad it was you and not me. Anyway, you ought to claim for the rail being dodgy when we get home. You could get good compensation for that."

"Not really," replied Margaret, "I shouldn't have been on that deck. If the company wanted to get funny, I suppose they could sack me. I think I'd be better forgetting all about it and saying nothing."

"I suppose you're right," said Chris. "Well, Maggie, I'd just nipped up for my ciggies. I left them in my other pocket. I'd better get back down." She gave Margaret a concerned look. "Did you want me to bring you something to eat at lunchtime?"

"No thanks, Chris, "I don't really feel hungry at the moment."

"Ta-rah then. See you later." Chris went out.

Margaret suddenly felt drowsy again – probably because the tablets hadn't fully worn off. She climbed onto her bunk and quickly fell asleep.

Her last thought before dropping off, was that she hadn't seen Ricky since he'd lifted her into the rescue boat. Why hadn't he come to see her…?

229

It seemed like moments later that a voice woke her. "Hello Margaret."

Ricky! She forced her eyes open and peered down from her bunk. But it wasn't Ricky – instead someone just as welcome.

"Ginger! Am I glad to see you? But how did you know I would be here?"

"I thought I would just pop up to the hospital to see if you were alright, and they told me you'd been discharged. I did go yesterday, but they wouldn't let me see you. They just told me that you were asleep."

Margaret sat up, while he perched on Eileen's bunk.

"How are you feeling now?" he asked, with a concerned look.

"Much better, thanks, Ginger."

"How did the accident happen, anyway?"

Margaret went through the whole story again, from the rail giving away, to being scared by the dolphin, to being pulled into the lifeboat.

Ginger just sat there, shaking his head.

"Would you like a beer?" she asked. He nodded, so she climbed down, gave him one from the cupboard, and climbed back.

Ginger opened it and took a sip. "Last time we met, you said you knew who the murderer was." He gave her an expectant look. "Who is it?"

Margaret took a steadying breath. Now she was finally going to share with Ginger what she knew. Hopefully he would believe her.

"George Bowder," she said. "The second engineer."

"George Bowder!" he repeated. "He's old, fat and sweaty, for sure. But a murderer? Why him?"

"Well," Margaret began, "it was the night that Peter went missing." Ginger flinched at the sound of the boy's name, then lifted his chin. "Go on," he said.

It looked like he was going to believe her.

Margaret told him about going into the wrong cabin and seeing the officer in a dressing gown and something being pushed through the porthole. "At the time I thought it might have been feet, but stupidly, I didn't put two and two together with Peter's disappearance.

"And that was George Bowder's cabin?" asked Ginger.

"Yes, it was him. You should have seen the look on his face. I thought he was going to kill me right there."

"Have you mentioned it to anybody else?"

"Only Ricky. But he said I was being too imaginative and I wasn't to tell other people, as I could get into serious trouble for malicious gossip. So I must keep it to myself."

The blood seemed to have drained from Ginger's face.

"Why didn't you mention this to me, Margaret, when I asked you in Barbados if anyone was out to get you? After the shark incident. Was that Bowder as well?"

She bit her lip and gave a small nod. "I should have told you, Ginger. I'm sorry. But after talking to Ricky I didn't want to say anything to anyone else."

"So how can you be sure it was definitely Bowder?"

"Because he tried to kill me again." She told him of the incident in the San Juan street. When she finished, Ginger looked quite impressed. "You ran past and hit him with your bag of boots?" She nodded. He gave a hollow laugh. "That's impressive. I wish I'd seen it!" He finished his beer. "So, that's when you became certain it was him?"

"Yes."

"So why are you only telling me all this now?"

She shook her head. "I didn't know where to find you alone, and whenever I did see you, either you or I were with somebody."

"You could have come up to my section."

"I was too frightened of getting into trouble."

Ginger raised his eyebrows. "More trouble than having a murderer stalking you around the ship?"

"I suppose when you put it like that…"

Ginger looked thoughtful. "So the railing the other day was him as well?"

"I don't know for sure, but it does seem likely. I always stand there, so if someone wanted me to fall in, that would be a good way to do it."

"Bowder has been quite the busy boy," Ginger observed. Then suddenly he gasped and put his hand to his open mouth.

"What is it?" she asked.

"The light switch!" He explained what had happened at his locker. "Martha said someone was hanging around. Now I remember what she said – it was an engineer!" His face went even whiter than before. "Oh my god!" he whispered. "Bowder's trying to kill me, too!"

"He's so dangerous," Margaret said. "Do you know, he was there. In that cable car in Rio when the lights went out. I thought he was going to try and throw me out."

"Oh Margaret!" Ginger exclaimed. "What do you think stopped him?"

"Well, Ricky was there, for one thing. And lots of other people too." She looked at him with wide eyes. "But next time he could succeed. He could kill either of us."

"Or both," said Ginger. He came over to the bunk and took Margaret's hand. "We'll have to look out for eachother," he said.

Just then there was a knock at the door, and Ricky walked in.

He stopped, taking in the scene. "I hope I'm not disturbing anything?" he said, his tone dripping with sarcasm.

"No," said Ginger, letting go of Margaret's hand and standing back. "I just thought I would pop down to see how Margaret was, and see if she would help with the make-up for the pantomime."

Ricky looked at him in a distasteful silence.

Ginger went to the door, then turned back. "Hope you don't mind, Ricky, but I thought maybe she would enjoy making us up for the pantomime."

Ricky nodded slowly.

"Don't forget, Miss Margaret," Ginger said as he was leaving, "I'll pick you up outside the Pig at nine-thirty tomorrow night."

When Ginger had gone, Margaret climbed down from the bunk and flung her arms around Ricky.

"Oh Ricky," she breathed in his ear, "I'm so glad to see you again."

He held her at arm's length, his eyes searching hers. "And there's nothing between you and that steward?"

"Of course not! He's not into girls, anyway."

He nodded. "If you say so, Margaret. Although you're pretty enough to turn him."

"Nothing, I swear."

He grinned. "Okay then." He took her in his arms, and gently brushed her cheeks with kisses.

CHAPTER 36

Tom came into the Pig, then scanned the tables for Eileen. He spotted her sitting with Chris, so after getting himself a beer, he went over.

Like most of the crew, they were talking about Margaret. "She was on the boat deck," Chris was saying. "I know the rail shouldn't have been faulty, but she really shouldn't have been on that deck."

"Somebody's head's going to roll," agreed Eileen.

Tom sat next to Eileen. "I suppose she will be having an early night tonight," he observed.

"Not too early," answered Eileen, taking a swig of her beer, "She said she's meeting Ricky in 'is cabin tonight for a drink." She winked at Chris. "Or whatever."

"Oh," said Tom, then he added as casually as he could. "What time's that then?"

Eileen shrugged. "Dunno. I think she said about nine-thirty, but I could be wrong. Why?"

Tom kept his tone casual. Paddy was promising him the newly diamond-encrusted comb later in the afternoon, so he wanted to make the switch as soon as possible. "It would be nice to have a drink somewhere other than in here, for a change."

"If the two of you want to be alone, I can always come up here tonight," said Chris.

"Okay," Tom said to Eileen. "I'll pop down around nine-thirty for an hour, luv," said.

About five minutes later Tom stubbed out his cigarette, drank the last drop of beer from his glass, and stood up. "I'd better get back to the restaurant." He gave Eileen a peck on the cheek. "See ya later, luv."

He made his way back to the passenger restaurant. So far, everything was going to plan. Now to check on Paddy. Tom found him by the silver locker.

"You'll definitely have that comb ready tonight, won't you?" whispered Tom, as he looked around to make sure nobody could hear him.

"By Jaysus," replied Paddy, loud enough for all the galley staff to hear him. "I told ye now, I'd have them for ye this afternoon."

"For God's sake, stop shouting, you idiot!" hissed Tom, adding in a sarcastic voice, "Why don't you go and announce it on the bloody Tannoy? Then everybody will know what we're talking about."

They agreed to meet later in the afternoon at the aft-end.

When Tom got there, Margaret was in a deck chair on the port-side, reading a book. He frowned. Trust her to be here at the same time. He went round to the starboard side, where Paddy was perched on a bollard smoking a cigarette.

"Have you got it, then?" Tom asked.

Paddy produced a small, wrapped package from his pocket, and handed it over with exaggerated surreptitiousness. "Am I glad to get this out of me way."

Tom checked no one was looking, then unwrapped it. He examined the comb, and had to admit that Paddy had made a good job of it. The piece didn't look too different from the way it was before, apart from maybe a bit more sparkle from the real diamonds.

He patted Paddy on the back. "Well done! I didn't think you had the brains to do such a fine job. It looks identical to Maggie's. She'll never notice the difference."

"Ye cheeky young devil," laughed Paddy. His laughter was infectious, and Tom found himself joining in. In a few moments they were both helpless with laughter.

236

Eventually they calmed down and became silent, catching their breaths.

Tom was taking one final look at the comb, when a female voice interrupted them.

"Hello Tom. Paddy. What's so funny?"

Margaret was standing beside them. "Oh!" she exclaimed, ignoring her own question. "I see you've got a comb like the one Ricky bought me. They're nice, aren't they? Did you get it for Eileen?"

"Um, yes." With the shock of seeing Maggie the words just came out.

Paddy shot him a questioning look.

"Oh golly! I'd better hide mine," Margaret said. "Because, knowing Eileen, she'll get them mixed up!"

Thankfully, Paddy had the presence of mind to change the subject. "And how are ye feeling now?" he asked. "Got over the shock?"

"Yes, thanks, Paddy," Margaret answered. "Mind you, I would hate to go through all that again."

"Well," said Tom, "you'll have to excuse us, Maggie, but we've got to get ready for work." He put the comb back in his pocket. "Coming, Paddy?" The two men walked away.

"That was close," said Paddy, as soon as they were out of earshot.

"I never saw her coming around," said Tom. "And did you hear what she said about hiding her comb, I only hope she doesn't do it before tonight."

At about twenty past nine, Tom came straight down to the girls' cabin from the restaurant and knocked on the door. Eileen opened it, and let him in. Margaret was pouting at herself in the mirror, as she finished putting on her lipstick.

"I'm just leaving, Tom." She smiled at him as she grabbed her keys from the dresser.

"See ya later, Maggie," said Eileen, as Margaret went out. "And what have you got 'ere?" she asked Tom, pointing at the bag he was carrying.

Tom took out two bottles of white wine and put them on the table. "Well luv," he said, "I thought I would treat you to these, after upsetting you last night. I've been to the doctor's and he said for me to take it easy. Turns out I do have a touch of the 'flu. So maybe now you'll understand why I don't feel too well."

He took out his hankie and blew his nose loudly.

"You couldn't get any ice for the bucket so we can chill them, luv, could you?" he said, pocketing his hankie. "I forgot to get some. If you nip down quickly to the galley, I'll open one up."

Eileen shrugged. "Okay." She paused by the door. "Oh, by the way, Tom, I was speaking to Maggie and she said that she saw you up on deck earlier with Paddy." Eileen came back over to him, "She said that you bought me a comb, just like hers."

Tom forced a smile. "Trust the girl to spoil my surprise."

"You got it with you now?" Eileen gave him a look that was half way between a smile and suspicion.

"I was going to give it to you tomorrow night?" tried Tom.

"And what's wrong with tonight?" Eileen snapped.

"Well luv, I was planning on surprising you with the wine tonight and your comb tomorrow night. Anyway let's not argue. The sooner you go and get the ice, the sooner we can enjoy our time together."

Eileen's expression hardened into pure suspicion, then she picked up the ice bucket and left him alone at last.

Tom was soon rummaging again in Margaret's drawer for her comb. There was a nasty moment where he thought she might have hidden it elsewhere, then his hand closed on it.

It was the work of a moment to swap it for Paddy's, and he had no sooner closed the drawer and stood, when there were footsteps in the corridor.

It was Margaret.

238

Maggie!" he exclaimed, "I thought you had gone down to Ricky's. You haven't had an argument already have you?"

"No, I just remembered my comb. I was going to lock it in the wardrobe, and I forgot. Now Eileen's got one, I don't want them to get mixed up."

Tom took a deep breath. "Wise girl," he laughed.

"You're back early, Maggie," said Eileen coming through the door with the bucket of ice.

"I was halfway down to Ricky's cabin, when I remembered that I had forgotten to lock my comb away. With Tom saying he had bought you one, I didn't want mine to get mixed up with yours," Margaret said.

"Bloody cheek," replied Eileen. "And what makes you think I want yours?"

Margaret just laughed as she locked the cupboard.

Tom smiled inwardly. With that turn of the key, his diamonds were even more secure.

"See you both later," Margaret said, with a wink at Tom as she left.

CHAPTER 37

Ginger was in Teresa's cabin, sitting in front of the mirror. His neck was aching; Margaret kept pushing his head too far back as she pencilled in black lines around his eyes.

He wanted to tell her to be a little more gentle, but he really didn't want to upset her.

No. They were in this together – both targets of the vile murderer, George Bowder. The man who had so cruelly taken Peter's life.

Such a sweet, innocent boy.

Ginger allowed Margaret to push his head round so she could do the outside of his eye.

He'd get his revenge on Bowder, if it was the last thing he did.

And Ricky. What was his part in all this? As Bowder's nephew and a married man, he had to be stringing the girl along. Keeping her under observation. At least Ginger hoped that was what he was doing. Not trying to murder her as well.

He shook his head. If Ricky was trying that, he would have had ample opportunities already. So no, he was just keeping an eye on her.

"Keep still!"

"Sorry."

Margaret added a few more strokes of the pencil, then stood back, frowning critically at his face in the mirror. Then she nodded.

"You'll do."

"Are you finally done?" asked Teresa, pushing his face in front of Ginger's, while trying to get his wig straight. "We've all got to get ready you know."

"I haven't even got any make-up on yet," said Lola with a pout.

"For fuck's sake, why don't you all stop moaning," groaned Sophie, a tall queen in a strawberry wig, He put down his razor having finished shaving his legs, then took out a pair of tights and started pulling them on. "Bugger!" he complained. "Bloody laddered them already!" He ripped them off and tried again with a fresh pair.

"Hey," shouted an elderly chain-smoker known as Fag Ash Lil, "mind your bloody language, there's a real woman in here."

"Sorry, Maggie," said Sophie. "With all us girls around I was forgetting myself."

Margaret smiled, "Thanks, boys… I mean girls," she said. "I'll do you next, Lola."

Ginger took one last look in the mirror, then stood up, Margaret had done an excellent job; his make-up looked pretty good.

"Can you zip my dress up, dear?" little Delores asked Sophie. Ginger grinned. Delores was only five foot two, and even in heels, looked tiny beside Sophie in his stockinged feet. Sophie bent over and struggled with Delores's fastener.

"Anybody for another drink?" asked Ginger, reaching into his locker for a bottle of vodka. "What about you, Maggie?"

"No thanks, Ginger, I'd better not be drunk in front of Ricky."

Blooming Ricky! Even the sound of the man's name was making him sick. Poor Margaret was so gullible. When she finally found out the truth about Ricky – as she must – it would break the poor girl's heart.

Lola sat down in the chair, and Margaret began working on him. She piled on the foundation and blended in the rouge. Lola kept leaning forward to examine his face.

"Not that I don't trust you, Maggie, but being the star of the pantomime, I must look my best."

"Listen to her!" cried Delores. "If it hadn't been for me saying you could be Cinderfella, you would never have had the part."

"And if I hadn't have been the best person for it," retorted Lola, "you would never have chosen me!"

"If I had my way, dear," Delores countered with acidic sweetness, "you would have been an ugly sister instead, and you wouldn't have had to be made up for it either. It was only Ginger who persuaded me to let you be Cinderfella."

"You fucking cow!" yelled Lola, jumping up from the chair and grabbing a hairbrush. He threw it at Delores, missing him by an inch.

"Any more nonsense from you," shouted Delores, "when we get back home, I'll get my six brothers and sisters on to you. They'll soon sort you out."

"Who was your father?" asked Fag Ash Lil calmly, as he slowly blew smoke from his mouth. "Brer Rabbit?"

"Stop bitching, all of you," interrupted Ginger, who was trying to push a couple of balloons down the front of his long red dress. "Sit down, Lola, and let Margaret finish your face, and you, Delores, calm down and pour yourself another gin."

Margaret started laughing, and laughed even louder when suddenly there was a loud bang. Ginger had burst one of his breasts.

When Margaret finished Lola's make-up, she fitted his long blonde wig, then brushed it straight so it would fall nicely over his shoulders.

"She looks quite nice," said Teresa, who was now sitting with a cigarette in one hand and a glass of gin in the other. His crossed, skinny legs were poking out of his long green lamé dress.

Lola stood up and began parading in front of the mirror, pouting and fluttering his eyelashes.

"Everybody ready?" asked Teresa, finishing his drink and stubbing out his cigarette. "We've only got a few minutes before the pantomime starts."

"Come on, Miss Margaret," said Ginger, "I'll take you up to the Pig." Then he whispered in her ear, "Remember wherever you are, make sure that you're never left alone. You know where I'll be if you need me."

"Same for you," she whispered back. "Never be alone either."

Margaret left Ginger at the door of the Pig. Ricky was sitting with the deckhands, so she went over and squeezed in beside him.

The Pig had been decorated with Christmas trimmings, while a makeshift stage had been put up at the far end of the room. It was draped with a slightly grubby red curtain.

Ricky passed Margaret a beer, just as Sophie stepped onto the stage, to wild cheering from the audience. He was wearing a blue sequinned dress, high-heeled shoes and long black gloves. His strawberry wig was done up in a bouffant style, setting off the bright scarlet of his lips.

"Ladies and gentlemen," he yelled, while his false eyelashes kept blinking to the movement of his mouth, "I would like to announce this year's pantomime, *CINDERFELLA*!"

The crowd cheered and banged their beer cans on the table.

Margaret laughed as all the actors walked openly into the room, then hid behind the curtain. A few minutes later, Teresa and another crew member pulled the curtain to one side, and the pantomime began.

Whatever could go wrong, did go wrong.

Lola kept forgetting his lines. Delores tripped over his stilettos and broke a heel, thereafter walking with a limp. Both Ginger's balloons burst, leaving him totally flat-chested. The two ugly sisters, who were pretending to be bitchy towards

244

Cinderfella, didn't have to do much acting. That seemed to come naturally.

But the audience appeared most forgiving, going along with the show, calling out the well-known panto responses and laughing hysterically at all the mistakes, almost as if they had been scripted.

Margaret was laughing along, when she was distracted by a sparkling flash in the corner of her eye.

It was Eileen, pushing her way through the crowd with a few cans of beer. The flash had come from her hair comb catching one of the overhead lights.

Ricky must have noticed it as well,

Margaret was shocked at how quickly his laughter became fierce anger.

"What the fuck is she doing wearing your comb?" he demanded.

"Oh no, Ricky," Margaret replied. "Tom bought one for Eileen." She nearly let slip that they had seen hers first.

"What? Why on earth did he get a comb like the one I gave you?"

"They do sell them in the shop, you know. You're not the only person who wanted to get one for his girl."

"That's a fucking joke. What if they get mixed up with each other?"

"I'll tell you why that's not going to happen," Margaret snapped back, feeling her cheeks flushing. "Because mine is locked away, and that's where it'll stay until Madeira, and after Madeira it will be locked away again until we get back home." She sat back. "Happy now?"

He gave an angry grunt, then carried on watching the show with folded arms and a face like thunder.

At the interval, Margaret had had enough.

"Listen. If you don't believe what I say about the comb, then why don't you come down to my cabin and I'll prove to you that mine is in the locker."

To her surprise, he agreed. So they left the Pig and went down to her cabin.

Margaret opened her locker and stood on her toes, running her hands along the top shelf to retrieve the package. With a smile of quiet triumph, she handed it over.

Ricky's relief was unmistakable, and, in Margaret's view, quite out of keeping with the value of the comb.

"I'm sorry, love," he said putting his arms around her shoulders and giving her a kiss, "I should never have doubted you."

She put the comb back, locking it safely away.

They both made their way back to the Pig, with Ricky's arm around her waist. When they reached it, the second part of the pantomime had already begun. This time even more of the actors forgot their lines. Sophie was so drunk that he had to be carried off stage.

At the end of the final act, the queens made their final bows. Teresa and Fag Ash Lil tried to pull the curtains together, but they must have pulled too hard. The frame fell over, leaving the whole cast flapping about under the material.

The whole Pig screamed, stamped their feet and roared with laughter.

"I think that's the funniest thing I've ever seen," laughed Margaret, feeling more relaxed now that Ricky was again in a good mood.

Later that evening, Margaret was at her table in the Pig when Eileen and Tom staggered past on their way out. Eileen's hair was falling half over her face, and her comb was hanging precariously loose. As she passed where Ginger was sitting, it fell out, and clattered to the deck.

Ginger picked it up. He studied it curiously for a while, turning it in the light, then handed it back to Eileen.

She took it from him with a few slurred words of thanks, then stuck it back on the top of her head. She and Tom then staggered out, weaving precariously from side to side as they went.

"At least you know," Margaret said, giving Ricky a hard stare, "your comb will be better looked after than that one."

CHAPTER 38

It was Christmas Day morning, and Mick was on the warpath.

The lack of information from Tom about how he was going to get the diamonds ashore was eating him up; if he didn't hear something reassuring soon, he'd explode.

He'd spent the whole of Christmas Eve in the Dolphin Lounge with his mind on the diamonds rather than the drinks he was supposed to be mixing for the passengers. Instead of Tom Collins and Bloody Mary, all he was seeing were diamond disaster scenarios, such as the stones being lost, stolen, or worse still, seized by Customs…

All because he had trusted them to a moron like Tom. How had he been so stupid? Not only was there a significant amount of money at stake, but if it all went pear-shaped, there was a risk to life and limb as well.

It was at the crew pantomime that his fears really took off; moving from general concern to full-blown panic.

He'd missed the actual show; he had no wish to watch a bunch of effeminate stewards prancing around in drag, but had gone up to the Pig after it had all finished.

That's when he'd seen Tom and that bird of his staggering out of the bar so drunk that they were almost incapable of standing.

Mick had been dumbfounded. What on earth had possessed him to recruit a pisshead like that to such a high risk venture?

But that wasn't all. Tom's bird had been wearing a diamante comb in her hair, sparkling in the lights. Seeing it had triggered a wild thought. Surely that moronic waiter hadn't been daft enough to put the stones in a plastic woman's comb, hoping the girl would take them off the ship for him?

She was even so pissed that it dropped onto the floor. Hardly a good indication that she would it ashore safely.

If that was Tom's plan, it was an absolute disaster.

Mick strode through the ship towards the Pacific restaurant. Perhaps Tom was laying up his table? But it was empty, apart from a few commis waiters polishing the silver. He tried the galley, but there was no Tom; only the chefs and cooks rushing around getting the Christmas meal ready.

In truth, the best place to look for Tom was the Pig.

As could be expected, Tom was there, sitting with some other waiters.

Mick decided to get Tom on his own by using a diversionary tactic. He casually walked up to the table.

"Tom?"

The waiter looked up, his easy smile becoming a worried frown. "Yes?"

"It's about that rare bottle of wine one of your passengers ordered from the wine waiter. I've managed to find it. Do you want to come with me and collect it?"

"What bottle of wine?"

Mick gave him a hard stare.

"Oh. Ah, yes. That bottle." Tom squeezed past his companions. "I'll be back in a minute. Get me another pint while I'm away, Paddy." He followed Mick out of the bar.

"What's this all about?" asked Tom. "I was just having a few drinks before turning to." Mick didn't answer, but led the way up the stairs to the well deck. He stopped over by the ship's rail.

"I need to know about the diamonds, Tom. You've not told me anything, and I am getting seriously concerned. Especially when I saw your girlfriend wearing some fancy comb in the Pig the other night. You weren't stupid enough to put them in that, now were you?"

Tom's went white, then gave a loud laugh. "Good heavens above," he said, "you certainly don't have much faith in me.

D'you think I would be daft enough to do a crazy thing like that? To give them to Eileen?"

"So where did she get that comb from?"

"They sell them in the ship's shop, okay?" Tom gave him an intense stare. "It all started with young Maggie. We were having a drink down in her cabin when she walked in with this comb. Ricky had bought it for her. When Eileen saw it, she, um, kept pestering me for one, so to keep her happy I went up to the shop and got her one. Does that satisfy you?"

To be honest, Mick thought the explanation was a little too elaborate. Maybe too detailed. He said nothing.

"You must stop worrying about them, Mick," Tom continued. "Like I said a hundred times over, they're safe with me. I have it all planned. How I'm going to get them off the ship. And believe me they certainly won't be going in a cheap, plastic comb."

"Are you sure?"

"Of course."

"And you'll tell me what the plan is?"

"In good time, of course." Tom leaned closer. "Best you don't know for now, eh? What you don't know, you can't tell." He tapped the side of his nose and winked like some dime-novel spy.

Mick took a deep breath. "Okay," he conceded. "But nothing stupid, you hear?"

"Absolutely not."

Mick nodded. "They're worth a fortune, Tom. If anything goes wrong, we are all in the shit."

"I do know that." Tom paused. "Do you fancy a quick drink down in the Pig? It'll do you good."

"No." Mick checked his watch. "I'm running late, I must get back to the bar."

They went back inside. Mick was just about to leave Tom outside the Pig when Eileen came up. She still had the comb in her hair.

"There you are, Tom! Where the hell 'ave you been?"

"Sorry about that, Eileen," said Tom. "I had to see Mick about some wine."

Eileen grabbed hold of Tom's arm and led him back into the bar.

As she left, Mick caught sight of her comb again.

The stones did look very realistic.

Maybe… just maybe… it wasn't such a bad idea after all?

CHAPTER 39

It was Christmas Day on the *Ocean Star* and Margaret was determined to put her worries out of her mind.

She wanted to have a jolly good time.

George Bowder? Ignore him.

Although best not to be alone outside the cabin.

Ricky and his anger over the comb? Focus on how he makes her feel when he is being nice. See the good in him, not the bad.

There. Now she could concentrate on enjoying the day.

The fun started at ten o'clock, when Freddy closed the laundry early and invited everyone up to his office for casual drinks.

Eileen also seemed to be in a good mood. She was parading around with her hair up in a French roll; the comb holding it in place. Margaret was right beside her at one point, and couldn't help noticing how much the piece sparkled. Just like her own, really. They were both very authentic-looking.

Then there was lunch.

In keeping with an old Christmas tradition, the officers became the waiters – which seemed a great way to bring the crew together. Margaret enjoyed being served by some quite senior officers, although she did keep an eye out for Bowder. Thankfully he wasn't there – probably unable to lower himself to being a waiter, even for fun on Christmas Day.

As she was starting to tuck in to her turkey, a young officer in a waiter's uniform leaned over her shoulder. He was holding two bottles of wine.

"Red or white?" he asked.

"White, please."

As the officer moved away, Betty leaned over and said, "Look at him walking around with those bottles in his hand.

Why can't he leave them on the table? Doesn't he trust us or something?"

"You're right there, kid," said Owd Rosie. "He must think we would finish the whole lot off."

And they would, thought Margaret, *and lots more besides*.

After a very fine Christmas pudding, Margaret excused herself, She wanted to tidy up her hair before seeing Ricky. She could hear Christmas carols playing from various record players as she walked towards her cabin through the crew quarters.

Maureen, the bathroom attendant, poked her head out of her cabin as Margaret passed by.

"Coming in for a drink, Maggie?" she asked.

"I was just going to get ready before going down to Ricky's cabin."

"Go on, have one for the road," shouted another voice.

"Billy! What are you doing in here?" Margaret exclaimed.

Johnny and Joe's heads appeared round the door.

"Wherever there's a party, that's where you'll find all of us," Johnny replied with a wink.

By the time Margaret left, she was a little unsteady on her feet.

After a couple of false turns, she made it to her cabin. She quickly retrieved her present for Ricky, combed her hair and set out for his quarters.

Ricky's door was wide open, with a party in full swing. Deckhands and greasers were everywhere, with empty beer cans piling up on every surface. The men were all wearing paper pirate hats, and some had painted black moustaches on their faces. Others, including Ricky, had clip-on beards.

"Come in and have a drink," Ricky slurred, giving her a beery kiss.

---0---

254

A few hours later, Margaret woke up in Ricky's bunk. His arms were clamped around her, and something was tickling her face.

She eased herself free to the sound of him snoring and grunting, then got out of bed. She picked her way through the can-littered floor to the mirror. The tickling was from his false beard, which somehow she was now wearing. With a pained frown, she ripped it off.

The cabin looked as if a tornado had hit it. There were cans everywhere and cigarette buts in every possible receptacle as well as liberally spread across the floor. A forlorn party hat was hanging over the light fitting and a couple of deflated balloons were taped to the wall.

With a groan Margaret perched on the side of the bunk and rubbed her temples. For some reason they appeared to be under attack from a pair of hammers.

There was another grunt from Ricky, then a movement behind her. She twisted round. He was sitting up, looking slightly green.

"That was some party," he said. "I think I could do with hair of the dog. Pass us a can."

Margaret scanned the room. "Sorry, Ricky," she said. "It looks like they're all empty."

He leaned forward, and she caught a blast of his morning breath. It smelt as if he had swallowed a sewage tank.

"I'll tell you what," he said. "I'll pop up to the Pig for a few cans. I'll also grab some food from the crew galley."

"That sounds like a good idea."

Ricky quickly dressed. "You stay here. I'll only be a few minutes."

An hour later, he had still not returned.

---0---

255

Tom grabbed Paddy's arm as they sat in the Pig.

"Don't forget to go to the shop and get one more comb," he hissed. "We'll need it to swap with Maggie's when we get to Liverpool."

Paddy just nodded and carried on drinking.

Eileen came in with Chris. She waved across the room, gesturing 'want another drink?' Tom nodded with a smile.

Ricky walked in behind Eileen, and went over to the deckhands' table, where there was a lot of raucous shouting and singing.

Eileen and Chris came over with a couple of pints each.

"Can't stay too long, luv," Eilen said as she sat. "I've got to turn to in a few minutes." For once her hair was neatly pinned back.

"I see you've found your hair comb again," Tom observed with a slight edge of sarcasm. "I only gave it to you a few days ago, and you must have lost it about a hundred times already."

"I'm still dead chuffed with it, and at least I keep finding the bloody thing." She laughed. "Proves how much I look after it."

"I think the combs are quite nice," said Chris. "I wouldn't mind treating myself to one. They sell them in the shop, don't they?"

"Yes, they do," replied Paddy, "There weren't many left when I got one." Tom gave him a sharp kick under the table. "Hell, Tom! What was that?"

"Sorry, mate," said Tom with a glare. "Foot slipped."

"What did you go and buy one for, Paddy?" asked Eileen with a surprised expression. "It would look blooming stupid in your hair."

"For his wife," said Tom quickly.

"Wife?" Paddy spluttered. "Ye know I don't have a wife, Tom."

"I mean," Tom said with an even darker glare, "your girlfriend."

There was a difficult silence, then Chris leaned forward. "You're a dark horse, Paddy," she said. "You never mentioned you had a woman. What's her name?"

Paddy went a bright red, but before he could say anything, Tom cut in with a quick change of subject.

"Is Maggie still in her cabin? I've just seen Ricky coming in without her."

"Strange they're not here together," said Eileen. "The silly bitch is usually glued to his side," She opened up a packet of cigarettes. "She's potty over 'im." She shook out the packet, but it was empty.

"Here you are, luv," Tom said, offering his. "Have one of mine."

"That's okay, Tom, I must get another packet." She jumped up from her seat and went over to the bar. A few minutes later she was back.

"Well luv," Tom said. "I'd better get back to the restaurant and show willing."

Just as he stood up, Ginger came over to the table.

"I think you dropped this," he said to Eileen, passing over her comb.

"Thanks, Ginge," Eileen replied as she took it. "The thing won't stay in my hair. I think I'll leave it in my pocket for now."

"One hundred and one times," muttered Tom, dialling up the sarcasm again.

---0---

An hour later, Margaret was nearly in tears as she sat alone in Ricky's cabin.

Should she go up to the Pig and see if he was there? No, it would make him look a fool in front of his mates.

Maybe she should stop waiting like a daft cow, and go back to her cabin? He could come and find her there, if he felt like it.

257

Her cabin was empty when she got there. So there was nothing else to do but change into her pyjamas and get into bed.

There were the sounds of parties going on down the alleyway. These made her feel even more alone. She could hardly get up again and join one. What if Ricky did happen to come down? He would miss her – and anyway, she'd probably just shout at him for leaving her.

But when there was a knock on the door, her heart missed a beat. It must be Ricky! He had come to see where she was!

"Come in!"

The door opened and her heart dropped. It was Tony, the mess man.

"Can I leave these rolls here for Chris and Eileen?" he asked. "They asked me to make some for them, as they missed their tea."

She nodded. "Of course."

He put a bag down on the table, then came closer to the bunk. "Why are you in bed on Christmas night Maggie? I thought you would be in the Pig with Ricky."

"Have you seen him then?"

"Oh yes, he's up there with the rest of the deckhands. They're all pissed out of their heads, but they seem to be enjoying themselves. You should go and join them."

"Yes, I might do that," said Margaret, with no intention of doing anything of the sort.

Margaret was still awake when Eileen and Chris came in with Tom, although she pretended to be asleep.

"Shh, she's in her bunk," Chris said in a loud whisper.

"It's unusual for her not to be flopping around Ricky," said Eileen. "Mind you, he did seem to be enjoying himself, and he didn't look like he was missing her." There were some girlish giggles.

"Shh," Tom hissed. "Anyhow, what about getting the beer out?"

There was the sound of the locker being noisily opened, but no sound of it being closed. The door started banging with the motion of the ship.

"Oh look, there's the rolls from Tony. I could eat a horse."

"Sorry. I asked for ham."

There was laughter as the bag was opened, accompanied by loud rustling.

Margaret lay awake, listening to the whispering, munching and drinking, which seemed to go on for ages.

How could she sleep with all that noise?

CHAPTER 40

It was Boxing Day, and Margaret was busy at the hot calender.

"You don't look very happy today, Maggie." This was Billy, who was working with her. "Suffering from a hangover? I didn't half enjoy myself, though; I think I must have been drunk the whole day. I went to a few good parties. I'm certainly going to have an early night tonight."

"I believe we're in Dakar tomorrow," said Margaret, trying to put the misery of Christmas Day out of her mind.

"Going ashore with Ricky tomorrow night?"

"I don't know yet. I'll have to wait and see." Of course, when she did see him, there would be a hell of a row.

Margaret kept looking at her watch. The time seemed to drag by. Would twelve o'clock never come?

It seemed like an eternity down in the hot, sticky laundry. Finally the machine stopped and everybody made a big rush towards the stairway leading out of the laundry.

When Margaret reached the top of the steps, Ricky was standing there, looking down at her.

He must have known from her face how angry she was. "Sorry about last night," he muttered. "I suppose I got a bit carried away."

"Carried away?" she snapped. "And what about me? I was alone all night. You didn't even have the decency to come and see where I was."

"Listen, Margaret," he said, raising his hands in a gesture of conciliation. "Don't let's argue here." He looked pointedly at the others, who were standing behind her on the stairs, clearly listening. "Come down to my place for a few minutes."

She followed him silently to his cabin, her blood boiling.

When they got inside, instead of sitting down on his day bed, she stood by the door with her hands on her hips.

"Why didn't you give a thought to me, sitting here all alone for hours? 'I'll be back in a few minutes' you said!"

"Well, why the bloody hell didn't you come up to the Pig?" Ricky snapped, his own anger showing. "You knew where I'd be!"

"But if you had given me any thought at all, I wouldn't have needed to go up there after you! Not on Christmas bloody Day!"

"Oh for God's sake, Margaret, what are you? Some little puppy that must have all my attention every five minutes?"

She couldn't stand his hurtful words any longer. With this, and all the worries she had, she suddenly burst into floods of tears. This seemed to soften Ricky's anger. He put his arms around her shoulders and guided her to the day bed.

"I'm sorry, love," he said. "Don't cry. I was just going into the Pig to get our drinks when I passed by the lads' table. They saw me and called me over." He paused, and squeezed her shoulders. "I told them I had to get back to you, but you know what they're like. 'One for the road', they kept saying, and I'm afraid that's what happened."

She looked back at him through misted eyes, as her sobs began to slow down. Maybe he was right. It was always difficult to get away from a crowd of people.

Ricky held her at arms' length and gave her one of his big smiles. "That's better, love." Then he added a kiss on the cheek.

He went over to his locker, as she wiped her tears and blew her nose. "Hey, I say, I forgot to give you your Christmas present." He pressed a little square box wrapped in shiny red paper into her hand. "For you, Margaret, I'm sorry I didn't give it to you yesterday."

Her hands began to shake as she unwrapped the package. In it was a small oval-shaped aquamarine pendant.

"Oh, Ricky, it's beautiful!"

262

This time he kissed her on the lips.

"Did you like the present I gave you?" she asked after they had broken away.

"The jumper fitted perfectly," he said smiling back at her.

She frowned. "I still haven't fully forgiven you, you know. And if you get stuck in the bar again, have the decency to tell me. You must have known I would be upset, especially it being Christmas."

---0---

George Bowder was ensconced in one of the comfortable chairs at the polished mahogany table in the officers' wardroom, enjoying his third whisky of the day.

He'd met with Ricky on deck a few hours before. After the lad had filled him on some argument he'd had with that steam queen, their talk had naturally turned to the diamonds.

"Not long to go now," Bowder said. "Just think, when we get back home, the money we should make on those stones will mean it's all been worthwhile." He smiled. "This time next year you could even be sitting at a beach bar, with the sun streaming down, eating lobsters or something exotic with Babs and the kids."

"You keep telling me that. We need to get the comb off and through Customs first."

"Talking of combs," Bowder said, "I saw that other laundry maid yesterday. You know, the one that goes out with the waiter. She was wearing a comb similar to the one I gave you."

"Oh, I know the maid you mean," said Ricky, "That's Eileen. She cabins with Margaret. Tom, her boyfriend, bought it from the shop as present for Christmas."

Bowder gave Ricky a serious glare. "I trust there's no chance of them getting muddled up?"

"Not a chance, George, Ours is safely locked away. I checked." He grinned. "You do realise that the more crew members go through Customs with them, the less they'll suspect anything from ours?"

He was right of course.

George finished his drink and was about to get to his feet, when The Chief Office came in, and sat at the table.

"We'll be in Dakar tomorrow, old chap," he said. "Are you going ashore?"

George shrugged. "I might."

"You should. Senegal is a beautiful country." The Chief Officer sipped his drink. "It was a French colony until 1960. Now it has its independence. In fact that's where I learnt to speak French fluently. Mind you it's always a bit dodgy around the port areas, especially in Dakar. Bloody awful city for thieves; the worst in West Africa actually." He gave a chuckle. "Of course, most of them are just pickpockets, but they can turn nasty. Especially with a single female tourist whose got some jewellery."

"Sounds…" George paused. "Interesting."

"You'll be alright, old chap. Just be cautious around Place de L'Independance, Sandaga market and along Avenue Pompidou. That's where knives can be used. Particularly at night. Stay away from those places, and you'll be fine."

But it wasn't his own safety that concerned George.

No, it was Margaret's.

CHAPTER 41

The *Ocean Star* docked early in the port of Dakar, two days after Christmas.

Margaret stood on the poop deck looking down on the quayside, before starting work in the laundry. The vendors were setting out their goods, getting ready for the passengers to disembark. She could see all sorts of carved figures and beautiful paintings on display.

"Freddy's letting us finish at two today, kid," observed Owd Rosie beside her. "We can take half an hour for lunch and go early. Fancy going to one of them markets?"

"Yes, that's a good idea, Rosie, I love markets."

Ricky had told her the night before that he would not be going ashore in Dakar, because he had a lot of work to catch up on.

"Do you mind if we come and join you?" asked Billy, who was standing next to Johnny and Joe. "We could either share a taxi or walk."

"Why don't we walk through the town a bit then take a taxi to the market?" said Johnny with enthusiasm.

"The Kernel is the nearest one to the port," said Joe, "that's within walking distance."

"We'd better get down to the laundry or we're all going to be late," said Margaret, checking her watch.

"Right then," answered Johnny, "we'll all meet down on the quayside at two-thirty prompt."

When Margaret and the rest of the laundry crew finished for the day, she hurried back to her cabin to get changed in good time. Owd Rosie was not far behind.

There was an envelope on the floor of her cabin. It had one of Ricky's typed notes inside, explaining that he was going to take her ashore after all, but she must – really must – keep it a secret so he didn't get into trouble. He gave her instructions on where they should meet in town, travelling in separate taxis so as not to raise suspicion. He named the bar and the street, and said they should meet an hour earlier than they had originally agreed, at eight.

It seemed like he'd planned it all out. After their earlier argument, maybe he was trying to make it up.

"I thought that you were supposed to be in a real hurry?" Eileen said, poking her head round the door.

"Yes, I…" Margaret stopped herself from mentioning the note from Ricky. "I was just thinking of what to wear."

"Blinking well get a shift on, wear something, and bugger off," Eileen said as she came in. "I want to put my head down for a couple of hours."

Just as Margaret was pulling on her jeans, Owd Rosie came in. "Aren't you ready yet, kid?" she asked. "It's nearly two-thirty, I don't want them to go without us. I don't feel safe wandering around on my own in this port."

"You were the one to suggest it," said Margaret.

" I know, kid, but we were going to take a taxi."

"I'll tell you what, Rosie, you go ahead and I'll be down in a few minutes."

Margaret walked down the gangway. Owd Rosie was easy to spot in her bright yellow dress and red shoes, surrounded by the laundry boys.

Before making their way outside the dock, they lingered for a while to look at the some of the carvings.

"Here, lady, you want wood camel?" said one of the traders, grabbing at her arm and holding up a carved piece.

"I'll think about it when I get back," she replied.

"Think? Don't think! You buy now! For you I give special price. Three pounds!"

"No thanks," said Margaret. The man's persistence was making her uncomfortable.

266

"I'll tell you what," laughed Billy, grabbing Margaret's other arm, "how much for this beautiful English lady?"

The trader eyed her up and down, his expression a little too serious for her liking. "I give three of these carvings," he said.

"Oh, thank you very much!" burst out Margaret, "I'd have thought I was worth more than that."

"Come on all of you," said Johnny, half laughing, "let's get on our way. We haven't got all day."

As they all walked away from the man, Margaret could hear him shouting after her. "Okay mister! I give you four carvings!"

They asked the way to Kernel Market, and were told it closed at one o'clock.

"We'll grab a taxi," said Johnny, "and go to another one. The bloke said the Medina Market, in Avenue Blaise Diagne."

Margaret stopped briefly. The name Avenue Blaise Diagne rang a bell. Surely that was around the place where she would be meeting Ricky tonight?

The market was busy, colourful and vibrant, packed with stalls selling all manner of foods, pots, pans, clothing and souvenirs.

Margaret pushed her way in, past the tourists and locals clustering round the stalls. She kept an eye out for something to buy for Ricky, now their relationship was back on a more even keel.

It was good of him to say he would slip off the ship with the chance of being caught, just so that he could take her for a drink ashore.

A portly figure in white caught her eye, standing at one of the far stalls. She leaned round to check, and her blood froze.

It was the second engineer, George Bowder.

Margaret searched across the stalls for Johnny. She could not be alone with Bowder around. With a small cry of relief, she spotted her friend at a pottery stall, and quickly pushed her way over to him.

"Hello," he said with a smile. He was turning an earthenware pot over in his hand. "What do you think of this?" he asked. "I might buy it for my mum."

They spent a few more hours exploring the market. Margaret kept scanning the crowd for Bowder, while sticking to Johnny like glue. Thankfully, she did not see the second engineer again, and it was with some relief that they found a taxi and made their way back to the ship.

Margaret eased open the cabin door. It was still in darkness, with some heavy breathing and light snoring sounds. Eileen, Chris and Kitty must still be sleeping. After her time ashore in the sun, and the shock of seeing Bowder, that seemed like a good idea. She climbed into her bunk for a quick rest before her evening with Ricky.

A bell sounded, loud enough to wake the dead, and Margaret sat bolt upright. Her immediate thought was that there was another fire – but then there was a crash of an alarm clock hitting the floor, and a curse from Eileen.

"Bloody 'ell," she said. "It's six-thirty already! Gotta get up, or we'll miss tea!"

They all dressed quickly while Eileen stood by the mirror, putting her hair up into a French roll and pinning in the comb.

"I'm just nipping down to the quayside for a minute," Eileen announced. "I want to buy one of them wooden carvings. I'll see you all up in the mess room later. Tah-ra." She left, banging the door behind her.

After Chris and Kitty had left as well, Margaret went down the alleyway for a shower. Thankfully none of the girls had asked what her plans were for the evening. Ricky's note had made it clear she was to keep it a secret. A romantic evening, just for the two of them.

She came back to the empty cabin, and picked out her favourite dress. She had another quick look at her comb. Should she surprise him and wear it tonight? On second thoughts, no. She didn't want any more trouble. Save it for Madeira.

At seven-thirty, Margaret locked the cabin and headed towards the gangway. As she walked through the passengers' accommodation, she bumped into Ginger coming out of a cabin.

"Well hello, Miss Margaret," he said. "You are looking very smart. Where are you off to tonight?"

"Keep it a secret Ginger; I shouldn't be saying anything, but I'm meeting Ricky ashore. He's supposed to be working so I don't want to get him in trouble. He's going to meet me at this place at eight o'clock." She showed him the typed note with the address of the bar. "Anyhow, I'll be late if I don't hurry."

She took the note back from Ginger and trotted away.

Ginger stared after her with a look of deep concern.

---0---

Margaret jumped into the back of a cab and showed the paper to the driver. He handed it back with a brief nod, then set off.

After a couple of minutes she noticed that the meter hadn't clicked on. She tapped him on the shoulder, and pointed at it. The man turned and glared at her, almost as if it was her fault, then switched it on. Margaret sat back; for a moment there, it looked as if he would turn nasty. So much for trying to be honest.

The taxi drove through the modern part of the town, then towards the market she'd been to earlier with Johnny. Maybe the driver was taking her the long way around, to punish her for pointing out his mistake? It was dark by now, and everywhere looked different at night.

Margaret checked her watch; it was just eight o'clock. She hoped she wouldn't be too late for Ricky. The car took a turn off the Avenue Blaise Diagne down a cobbled side street, then stopped abruptly.

"Here is place you want, miss."

Margaret got out of the taxi and paid the driver. He gunned the engine and drove away fast, leaving her on her own in a strange street, lit only by a single dim lamp.

It was quiet. There was no one around.

A chill ran down Margaret's spine.

She had assured Ginger she would never be alone at any time – and here she was, in a strange place, in a strange city. At night. Quite alone.

She looked up and down the street. There was no sign of any bar; only shabby houses, most of which looked derelict. None had lights on, or indeed, any signs of life.

Where was Ricky? Why wasn't he here to meet her? To protect her? She had followed his instructions to the letter.

The letter!

A frightening thought occurred. What if that note hadn't been from Ricky at all? What if it was a trick to lure her here? What if it had been typed by someone else?

By the second engineer?

As if on cue, a large dark shape stepped into the pool of light from the lamp. The light shone on his face.

It was the face of the man she never wanted to see; the man who made it clear he was out to kill her.

George Bowder.

With was a glint of steel in his hand.

Margaret backed away, but her heel caught on a cobble and, with a scream, she fell backwards.

Bowder loomed over her, as she tried to shuffle away.

"You little bitch," he snarled. "You've been lucky too many times. But not now. I've got you this time."

The blade rose, glinting in the light.

She lay helpless beneath it.

Margaret screamed again, as the knife swept down.

CHAPTER 42

Margret couldn't breathe.

There was such pressure on her chest that it pushed all the air out, and try as she might, it wasn't possible to draw in another one.

Nor was it possible to scream for help; you need to be able to breathe for that. All she could manage was a small whimper from the back of her throat.

She opened her eyes.

George Bowder stared back, his ugly, snarling face just inches from hers.

She whimpered again. The man must have stabbed her in the lungs, which was why she couldn't breathe.

Any minute she'd be dead.

He'd won.

She closed her eyes and tried to draw a final breath. Anything to prolong her life for just a few more precious seconds.

"Miss Margaret?" said a voice from somewhere.

It sounded like Ginger. Her dying brain had conjured up Ginger. Funny how the brain plays tricks. They say those who really love you appear in your dying moments.

Ginger.

Why not Ricky?

"Miss Margaret?"

She opened her eyes again. Bowder's expression hadn't changed; his eyes still wide open with a look of shock.

Then suddenly he moved away.

The air rushed back into her lungs, making her sob and retch.

Ginger's face appeared.

"Miss Margaret?"

"Ginger?"

"Are you all right?"

"He stabbed me. I'm dying."

Ginger smiled. At a time like this, he actually smiled. "No." He shook his head. "No, he didn't. I stabbed him in the back. He fell on top of you."

"I couldn't breathe," she whispered. "Now I can."

"I rolled him off you."

"He was going to kill me."

"Luckily I got him first." He cupped her face in his hands. "I got him, Miss Margaret. He didn't kill you." He stroked her cheek. "We won! Bowder's dead, not us."

Suddenly the enormity of what had happened took Margaret's breath away once more. "He's dead?" she gasped, once she could speak. "Not me?"

Ginger nodded, then helped her to her feet.

George Bowder was on his side, a large knife handle protruding from his back. He still had the same shocked expression that she'd first seen. Now she knew it was the look he'd had as he died. As Ginger's blade went deep into his heart.

Another knife was on the cobbles by his side, its blade clean. She put her hand towards it.

"Don't touch it," Ginger said. "His prints will be all over it. They'll know it was his, and assume he was about to use it."

"He was."

"True. But this is a rough area. It will look like maybe someone was trying to rob him."

Margaret nodded. This made sense. "Then take his wallet. It will make it look like a robbery for sure. And harder to identify him."

Ginger reached into Bowder's pocket and eased out the wallet with just his thumb and finger. "Come on," he said as he slipped it into his own pocket. "We had better go."

They headed past the lamp towards the Avenue Blaise Diagne.

272

"Try and look casual as if nothing has happened," Ginger suggested. "We'll go back in a taxi together. I'll get him to stop just before we reach the ship. You get out first and go to the souvenir stalls. Act like you have just popped down to the quayside to look for gifts. I'll follow on after you, and do the same thing." He was silent a moment. "Margaret," he said, "don't mention anything about this to anybody, not even Ricky. It will be seen as murder. So it's very important that nobody but you and I know what has happened." He gave her a worried look. "You promise?"

She put her hand on his shoulder and looked him in the eye. "Ginger, I promise."

They walked a few more streets, until they were in a busy, well-lit area with shops and bars. A taxi drove slowly past with his light on, so they flagged him down and got in the back.

"Ginger?" Margaret whispered softly so the driver wouldn't hear, "How did you come to be there?" Then she added, "Not that I'm complaining, mind."

"When you showed me that letter from Ricky," Ginger replied, "I had just seen him in the Pig, in the queue to get some beers. So I wondered why he was giving you such detailed instructions to meet him ashore, when he clearly wasn't going himself. And it was a weak excuse to say he couldn't be seen going ashore with you. That seemed very odd, so I realised I had do something. I got Martha to cover me, and came ashore."

"So I was right – it wasn't him who wrote that note?"

"No." Ginger replied. "It must have been that murdering Bowder." He paused. "And it was typed, too."

She nodded. "Ricky often types his notes to me."

"So Bowder could make you think it was Ricky who'd sent it." He gave a grim smile. "And the address you showed me was one of the dodgiest areas. So I put two and two together – and realised you were in big danger. I grabbed a ten-inch knife I'd once bought a few trips back and kept in case I ever needed it,

273

then got a taxi to where Bowder sent you. I got out a couple of streets back, then ran on. And luckily, I was just in time to come up behind him as he was about to stab you."

"Thank you Ginger. Thank you, thank you, thank you."

---0---

The cab stopped two streets before the port, and Margaret got out. She headed for the stalls, and was soon innocently mingling among the passengers and crew browsing the stalls.

"Hello pretty lady, you come back for this beautiful carving? For you, just two pounds."

It was the trader from that morning. Good. He'd remembered her, so would say he'd seen her if asked.

She handed over two pound notes, and took the wooden camel from him.

As Margaret headed back to the ship, she was pulled to one side by a hand on her arm.

She spun round, ready to run if it was a policeman. How quickly could they have found the body and traced the murder back to her?

But it was a little old lady, with a broad smile.

Margaret let out a long breath. "Can I help you?" she asked.

"I believe you already did," said the woman. "Aren't you the young lady who prevented me getting trampled by the crowd on the stairway? When there was a fire after we left Rio?"

Margaret nodded slightly vaguely. That all seemed so long ago.

"I'm Miss Pike. I thought it was very brave of you. I just wanted to thank you again. Your name is Margaret Hargreaves if I recall correctly?"

"Yes it is."

"Well, Margaret, you very possibly saved my life."

They walked towards the ship, with Miss Pike chattering away, until they saw Ginger and Miss Pike excused herself to greet him.

---0---

Margaret reached Ricky's cabin about twenty minutes after nine. He was sitting on the day bed with a beer.

"Hello Ricky," she said, in as casual a voice as she could manage."

"Where have you been?" he demanded. "And why are you all dressed up? I told you we weren't going ashore tonight."

"Oh I know, Ricky, I just thought I would wear this dress to look nice for you. I nipped down to the quay to buy some souvenirs. I'm sorry I'm late but I met with one of the passengers. She insisted on talking to me for ages. I got away as quick as I could." She held up the wooden camel. "Do you like this carving I bought for my mum? I only paid two pounds for it."

Ricky nodded in approval, and opened her a can of beer.

"We've got time for a few. I'm due on deck in an hour as we're sailing soon.

At a quarter past eleven, Ricky walked Margaret back to her cabin.

She had just climbed into bed when there was an announcement from the officer on watch, saying that the departure would be delayed for some time.

Presumably because George Bowder had not returned.

She lay in her bunk, unable to sleep.

What a nightmare. Bowder was no longer a threat – but now Ginger was at risk of being up for his murder.

Eventually she must have dozed off, because at some point she became aware that there was the familiar feeling of movement through the waves.

She turned over and went back to sleep, as the ship sailed on.

CHAPTER 43

Margaret followed the other women along the working alleyway down to the laundry.

"Yes, girl," Betty said to Lil, "I believe the second engineer missed the ship last night. Departure was delayed for I don't know how long."

"Never did like the man," said Eve. She turned to Margaret and asked, "What does your Ricky say about it?"

Margaret stopped. "Ricky?" she asked. "What's Ricky got to do with the second engineer?"

"Oh aye, girl, didn't you know? Didn't Ricky tell you George Bowder was his uncle?"

Uncle? Margaret felt knocked sideways. Ricky's uncle?

"No," was all she could say in a small voice.

"Really? 'Ee's a dark horse if ever there was one."

Margaret didn't say any more, but just carried on to the laundry.

Even the heat and monotony of the calender couldn't stop Margaret from going over what she'd learned that morning. It was almost more appalling than her near-death experience the night before – because it meant everything she knew, or thought she knew, about Ricky was now up in the air.

Ricky was Bowder's nephew.

Of course! That was why Ginger hadn't wanted her to mention anything to Ricky. Ginger knew they were related, and he hadn't told her.

So much for her blushing saviour.

And did Ricky know that his uncle had murdered the bellboy? When she had told him of her suspicions, he had immediately advised her not to mention a word to anybody about it.

A sheet snagged on the calender and she cleared it without conscious thought.

Was Ricky only going out with her to cover for his uncle?

Or even – was he another would-be murderer? Had he been part of his uncle's plot to kill her?

This had to be resolved. Ricky might be innocent, or he might be in it up to his neck. She decided she would see what happened in Maderia, when the ship was there in a few days for New Year's Eve. In the meantime, she would play along with Ricky. Say nothing, but watch him carefully and see if she could decide where he stood.

---0---

The next few days were a nightmare, as Margaret could not deny her love for Ricky, while also trying to dispassionately assess if he truly loved her in return.

It was now common knowledge across the whole crew that George Bowder had been killed in a robbery gone wrong, as his wallet had been taken. (As agreed with Ginger, Margaret had dropped it over the side early the morning after in a weighted bag).

She took very careful note of how Ricky reacted to the news. She decided he was genuinely distraught, but was trying very hard to conceal this from her.

"I think there will be an inquest when we get back to England," he said in his most matter-of-fact tone. "What with his murder being abroad, it will be practically impossible to find the killer."

"Poor man," she said calmly, then changed the subject.

Maybe he wasn't the only one able to hide their true feelings.

On New Year's Eve, the *Ocean Star* dropped anchor in Funchal harbour in the beautiful island of Madeira.

Margaret, along with the rest of the laundry crew, were watching from on deck. She admired the city and beyond, spreading out like a fan, the steep sides of the mountains rising behind the red-roofed buildings. The view was breath-taking. Now the cruise was coming to an end, she wanted to make sure all these lovely views were etched into her memory.

At least she could enjoy them freely, without having to worry about George Bowder's murderous plans.

The laundry would finish early again that day, so Margaret was going ashore with some of the laundry boys for a few hours that afternoon. Owd Rosie felt too tired and said that she would put her head down when they finished work, and save herself for New Year's Eve.

Ricky's plan for the evening was to take Margaret to a hotel for drinks and dinner.

At two-thirty, Margaret met Johnny and Billy at the bottom of the gangway.

"We can get a little boat that will take us to the other side of the harbour," said Johnny. "It leaves from the side over there." He pointed towards the bow of the ship.

After waiting for about ten minutes a little boat pulled alongside the quay, picking up a few passengers, including Margaret and the laundry boys.

It all seemed so normal, as if George Bowder hadn't ever tried to lure her to her death. As if Ginger hadn't managed to stab the man just in time. Life on board had settled back into the usual routine for Margaret, and she sometimes had to pinch herself to remember that nothing was normal any more.

Not when a murderer had died on top of you, and nearly crushed you to death.

Margaret had only seen Ginger once since the fateful night in Dakar.

She had been standing in a queue at the crew bar, waiting for a few cans of beer to take down to Ricky's cabin. Ginger was right behind her. Margaret had turned to speak to him, but he just smiled at her in a friendly way. A little while later he had whispered in her ear, "I'll see you after Madeira." He then turned to Lola, who came up to ask him what he wanted to drink.

The boat pulled in at the jetty and everybody went ashore. Margaret stood on the waterfront of the beautiful Portuguese island, gazing all around. Steep cobbled streets ran up from the harbour, while the city stretched northwards beyond them, up the hills into the mountains.

"Oh, look over there," said Johnny, pointing over to some ox-carts. The carriages were on wooden runners instead of the conventional wheels. "Let's see how much it is to go on one of them."

Johnny began talking with one of the men standing by the two oxen. He turned back to the group. "He says that they're called Carros de Bois sledges, and he will take us on a tour of the surrounding peaks and beauty spots. Then we climb into wickerwork toboggans for an exciting trip down the steep road into Funchal."

"Okay, let's do that!" Joe exclaimed. Billy added, "Yes, let's."

"It's quite expensive." Johnny told them the price and their faces dropped.

"I've just got enough on me," said Margaret, looking in her purse.

Too bad she'd left Bowder's money in his wallet when disposing of it, but she and Ginger had agreed it was too risky to keep.

They found enough between them and jumped in the carriage. The sledge took them up the narrow streets, passing churches and monasteries faced with ancient, dark volcanic stone, contrasting with whitewashed walls and bright-shuttered windows. Houses with colourful doors and awnings set off the

280

reds, blues and greens of the flowering plants that pervaded every nook and cranny.

Later they climbed into wickerwork toboggans, locally known as the Carros de Cesto, for an exciting ride down to a couple of thousand feet below. The sledge would only hold two so Margaret shared it with Johnny. It was steered and controlled by two operators using ropes to restrain the craft on its downward flight. The drivers in their traditional garb ran alongside. At the end of the ride they all jumped out laughing.

"I know what we'll do now," said Billy. "Let's go wine tasting. The Madeira Wine Company Lodge has tasting rooms."

"You lot go," said Margaret. "I'm going out tonight with Ricky, so I'll go for a walk by myself."

"Will you be alright on your own, Margaret?" asked Johnny,

"Don't worry about me, I'll be fine on my own, believe me."

Margaret left the three boys and began to walk around the narrow streets, admiring some of the quaint churches as she took photographs of the varied surroundings. She walked around Praco do Municipio the main square of Funchal, then eventually came across some public gardens called Jardin de Sao Fransisco and sat down on a bench, admiring a fountain in a pool with a trickling waterfall.

She was just starting to feel at peace.

---0---

That evening Margaret and Ricky walked down the gangway together.

"You don't need to keep patting your hair," he said.

"I'm just checking the comb is still there," she replied. "This is the first time I have worn it."

Ricky hailed a taxi to take them to Reid's, one of the most famous hotels on the island.

Ricky found a seat in the cocktail bar and ordered a couple of drinks. Margaret noticed how quiet he was. In the end she suggested they went out on the veranda.

Outside, the view across mature sub-tropical gardens was breathtaking, with the lights of Funchal spread out like a magic carpet to the east.

"Sorry, I'm quiet tonight," Ricky said. "I don't really feel very well. I think I must have caught a stomach bug or something."

"We won't stay out too long then," she answered, with a slightly terse edge to her voice.

Was this genuine? Did he really have a bug – or did he have some other plan?

"Will you be going straight to bed, then?" she asked.

"Most likely. I'll see how I feel."

Keeping his options open?

"Don't forget to take care of that comb you're wearing, Margaret," he said, looking at it for about the hundredth time. "I still want to exchange it for that diamond ring."

She smiled back at him, and squeezed his hand. Those words were like magic to her.

Or were they just an illusion, like a magician's trick?

"Do you mind if we leave after these drinks. I know its New Year's Eve, and I don't want to spoil your evening."

"Don't worry, Ricky, I do understand."

At ten o'clock they left Reid's Hotel and took a taxi back to the ship. Ricky saw Margaret to her cabin and gave her a quick kiss, saying, "If you want to go to any of the parties, do go. I don't want to spoil your night, but do put that comb away safely first."

He left her outside the door.

Kitty and Chris were seated on the bunks having a drink when she got in.

"You're back early," said Kitty, in surprise. "Had an argument with Ricky?"

"No, he just doesn't feel very well."

Chris grabbed her arm. "Don't worry about him, Maggie, it's New Year's, and there's a party up on deck. I think Eileen's gone ashore with Tom. You can't be alone on New Year's. We're just going up there now; come and join us."

Margaret did just that. She drank every drink she was offered, and at twelve o'clock, leaning over the rail, watched the traditional Maderia fireworks display.

Then she drank some more. She got so drunk that she did not remember going to bed. But in the morning, one small bit of memory returned; she had forgotten to put the comb back in her locker. She felt her hair.

It was not there.

She must have lost it.

CHAPTER 44

Margaret searched the whole cabin, looking in every place she could think of, that the comb might have fallen.

Then she searched it again.

Throughout all this Eileen was asleep in her bunk; her own comb still in her hair and clinging on, as if to taunt Margaret with its very presence. How unfair; Margaret had worn hers once and lost it, while Eileen had lost hers hundreds of times – yet there it was, still in her hair.

Margaret even leant over and took a closer look at Eileen as she slept, in case for some drunken reason she was wearing both combs.

With her head pounding, Margaret went up on deck, and searched the area where she'd been partying the night before. After a fruitless time walking up and down by the rails, she stopped and leaned on them, gazing out to sea.

This brought a flashback to the night before, when she had been leaning in the same place, watching the fireworks.

Which led to the only possible conclusion; the comb had fallen into the sea.

She decided not to say a word to Ricky, or even the girls. The only thing now was to go up to the ship's shop and buy another one. Hopefully he would not notice the difference.

Later in the shop, Margaret looked around at all the fancy goods, but couldn't see another comb anywhere. She asked one of the assistants.

"I don't think we have any left," the girl said with a rueful shake of her head. "There's been quite a run on them. Surprisingly popular with the crew this trip."

Margaret gazed at the girl. What would Ricky say? If he was innocent, and did love her, this would be the end. She felt a tear run down her cheek.

"Oh gosh, I didn't realise how much it meant to you," the girl said. "Look, I'll tell you what; I've got one put away for myself. You can have that."

"Oh, thank you!" Margaret said, "you're an absolute gem."

The girl bent underneath the counter, brought out the comb and showed it to Margaret.

"Yes, it is the same as the one I've lost. Thank you so much, it's so kind of you."

When Margaret got back to her cabin, she had another quick look at the new comb. It was similar to the one Ricky had bought, but it didn't feel quite as heavy, or sparkle as much. Hopefully, he wouldn't know the difference. The only thing that mattered was that she had got one, and if all was well, she'd be able to swap it for that diamond ring of Ricky's.

---0---

The ship was rolling heavily as it ploughed through the high waves of the Bay of Biscay.

Ginger strode up and down the alleyway. He was frustrated; the heavy seas meant his passengers were stuck in their cabins, so he couldn't service them.

It was now a few days since Dakar. Thankfully, there didn't seem to be anything to connect him to the killing; no-one saying they'd seen him getting into a taxi, or coming back with Margaret. He'd bumped into Miss Pike on the quayside when he got back, and let her prattle on a while – giving him something of an alibi. And the knife was one he'd bought years ago and kept hidden, so should be untraceable. Especially as he'd been wearing gloves when he'd plunged it into Bowder's back.

Which was as much for young Peter as it was for Margaret.

Poor Margaret, besotted with that rogue Ricky. Tomorrow night was Channel night, so they'd be home within a couple of days. She needed to know that her thing with Ricky was never going anywhere, so he'd tell her tomorrow.

One of the cabin doors opened. It was Miss Pike.

"Oh there you are, steward, I've got a little something for you." She gave a giggle as she popped a brown envelope into his hands. "I thought I would give it you now."

"Thank you, Miss Pike," Ginger said in his most polite voice. "I do hope that you have enjoyed your cruise."

She nodded at him, still giggling as she walked away down the alleyway.

He hefted the envelope. It felt very light; no coins. As soon as Miss Pike was out of sight he ripped it open, expecting there to be maybe a fiver or two. Poor reward for all her bother.

To his surprise Ginger pulled out two fifty-pound notes.

---0---

Mick gave Jill a peck on the cheek – knowing the relationship would shortly be over. Jill was nice, but he'd soon be back in England with his wife. He smiled at her as he handed over a drink. Clinking his glass with hers, he said, "This is for the lovely time we've shared together."

Aside from his time with Jill, it had certainly been a trip with a difference. He had never known so many things happen on one cruise. The death of the bellboy, the fire, Margaret the laundry girl falling overboard, and now the latest news; George Bowder being found ashore, killed in a robbery.

At least he had the income from the diamonds to look forward to. Mick could picture himself counting all the money he would get for them.

Tom kept assuring him that they would be taken ashore safely.

"You must trust me," Tom had said.

Well, he would just have to have faith in the man.

---0---

The last laundry of the cruise finished at two o'clock, and Margaret allowed herself to enjoy the moment. No more heat, sheets, sweat and toiling at the calender. How lovely!

She'd arranged to see Ricky that evening before meeting up again in England. Was he genuine? She still wasn't sure either way, He had been very civil to her since Madeira, and kept talking about how he was looking forward to meeting her at her home in Lancashire. As soon as he had spoken to his wife Babs, he told her, he would be looking for a diamond ring to swap for the comb.

Margaret wanted to believe him, but there was this little voice in the back of her mind that kept telling her to be cautious.

And it was a little voice that was getting louder.

She was just coming up from the laundry when she spied Ginger standing at the top of the stairs. He beckoned her over.

"I haven't seen you since we were in the Pig," Margaret observed with a smile.

"Yes," he replied with a serious look. "I need to talk to you. I'll see you on the well deck in twenty minutes. Wear something warm; it'll be cold up there."

Margaret nodded and popped back to her cabin to put on a coat.

Was she going to find out more about Ricky? Although if it was about him being George Bowder's nephew, she already knew.

A little while later she stepped out onto the open deck. It was cold and the sky looked grey. Ginger was sitting on a pile of ropes on the lee side of the ship. He had a few beers at his feet.

288

"Here you are, Miss Margaret," he said, passing an open can to her.

"I know what you're going to tell me," she said, without giving Ginger a chance to speak. "Ricky was George Bowder's nephew. I know because one of the women told me."

"And I suppose that you love him, and you're going to forgive him?" said Ginger dryly.

"I think so. I want to, but…."

"But?" He raised an eyebrow.

"I still don't know if I should trust him."

"I see."

"Do you think I should, Ginger? I've been thinking about it a lot."

Ginger took a swig of beer, then a deep breath. "Absolutely not," he said.

Margaret felt an icy chill, and shivered despite her warm coat. "Oh," she said. "Why?" She dreaded to hear, but after all they'd been through, she trusted Ginger. If anyone was going to tell her the truth, it would be him.

"Because he's never going to give up his family." Ginger considered her with a concerned expression. "He's been doing what all the married men do on board; have a fling with a girl during the trip, then go back to their family. Do you really think that he is going to give his wife and children up for you?"

"Children! What children?" Margaret whispered. "He said he didn't have children." A blast of cold wind brought tears to her eyes.

"Just like he didn't tell you about his uncle?"

"Which is understandable, given his uncle was a murderer."

"You're still defending him?" Ginger asked softly. "When you said you weren't sure? Why?"

"Because I so want it to be true," she said. "He wants to see me again in Lancashire, and swap my comb for an engagement

289

ring." She stopped, with a hand over her mouth in shock at what she'd just said.

She'd given away Ricky's secret.

"What comb? For heaven's sake, Margaret, whatever are you talking about?"

In the end Margaret explained everything about the comb, and Ricky's promise. The only thing she didn't mention was that she had gone and lost the original.

The effect on Ginger was like a dam bursting.

"You silly little fool," he exclaimed. "Seriously? And you believed him? Come on, girl, wise up! The man was leading you up the garden path!" He stood up from the pile of ropes, and paced away, then turn back with an angry frown. "I should imagine in the first place he only went out with you to protect his uncle. After all you did tell me that he had said, 'Promise not to tell anybody about Peter'. He must have known all along that his uncle had murdered the lad! Why he insisted on seeing you again in England I will never know. Maybe it's another cover-up." He sat down again. "Don't you see how daft it sounds, swapping a diamond ring for a silly cheap comb?"

Ginger was right, of course. It was all a daft story.

How on earth had she swallowed it all?

Blinded by love?

Suddenly Margaret couldn't control herself. She held her head in her hands and sobbed her heart out.

All her doubts about Ricky – they had been real.

Ginger put his arms around her shoulders, and held her close to him. "I'm sorry, Miss Margaret, I didn't mean to hurt you, but I don't want you to be fooled."

Oh yes, she had been a stupid fool. A fool to herself.

Margaret broke away. "I need… need… some time alone… Ginger," she managed to say. "Thank you, but I'm going down… down… to my cabin now."

290

"Okay. If I don't see you later I'll be around tomorrow sometime after sign-off. We can go for a quick drink, and then I'll see you safely to the station.

"Thanks, Ginger… thanks." Still crying, Margaret staggered down the stairs and along the working alleyway. She passed a few of the crew, and could feel that they wanted to ask why she was crying – but she ignored them and made her way to the cabin.

Thankfully it was empty. She grabbed the comb and slipped it into her pocket, then made her way to Ricky's cabin, which was unlocked and empty.

She placed the comb on his bunk, together with a short note scribbled on a scrap of paper she found. It helped her to get it all out; to let him know she'd discovered all his lies. Plus the added emphasis from the blots caused by her falling tears.

CHAPTER 45

On the way back to her cabin, Margaret felt that her heart had ended up in the pit of her stomach. She had lost her lovely Jim through death, and at the time she thought that she would never get over him. But death was final, a broken heart wasn't. It was worse. You knew that somebody you loved was still walking around, and would be in another person's arms.

Deep down she was hoping for a miracle to happen. Ricky would get her note, then come rushing to the cabin, telling her it was all a terrible mistake and that he still loved her more than anything else on earth.

Wishful thinking.

When Margaret reached her cabin again the door was unlocked. Chris was sitting alone on her bunk.

"You all right, love?" Chris asked, looking concerned. "Have you been crying?"

The soft words started Margaret off again. Chris sat beside her and enveloped her in strong arms. It was both reassuring and comforting – like having a hug from her mother. Margaret snuggled back into Chris's arms.

"There, there," Chris whispered in her ear.

Then Margaret stiffened, as Chris's hand dropped down onto her breast and began to fondle it.

Margaret pulled away. "What the heck do you think you're playing at?" she demanded. Chris said nothing, but her expression was a mix between hope and anguish.

"I'm sorry," she said. "I thought…"

"You thought wrong."

Just then the door shot open and Eileen strode in, her comb hanging from her hair.

Chris jumped up and left the room quickly, leaving Margaret and Eileen alone.

Eileen frowned. "Why are you looking so guilty?" she demanded.

"She tried to feel me up." Margaret said.

Eileen gave a crowing laugh. "Oh, that's priceless! Didn't you know the woman was a bloody dyke?"

"Chris?" Margaret stood up.

"Come off it, Maggie, she's had the hots for you since the start." Eileen observed her for a moment. "You're so blinking naïve. No wonder Ricky doesn't want you."

Margaret felt a cold flush, like she'd fallen in to the sea again. "What on earth do you mean?" she asked.

"Everybody knew he was only using you. A good lay while he was away from his wife." Eileen was standing with her hands on her hips, a look of unpleasant triumph twisting her mouth.

After all she'd been through over the past few days, this was enough. Something in Margaret snapped.

"At least," she said softly, making each word clear, "Ricky didn't have sex in the middle of a dance floor with a prostitute, like your man."

The colour drained from Eileen's face. "What the fuck do you mean by that?"

Margaret took a deep breath. "Your Tom was with a woman in a bar in Barbados, and everyone was watching them. And I know it's true because I saw it with my own eyes."

For a moment Eileen was still, her mouth working. Then suddenly she flew at Margaret like an alley cat, her hands reaching for Margaret's throat.

At which point Margaret's judo training kicked in.

It was if her Jim was standing just behind her, whispering his teaching instructions in her ear.

"*Osotogari is the throw to use here*," he seemed to be saying.

She stepped to the side, taking hold of Eileen's arm, then using her right leg to flip Eileen over so the girl fell with a shriek. Margaret kept hold of Eileen's arm and followed her down, then pinned her to the floor.

"You don't like the truth any more than I do," she whispered in Eileen's ear. "But it's not my fault Tom is a lying rat." The other girl struggled a little, but said nothing. "The truth is, we've both been had."

"You're hurting my arm," Eileen muttered.

"And I'll hurt it more if you come at me again."

Margaret let go and stood. Eileen struggled to her feet, then grabbed her comb from where it had fallen on the deck.

"Wait till I see him," she snapped, pushing it back into her hair. Then she stormed out of the cabin.

---0---

Tom knocked back the last of his beer and wiped his mouth with his hand.

Life was good.

The diamonds were safe with Margaret. Paddy had the substitute comb, ready to swap on the train. Mick seemed to have decided to trust him – finally – and had stopped his pestering. Even Miss Pike, after all runaround she'd given him, had slipped him a tip of hundred pounds. And to cap it all, he'd been given the all-clear by the doctor. Yes, the future looked bright.

"You fucking bastard!"

The door was flung open, and Eileen stormed in.

A few heads popped up from around the curtains.

"I've just been told what you was doing in some Barbados night club with a whore!" she yelled.

"Who told you that?" stammered Tom.

"That bitch, Maggie." Eileen stood in front of him with her hands on her hips, her face red. Her comb was hanging from her

295

hair, looking like it would fall off at any moment. "Is it true? Is that why you didn't want to make love with me? Because you got a dose?"

Tom indicated the watchers. "Shh, Eileen, please!"

"Don't you 'shh' me, you bastard! Is it true?"

Tom opened his mouth, but no words came out.

"Right," she snarled. "I'll take that as a 'yes'.

Tom tried to talk once more, but again, couldn't find the words.

"Here take your bloody comb!" Eileen ripped it out of her hair. "Maggie's given her feller his back, you might as well 'ave yours."

Tom found his voice. "What did you say?" he gasped, going as white as a sheet.

"Maggie's given Ricky his comb back, and you can have yours back as well."

"I don't want mine back," screamed Tom. "Keep it!

Eileen shoved it back in her hair and stormed out, leaving Tom the centre of many unwanted gazes.

That evening Tom did not feel like going to the Pig, preferring to stay in his cabin. A couple of the other waiters came in to keep him company – and, it seemed, to have a laugh at his expense.

"What's this about you screwing one of those whores in Barbados?" asked one.

"By God, Tom, your bird certainly has a temper on her," joked another.

But Tom was hardly listening to them.

Did he hear Eileen right? Did she say Margaret had given back the comb? Tom felt faint.

Their diamonds were in it, and now Ricky had them.

He must see Paddy as soon as possible. He knew that Ricky would be going home straight away tomorrow. Normally he would stay on board until all the passengers had disembarked, then take the boat as it sailed from Pier Head into dry dock with the rest of the deck hands. But with his Uncle killed in Dakar there would be a lot of questions to answer.

He and Paddy must follow Ricky and get the comb with the diamonds from him. At this very moment he did not have a clue what the plan would be, but he certainly wouldn't be telling Mick.

---0---

Margaret put her suitcases in the corner by the bunks, then her open hand luggage bag on top, ready for her make-up and wash things to go in the next morning.

Johnny and Billy poked their heads round the door.

"We're going to the Pig," said Johnny. "You coming?"

"I don't think so," Margaret said, turning away so they didn't see her teary red eyes. "But I'll see how I feel later."

"Okay." Their heads disappeared.

A few minutes later, Eileen stormed in. "That sodding Tom," she snapped. "That unfaithful, poxed-up, lying little toe-rag. I've ruddy 'ad it with 'im."

"As I said, it looks like we've both been had by our men," Margaret agreed.

"Why do they do that?" Margaret asked.

Eileen shook her head firmly. "That's what they do, kid. Keep your eyes and ears open. That's what I say."

"Thanks Eileen."

The other girl stood up. "You take care, I'm going to the Pig for a last one, if you fancy it."

"Perhaps," Margaret said as Eileen swept out, leaving the door ajar.

Margaret frowned. Something seemed different. Didn't Eileen have her comb in her hair when she came in?

297

A minute later, the door was flung open and Ricky marched in.

For a moment, her heart missed a beat.

"Why the fucking hell are you giving me this cheap comb." He shouted at her. "I want the one I gave you back."

Margaret was a taken aback.

"I want the original comb," he hissed at her.

"How do you know that it isn't the original one." asked Margaret, feeling rather shaken.

"Because the original one had real stones in. Now what have you done with the other comb."

Margaret was beginning to put two and two together. Ginger was right, he was only using her.

"I'll tell you what happened to it," she shouted back. "I wore it New Years Eve in Madeira. When we came back to the ship you went back to your cabin and I went up on deck, had a few drinks and whilst leaning over the rails it must have fallen out of my hair and dropped over the side into the water, I bought another from the shop the following day to replace yours thinking they would both look the same. It'll be at the bottom of the deep blue sea by now." She added sarcastically.

Next minute he gave her such a hard slap across her face, that she almost lost her balance. The pain was excruciating.

"You stupid fucking bitch!" he screamed.

She felt so startled at his insults that she quickly thrusted her knee into his crotch.

Ricky doubled over in pain.

"How dare you! Get out my cabin, you deceitful bastard," she yelled at him, "Your uncle tried to murder me! You have deceived your wife and children. Now get out, and don't you ever dare come near me again, or I will be going straight to the police and will also be telling your wife." At that she pushed him through the door and slammed it shut, locking the door from the inside.

Margaret did not go to the Pig that night.

Kitty, was first the women to come back to the cabin, rather intoxicated giving Margaret a strange look, after having to be let into the room, she then flopped onto the bottom bunk, out for the count.

---0---

The following day the Ocean Star docked in Liverpool, and two significant things happened to Margaret to end the cruise.

The first was when she was waiting in the long queue to sign off. There was a Tannoy announcement asking her to go to the bureau. Margaret wondered if this could have anything to do with Ricky. As soon as she signed off she went to find out.

"There's an envelope for you," said the Purser, smiling as he handed it over to Margaret.

When she opened it up she found a little thank you card and two fifty pound notes. It was from a Miss Pike thanking her for helping her when the ship had caught fire. She was about to go down to her room when Ginger came up to her. "I will see you at the bottom of the gangway as soon as you disembark Miss Margaret, I know a nice little pub we can go to before you catch your train to go back home." Margaret nodded then went down to her cabin.

She found the room empty. Everybody must have gone. Then she remembered that she should have stripped off her bed.

She climbed up and began pulling off the sheets and blankets. She tossed the blanket on the floor, while she folded each sheet. Then she shook the blanket out to open it before folding.

As she shook it, the second significant thing happened. Something brown and sparkly flew across the room, landing with a clatter in a corner.

Margaret put down the blanket and picked the object up.

It was her original comb.

Margaret broke into a wide grin. So it wasn't lost at sea! It must have fallen off as she collapsed drunk into bed, then got caught in a fold of the blanket, so she missed it when searching!

She studied it closely. Now she looked, some of the stones did seem to sparkle a bit more deeply. And it felt heavier than the one she'd bought to replace it from that nice young woman in the shop.

Suddenly the words of the girl in the jewellery store in Rio came back to her, explaining how to tell a real stone from a fake. "Rub the stone fast against your skin, then feel it. If it is warm, then it is glass. Stone will not heat up."

Margaret rubbed the comb against her cheek, then gingerly touched one of the larger stones with her finger.

It was cold.

They really were real!

And Ricky had wanted her to carry it through customs for him.

She dropped the comb in her bag. Yes, she would carry it through, for sure.

But not for him.

Oh no, she'd do it for herself.

---0---

As Margaret waited in the queue in the customs shed, she spotted Ricky on the dockside beyond. He had his arms around the shoulders of a tall, good looking woman, while she held on to two children.

While Margaret watched, the family started to walk away. She was interested to see that Ricky was walking rather stiffly.

Tom and Paddy were just ahead of her, holding up the queue while the officers searched their bags very thoroughly. But eventually they were allowed through.

"Anything to declare?" asked the officer when it was her turn.

"Just a bottle of whisky for my mother and two hundred cigarettes for my brother-in-law. Also this comb which was bought from the shop." She held it up, but the customs officer barely looked at it.

"Oh don't worry about that, miss. I've seen quite a few of them today." He began to chuckle. "We only stop people with high value items, like diamonds or gold." He laughed again, "Enjoy your leave."

"I certainly will," she said, laughing along with him as she put the comb back into her bag.

She walked out onto the dockside, and met Ginger as arranged. He led her to the little pub. They settled in a quiet corner overlooking the docks.

"Oh Ginger," she said when he brought over some drinks. "Ricky really was dreadful. He only gave me that comb because it had real diamonds, so I'd get it through customs."

"I thought so," Ginger replied. "I thought they were real." Then he frowned. "No, wait a moment – that was Eileen's comb, not yours."

Margaret said, "It was mine. I'll show you." She pulled the comb out of her bag and handed it to him. "I did get it through customs, but not for him. For me."

Ginger smiled. "Well done you, Miss Margaret." He handed it back. Margaret opened her bag to drop it in, then did a double-take.

There was another, identical-looking comb inside.

"What on earth…?"

She pulled it out and put them side by side on the table.

For a moment they both sat in silence, looking at the two combs.

Ginger picked them each up in turn and studied them closely.

301

"Well, Miss Margaret, I'd stake my life on it, these are both set with real diamonds." He looked up. "Where did you get the other one?"

"I don't know," she answered slowly. Then she had a sudden image of Eileen sitting on the bunk with the comb hanging off her hair. She'd been next to Margaret's bag, and it had been left open. Margaret laughed. "I think I know," she said. "I think it fell off Eileen's hair once too often."

Ginger nodded. "Then I reckon there were two separate plots – one by Ricky and presumably his uncle, and the other by Tom – to smuggle diamonds off the ship."

"Why Tom?" she asked.

"He gave a comb to Eileen, just like Ricky gave one to you. They must have had the same idea. I heard Tom and Paddy discussing something about diamonds at the beginning of the trip."

"Then the combs got all muddled up!" she said.

"So they did," Ginger said, "And there's going to be some very sorry people going home today, Miss Margaret. These are worth a fortune."

Margaret pushed one of the combs across the table.

"You saved my life, Ginger. You have one and I'll have one."

He was silent a moment, then he nodded and slid the comb towards himself. "Thank you, Miss Margaret." He dropped it into his pocket.

Margaret put her own comb in her bag. "Thank you Ginger, for everything."

He smiled. "Well, I have one more job to do, then."

She raised an eyebrow. "What's that then?"

"I'm not letting you travel on your own carrying all that fortune. We'll ring your mother and tell her you're taking a taxi back instead of the train. And I am coming with you."

They finished their beers and went out onto the dockside, just as there was a loud toot from the Pier Head.

302

"It's the *Ocean Star* casting off," said Ginger. "She only has a short trip, into dry dock. Come on Miss Margaret, we need to go now."

He squeezed her hand and they grinned at eachother, as the ship sailed on.

THE END

ABOUT THE AUTHOR

Valerie Lawson was born in Accrington Lancashire. Her childhood was spent in a number of different places; at the age of five, she and her family moved to Criccieth in Wales. After two and a half years, they moved again, this time to a town called Tawa, near Wellington in New Zealand. They then moved back to Lancashire and settled in Southport when Valerie was in her mid-teens.

It was in Southport as a young woman that Valerie met and married her husband. The marriage did not last long, and Valerie got a job working on the Isle of Man ferry out of Liverpool. From there she got work on various cruise liners, sailing all over the world.

It was this which inspired her to use her knowledge and experience as the background for an adventure story set on the high seas.

Valerie now lives in south west England and divides her time between writing, country walks and gardening.

Winter & Drew Publishing Ltd is a publisher of historical action and adventure – with a difference.

Winter & Drew Publishing specialises in helping independent historical fiction authors publish their books under the Winter & Drew imprint.

Do you have a historical action adventure novel of your own – and are looking for options to have it published?

Visit the website to find out more.

winteranddrew.com

Printed in Great Britain
by Amazon

38535076R00172